Internal Affairs

BOOKS BY JILL TWEEDIE

In the Name of Love
It's Only Me
Letters from a Fainthearted Feminist
More From Martha
Bliss
Internal Affairs

Internal Affairs

Jill Tweedie

Heinemann : London

William Heinemann Ltd
10 Upper Grosvenor Street, London W1X 9PA
LONDON MELBOURNE TORONTO
JOHANNESBURG AUCKLAND

First published 1986
© Jill Tweedie
ISBN 0 434 79984 X

Printed in Great Britain by
Mackays of Chatham Ltd,
Chatham, Kent

For Alan

Part One

'But I don't *want* a man,' Charlotte Macanally said.

Unnerved by her own vehemence, she looked down at her hands. The sight of them brought her no comfort. Pale, plump and freckled, they were as unappetizing as the breakfast she had just eaten, pork bangers undercooked by her mother. She gave a furtive tug at her wedding ring but again it would not budge, sealed in by a pad of flesh that had been less obdurate eight years ago. You're twice the woman I married, Bruce had said recently and Bruce wasn't a man given to jokes, even old ones.

'I'm afraid,' Pat Wilshaw said, removing her glasses the better to probe an inflamed pustule on her right eyelid, 'that a man is de rigor. Have you got a mirror?'

Charlotte rummaged in a stained leather bag, detached a round object from its nest of stray hairs and tobacco shreds and handed it over.

'Charming,' said Pat.

'Sorry,' said Charlotte. She watched Pat scowling at herself while she wondered whether this sudden appearance of a man constituted a last straw. Other people seemed able to recognize last straws the moment they saw them. This is *the last straw* they said authoritatively and convinced all who heard that they had indeed been driven beyond human endurance. Whereas Charlotte knew in her bones that if she ever claimed the same, she would convince no one. They would smile vaguely and change the subject or point out what she already knew, that worse things happened at sea. She had once attended a friend's birthday on a boat and had had to be carted off half an hour later in a dreadful state. The friend had been

3

unsympathetic. 'We're still tied to the quay,' she had cried over her partner's shoulder and tooted heartlessly on a toy trumpet.

Her face distorted, Pat Wilshaw tweaked at an eyelash and let out a low moo. One red eye glared at Charlotte, who clucked and said, 'Golden Eye ointment, that's what you need.'

'I've got it on,' Pat snapped. 'Do you think my eyes naturally ooze yellow grease?'

'Sorry,' Charlotte said again. She lit a cigarette. If this man was indeed a last straw she had better say so now, while there was still a faint chance of finding someone to replace her. But even as she thought this, the chance guttered and died. It had to be faced – she *was* the replacement. They had wanted Pat to go and Pat had suddenly (and most unselfishly) offered the trip to her. Since then she had endured all the symptoms of Delhi Belly without venturing further than Kentish Town, yet still she had hesitated to turn such an opportunity down, wanting desperately not to go but equally desperately *to have been*. She dreamed at night of showing an envious audience snaps of herself in exotic locations: 'Me on the edge of a live volcano; me' – a modest cough here – 'surfing in shark-infested waters.' Towards dawn, the dreams turned to nightmares as the live volcano blew her into titbits which were then dined upon by the sharks.

'The thing is,' Pat said, 'without this man, how would you communicate?' She peered at Charlotte. 'You know, anyone else but you would be jumping at the chance.'

'I know,' said Charlotte.

'Me, for instance. I need some sun, I'm thoroughly run-down. What else is this' – and she indicated the offending zit – 'but a cry for help?'

Charlotte's heart went out to her. 'Then do go, Pat. Really. You should. It's you they want, not me.'

'True. But it can't be done.'

'Why?' Charlotte frowned, dimly recalling something Ursula had said a few days ago. 'Is it that trip to Peru in March? Would you rather go there?'

'Peru has nothing to do with it,' Pat said crossly. 'I simply thought that a look at the Third World would do you good, with your divorce coming up.' She shifted her voice into the neutral tones of the counselling room. 'I expect that's what's really worrying you. Some women become pathologically indecisive during the trauma of separation, it's a symptom one has often observed in clients.'

'I'm sure you're right,' said Charlotte, wishing she could believe that dithering, in her case, was not congenital.

'Anyway,' Pat said, reverting to the matter in hand, 'though there may be English speakers in the capital city, once you get out into the field, I promise you, *nada*.' And she shrugged in the Latin American way for which she was famous in Development circles, that part of the world having been for so long what she called 'her baby'. 'So you see, it is imperative to have an interpreter with you. Otherwise you won't do a good job and it is a job, remember, not a package tour.'

'Oh, I know,' Charlotte stammered. 'Of course it is.' She groped at the woollen neck of her sweater, pulling it away from the reddening skin. It occurred to her that she might be experiencing a hot flush. How frightful to have hot flushes in the tropics. With that double measure of heat, a person could spontaneously combust. But The Change wasn't on the cards yet. She had three years to go till forty and everything was ticking over as it had always done, even if it were to no purpose whatsoever.

'I suppose,' she asked off-handedly, 'they couldn't provide a woman instead?' She didn't feel off-hand. Several severe attacks of her wheeze were almost bound to be the consequence of three weeks' close proximity to any human being, and a man doubled the hazards. The provenance of these attacks, which left her red-faced and gasping for breath, was unknown; 'We call it,' the doctor had said, 'Onset of Adult Wheeze,' and had given her a Ventolin inhaler to suck on in moments of stress. She had just met Bruce at the time and their courting was intimately connected in her mind with urgent lunges for the small blue nozzle. On her wedding day she had wheezed as loudly as the decrepit church organ, which had undermined the sacramental quality of the marriage service. A bride whose lips were glued to an inhaler rather than to her groom was not the romantic figure with which the more sentimental members of the congregation could identify and there were few moist eyes amongst them. At the reception her mother, blinking from under a home-made hat, had attempted to defend her daughter's poor showing by remarking darkly to anyone who would listen that the groom *had his own problems.*

'No woman available,' Pat said briskly. Scrabbling among the papers that littered her desk she came up with a telex. 'This came from Banabalu yesterday. It says the man is fluent in English and the KNNA uses him regularly to escort foreign visitors. He's a KNNA official himself so he should know what he's doing. His name' – she glanced at the telex and rolled the words off with cosmopolitan ease – 'is Hariyono Premendongerum.'

The mottling on Charlotte's neck crept over her chin and lapped at the foothills of her cheeks. She took the piece of paper and, after a pause, said, 'Pemedo . . .' Then she said, 'Premender . . .'

'Ah well. Que sera, sera,' Pat said.

Charlotte closed her eyes. She had begun to feel extremely unwell.

'Sorry, dear,' said Mrs Wren.

As Charlotte's cries died away she added, 'In my day, people wore a black band if they'd had an injection. To warn other people, you know.'

'Black bands were for when someone died,' Charlotte said faintly.

'That too,' Mrs Wren conceded. 'I wore one for your father *and* for my vaccination. But you wouldn't remember.'

Having set her daughter to rights on this point, she began chopping up some parsley. Her voice rose in song.

'I'd like to get you on a slow boat . . . to ro-man-tic places . . . these foolish . . .'

Obscurely challenged, Charlotte said, 'I'm not going for fun, mother. I'm going to work.'

Mrs Wren gave an exclamation, dropped the knife and pushed past her daughter to the stove, where some chicken bones and particles of blackened vegetation were coming to a scummy boil. Charlotte cried out once more.

'Gracious, you *are* in a bad way,' said Mrs Wren. She moved the saucepan off its ring. 'Charlotte. You know that comfrey bush?'

Charlotte shook her head. The pain was subsiding.

'It was in Aunt Nesta's garden. The one she had before she moved to Norfolk, where she isn't, I may say, *at all* happy. Because of the sawmill. It's awfully good. You should get some.'

'Yes, mother.'

'I expect if you asked the man who delivered the coal, he'd know.'

'Know what, ma?'

Mrs Wren focused for a moment on her daughter and her soft voice became a little louder. 'Where the *comfrey* is, darling. There was some rhubarb, I think, at the back of . . .'

Charlotte had already lost whatever thread there had been in her mother's conversation. She was accustomed to this. Mrs Wren wandered through an intricate and overgrown web of unadopted roads on her way to a destination, her voice fading occasionally as if she had momentarily disappeared behind a hedge. It was no use hurrying her along or trying to lure her into a short-cut or leaping out to catch her at unexpected junctures. The best thing was not to listen much until she had arrived, though this was tricky, too, since if you weren't on the spot to greet her she could become quite peeved.

'. . . fuzzy leaves and a dear little blue flower,' Mrs Wren said. 'You boil it. I'll ask the coalman myself.'

Charlotte touched her mother's arm as one waking a sleepwalker. 'Why should I get comfrey?' she asked gently.

'For your sore bits, darling. I keep telling you.' Mrs Wren was growing slightly impatient. 'You put comfrey on them, it's marvellous. Jennifer had a dog once with a bad leg, what was he called? Beautiful eyes. So spiritual. He reminded me of your father. Hartley. *That* was his name. Silly name for a dog. Well, for anything, really . . .'

There was a ring at the doorbell. Charlotte went out and opened it on the milkman, bearing a three-week bill. She paid it and returned to the kitchen.

'. . . they won't last the winter,' Mrs Wren was saying. 'He said he'd come and do them but he didn't. Of course, he may have got his bad lungs. What do you think, darling?'

'I expect so.'

Drifting against Charlotte, Mrs Wren focused again. 'Have you been in bed?' she asked sternly.

'Yes, mother.'

'Well, you ought to go back. You don't look up to scratch.'

'I wanted to help you cook,' Charlotte said. As she eased herself into a basket chair as far as she could get from her mother's unpredictable movements, she acknowledged to herself that this was not strictly true. Her real aim had been to creep unnoticed into the kitchen to get herself a bowl of cornflakes. Her mother left her hallmark on her cooking as surely as any of the world's great chefs

7

and Charlotte doubted the capacity of the upstairs loo to absorb much more of it.

She shifted gingerly in the chair. Both buttocks, her left thigh and her head were throbbing in unison. She had had to take the day off work and Pat at the other end of the telephone had not welcomed the news, her gay laugh and her 'goodness and here's me envying poor you' had told Charlotte that. It was wretched, feeling ill and apprehensive when everyone expected you to feel tremendously excited, it let them all down. Charlotte tried to conjure up a spasm of tremendous excitement and failed.

Saucepan in hand, Mrs Wren advanced to the table. She dumped the saucepan on a trivet and proceeded to ladle its dung-coloured contents into a bowl. 'Have some of my soup, darling,' she said. 'It's got camomile in.' Her steamed-up glasses glimmered at Charlotte. Mrs Wren believed passionately in her soups as she did in her vegetable stews, her stoneground porridge and what she called her pot-lucks. 'You're potty if you eat them, lucky if you don't,' an uncle had once commented sourly.

Charlotte said, 'It smells . . . amazing. But I couldn't, really. Not just now.'

Mrs Wren sat down with a thump.

'I'm sorry, ma.'

'I don't understand,' Mrs Wren sighed. 'All those Clark's X-rays when you were little. And Marmite and Ribena. I don't suppose they have Marmite and Ribena over there, do they? *Or* shoes.'

'What don't you understand, mother?'

'What? Oh. Why you need all those injections for where you're going in case you drop dead. How, one wonders, do the natives cope?'

'They drop dead,' Charlotte said. 'Poor things.'

Mrs Wren took spoon in hand and began on her soup. Charlotte regarded her with gloom. There was a lot in what her mother said, if that's what she had said. It was ridiculous to have to have all those jabs plus the two kinds of malaria tablets she was already taking ('first dose one week before departure' the labels instructed) when the Sulanasians were presumably lucky if they saw an aspirin from one year's end to another.

Upstairs in the spare bedroom her Woolworth suitcase was already half-full of prophylactics, each one ticked off before packing from a list pinned to the door. Lomotil for diarrhoea: not the kind

8

she was now suffering, brought on by her stupid nerves, but the genuine tropical article, the Real Thing. Cicatrin antibiotic powder to dust on suppurating ulcers – the smallest scratch takes *years* to heal in that climate, Pat had informed her cheerily. Then there was the Autan Insect Repellent and three tubes of Anthisan for the bites of insects that hadn't found the Autan sufficiently repellent. She counted the rest on her fingers. Sterotabs to sterilize the gunge in foreign water. A plastic bottle to hold the sterilized water. Nitrozapam sleepers to get her through foreign nights. Valium, which she took anyway, or had done since she and Bruce split up. Glucose sweets for energy. Salt tablets to replace the salt lost through sweat. Ventolin, of course. Plus Anadin and sunburn cream and five packs of toilet paper and Rennies for indigestion. With all that on her, she could well get stopped at Customs for possession of noxious substances. Already her body was a kind of travelling zoo of viruses. The wild Cholera, the rare Yellow Fever, the Greater Spotted Typhoid, the Man-Eating Tetanus . . .

But it was wicked, Charlotte reminded herself, to make light of what other people suffered and died of. After a swift calculation, she decided that the Rennies were not absolutely necessary. Sulanasians probably went to bed hungry every day of their lives and would not warm to a fat white woman crunching indigestion tablets over them. Rennies – out.

Mrs Wren, who was now flaying a banana, said she thought Charlotte ought to inform Bruce about going abroad.

On the other hand you could get indigestion from nerves, even if you'd eaten nothing. Particularly if you'd eaten nothing. And the Sulanasians certainly wouldn't appreciate her having heartburn in their midst. Better include the Rennies.

'I said,' Mrs Wren said, 'you ought to tell Bruce you're going abroad.'

'Why?'

'Made out of seaweed, these,' Mrs Wren remarked, pulling the biscuit tin towards her. 'From Wales; your Aunt Nesta sent them. I can't think how, when she never stirs from home but . . .'

'You mean,' Charlotte guessed, 'because Bruce is my next-of-kin?' and she saw the plane drop like a bomb from the sky, flames licking at its wings. Halfway to earth it burst apart and silver fragments hurtled across the storm clouds, each containing a kin to be next-of. 'I'm not going to die, you know.'

'. . . always wore a *very* strange shade of lipstick. Deadly Nightshade, I used to call it. She was so annoyed. There was a shop in Hay-on-Wye that stocked it and . . .'

'I'll tell him,' Charlotte said. 'I'll call round tomorrow and tell him.'

Mrs Wren deposited the banana skin in her soup bowl, picked it up and pattered over to the sink, where she dropped it into the pedal bin. As its lid snapped shut, she said over her shoulder, 'Of course, I would have loved it but in a way, it's a blessing you and Bruce didn't have any children, with you leaving him and going off all over the world. Isn't it?'

'I suppose so,' said Charlotte. She got up and went to the pedal bin, where she retrieved the bowl. She could smell her own breath. It smelt exactly like her mother's soup.

The next morning, despite a still-hot forehead and clammy hands, Charlotte slipped into her poncho and holding its stiff folds well away from her punctured body set off for the Cotterstock Fertility Counselling Clinic. The clinic leased premises on the top floor of a dilapidated building in Clerkenwell that had once been a brewery. The wide uneven floorboards and narrow beams still gave off beery fumes on hot days, providing a sharp reminder to some of its present-day visitors of the circumstances that had contributed to their current plight.

The clinic had been founded by a Miss Ernestine Cotterstock, spinster of Bedford Square, and a bust of her stood on a plinth at the top of the rickety staircase, chained to the wall as a precaution against the lighter-fingered of the clinic's clientele. The chain, passing across the Founder's throat, gave her the appearance of being garotted, but the plump features retained a serenity that Charlotte, squeezing daily round Miss Cotterstock's likeness to reach the door of the clinic, felt might well evaporate were the lady to know that what she had christened the Cotterstock Refuge For Fallen Females now largely concerned itself with arranging abortions, its present-day clients having fallen less from grace than through the contraceptive net for one reason or another. Most of them sought an abrupt end to unwanted pregnancy, a solution that Miss Cotterstock, for all her advanced ideas, would never have countenanced. Charlotte did not much like it, either. When she had first joined the staff of the clinic six years ago, she had envisaged her job as one of helping women with what she vaguely thought of as 'emotional problems'. She had not reckoned on encountering so many clients who knew, in vivid contrast to herself, exactly what they wanted and desired her only to arrange the time and the place. Initially, she had assumed that such determination was simply a smokescreen for a welter of unresolved doubts and fears and had applied herself energetically to winkling out the wracked and vulnerable souls beneath. Soon, there had been complaints to the Director.

'What's she giving me all this shrink-talk for,' one spiky redhead pierced with the modish safety-pins of that year had screeched at Pat Wilshaw, 'when all I want is an abortion?'

Pat Wilshaw had had a little talk with Charlotte after that. 'They know they haven't got much time, you see, and it makes them nervous. I'd take their word for it, if I were you. Within limits, of course.'

Within limits, Charlotte now did. She had contemplated resigning but the days had turned into months and the months into years and inertia combined with a shrinking job market had kept her Cotterstock-bound. Now and again she came upon the odd vulnerable soul, a drooping violet among the hosts of blooming daffodils, to whom she could give sustenance, and this kept her reasonably content.

This morning, edging her way up the staircase past the usual assortment of men attending on their wives or girlfriends inside, Charlotte noticed that Ernestine Cotterstock had recently been sprayed an electric shade of green. The paint was still tacky and she turned beside the bust with some idea of remonstrating with the culprit.

'That's not very nice,' she said.

A youth with heavy muscled thighs and a T-shirt that said 'Pull This One' detached himself from the queue. 'What's that?'

'This,' repeated Charlotte, indicating Miss Cotterstock.

'What's wrong with it?' the youth asked. He wore, Charlotte noticed, one black and one brown boot. An indication, no doubt, of an agitated state.

'It's been painted green,' she pointed out.

'Green?' The youth craned a goiterous neck over her shoulder. 'I don't see no green. What you on about, missus? Anyone here see any green?'

The queue behind him shuffled uneasily. One or two snorted.

'Oh, never mind,' said Charlotte. She retreated through the door, carefully holding it away from her sore parts, and hung up her poncho in the hall cupboard. Then she entered the alcove that served as the Clinic Director's office.

'Ah. You got here. Muy bien,' Pat Wilshaw greeted her. An old gas heater hissed in the corner but it had not long been lit and Pat's breath steamed on the cold air. 'It's panic stations here, I can tell you. Ursula and Jean have both gone down with 'flu and Elspeth called to say her son's got measles. So there's only you and Isabel to counsel and the waiting room's full. I've got three AIs this morning, so I'm fuera de combate.'

She bustled across to a dumpy white barrel parked under the window and pressed down on its pressure-cooker top. The lid swung open and a plume of glacial smoke emerged. Fanning it aside, she dived into the interior and picked out three glass phials which she held up close to her spectacles before inserting them in a nearby rack.

'One of the clients is Asian,' she said. 'Is that a blue label or a red, I can never remember.' She riffled through an exercise book and looked up, grinning, at Charlotte. 'Brown. Appropriate.'

Charlotte had already lifted her scarf to her nose. It was an automatic reflex. The smell of semen as it began to thaw was a dense and overpowering odour that seeped into every corner of the clinic like the sea through a battered dyke, bringing with it mournful intimations of wrecked ships and the weed-encrusted bones of drowned mariners. Charlotte had often instructed herself that the clinic's artificial insemination activities were the best things it did, thoroughly life-enhancing, occasions for joy and celebration, deeply worthwhile. It was her misfortune that AI days made her feel sick.

'Are you sure you're all right?' Pat asked, peering through her glasses at Charlotte's wan face. The stye on her eyelid was nearing full term and the sight of its volcanic head did little to steady Charlotte's stomach.

'Fine,' she said. 'Thank you.'

'Then better get going. Isabel's in Number One and I'll need Number Two for most of the morning so take your pick of the rest.' Helpfully, Pat added, 'They're all cold enough to freeze the balls.'

In the hall, Charlotte groped her way into her poncho again. Elspeth Morgan, a part-timer on the clinic staff and an old hand at foreign parts before motherhood had grounded her, frequently boasted of having been the only constipated person in the length and breadth of India, and Charlotte had no wish to challenge her by becoming the only person on the Equator to go down with double pneumonia. To head off this eventuality, she filled a glass at the chipped sink and swallowed two aspirin and three tablets of Vitamin C. A month abroad would at least be a respite from the smell of semen. Parting with Bruce had eliminated the only other source. Counting these small blessings, she entered the waiting room.

Counselling Room Three was a windowless cubicle with hardboard walls that let through enough of the sounds next door to distract but never enough to enlighten. It contained two low chairs, a small table surfaced with cracked tiles and a rickety stool that held a large box of tissues. This enforced proximity of counsellor and counselled was considered therapeutic. Since the onset of the Adult Wheeze, Charlotte had found herself short of breath until her client was safely in the near-squatting position necessary to accommodate the proportions of the chairs.

To her relief, today's client sat down immediately, bundling herself up in a zebra-striped fun-fur and blowing on her mittened hands. She was a woman of about Charlotte's own age but short, thin and sandy with a gap between her two front teeth that gave her a vulpine air. She quaked visibly, though whether from stress or from cold was not yet clear.

'I'll switch on the fire,' Charlotte said. 'It'll soon get warmer.'

Her client regarded the heater on the wall without hope.

'Now.' Charlotte compressed her bulk as best she could and smiled her professional smile. 'Mrs Pauline Waterman. Is that right?'

The woman nodded.

Charlotte propped her elbows on her knees and leant forward encouragingly. 'How do you feel about your pregnancy, Mrs Waterman?' she inquired.

Mrs Waterman began to cry. Tears dripped from beneath the beige eyelashes and trickled down the sandy cheeks. Charlotte repressed the hope that this was a promising reaction – a lot of clients cried at first, before they asked where and when. She also repressed her usual urge to offer the box of tissues. At her two weekends of training in counselling techniques the teacher had dwelt at some length on the dynamics of the tissue box, emphasizing that to give tissues to distressed clients amounted to an unspoken command from the counsellor to cease crying and would be interpreted by said client to mean that tears were unacceptable, that *emotion itself* was unacceptable. Definitely not an impression we would wish to convey, would we, ladies?

Charlotte had thought that it was, though she had kept her opinion to herself for fear of failing the course. At the time she had imagined that crying was a barrier to a proper assessment of priorities and, anyway, more or less inexplicable in the face of such a happy event. Later, she had grown to view these outbursts with suspicion. Experience taught her that tears tended to defuse maternal instincts, allowing the tearful one to arise refreshed and demand ways and means out of her predicament. Nevertheless, conscience daily baulked her desire to lunge at the damp faces opposite and swab them down.

'Pass me a tissue, would you?' said Mrs Waterman, sniffing disagreeably.

Reaching for the box, Charlotte passed it over and watched with approval as Mrs Waterman blew her nose. Through the partition she could hear the lugubrious monotone of Isabel's client in the next cubicle.

'. . . it's not as if . . . never . . . he wasn't . . . didn't . . .' and, inexplicably but clearly, 'mauve is *not* my colour'.

The one bar of the heater on the wall glowed red in the reflection of its curved holder but made little inroad on the icy room. In five days, Charlotte thought, hunching her shoulders under the poncho, I shall be too hot. It was impossible to credit.

'He never wanted children,' Mrs Waterman said. 'He made that plain from the start. Nor did I, then. I was twenty.' She sorted through the shreds of tissue in her hand as if they might contain her lost youth. 'I'm thirty-six now and I've been off the Pill for four years. More. But he never misses, him. With the johnnies, I mean.'

'Your husband,' Charlotte said.

'Trevor,' Mrs Waterman sounded irritated. 'Yes.'

'And now you're pregnant.'

Mrs Waterman shrugged. 'I was out of the habit, wasn't I? It was only the once.'

Several questions occurred to Charlotte. She censored them in favour of the main theme. 'And Trevor doesn't want the child?'

Bruce hadn't wanted the child, either. When she told him, he had been on his knees in front of the cooker and he continued arranging the frozen chips in neat lines on the baking sheet while Charlotte blubbed. He had been very kind. 'There is no point in recriminations at this juncture,' he said as he closed the oven door. 'Blame is neither here nor there. Nevertheless we did agree, Char, if you'll remember. No kiddies till we're out of this flat and in a home of our own. And for that we need your salary. There's a nice development on the drawing boards in Esher, as it happens. Came across it when I was down there last week for a client . . .' Bruce's clients were prospective home-owners, Bruce was a surveyor. 'Executive residences for first-time buyers, one hundred per cent mortgages. Fresh air, patio doors, wall ovens, ceramic hobs. Char, *please.*'

But Charlotte was shouting through her tears. 'I spend all day fixing abortions, Bruce. How many kiddies must I kill before I can pay for one of my own?' She'd made a disgraceful exhibition of herself but Bruce had been forgiving. He had got her a cup of tea.

Mrs Waterman screwed up her eyes and squinted at the light bulb on the ceiling. 'It's not Trevor's,' she said.

'Ah,' said Charlotte. She felt a strong urge to smoke.

Mrs Waterman hit her knuckles together and stuck out both index fingers at Charlotte. 'I don't want no lectures,' she said. Her lips vanished. When Charlotte did not react, they reappeared, wobbling. 'All those years, you don't know. Him banging away. And what did I get out of it? Fuck all. Not even a kid. He thinks this one's his, shows how much he knows. *His.*' She snorted. 'He couldn't put a rabbit in the family way so he needn't think' – her finger jabbed the air – 'he needn't think I'm going to have it took away because I'm not. For me, it's now or never.'

Charlotte had not known, then, that it might be never. The now was bad enough. They had been very patient with her, considering. The doctor had given her ten days to make up her mind. Talk it over with your husband, he had said, take your time. The screen behind which she'd undressed had been covered with gambolling lambs and baby ducks. Bruce had been patient, too. I'm only thinking of you, Char. You and our future kiddies. When she had screamed for Christ's *sake* don't call me Char he had understood that it stemmed from her condition and he hadn't taken it personally. You'll be your old self once it's over, Char, he'd said.

15

She hadn't been able to go through with the first booking at the hospital. The taxi driver had taken her all the way to Denmark Hill and all the way back. Bruce hadn't been with her that time, he had had a busy afternoon at the office, but the next time, he was. He'd patted her hand while he and the taxi driver discussed the intransigence of London traffic and exchanged various theories on keeping it down – Bruce had been in favour of a tax on non-resident cars, the driver wanted them banned altogether. Once she was installed in the white bed, he'd stayed with her almost to the end of visiting hours. No point in my coming tomorrow, he'd said as he left. The doctor says you'll be too groggy. I'll collect you Tuesday. I'll cook a nice meal. Just the two of us, Char, and he'd winked.

It turned out, during the next minutes, that Mrs Waterman's dilemma was not whether to have the child but whether or not to tell Trevor the truth.

'You can't tell me what to do,' she said to Charlotte with a fading belligerence.

'No.'

'What difference does it make, Trev not knowing?'

Charlotte maintained a careful silence.

After a pause, Mrs Waterman said, 'I won't tell him, then. It'd only stir things up and what's the good?'

'And the real father?' Charlotte asked, as neutrally as she could.

Mrs Waterman wiped a finger under her nose and stood up. 'He'll be the other side of the world by now,' she said. 'He's a merchant seaman.' She smiled then, showing the gap between her teeth. 'Got a kid in every port, I dare say. He won't want to know.' Her smile grew foxy. 'He was all right, though. Know what I mean?'

Charlotte pushed her chair back and got to her feet, anxious not to hear how all right the merchant seaman had been. Mrs Waterman touched her arm with a mittened hand. 'Ta, love. I feel a lot better. I've sorted my head out, talking to you.'

'I'm glad,' Charlotte said, and she was. Mrs Waterman's child would make it out of the Waterman womb, full term and wanted. Lucky it.

At the door, Mrs Waterman took a step back, treading heavily on Charlotte's toes. 'What if the kid has red hair? His dad did.' She considered this eventuality for a moment. 'Naa . . . Trev's got an auntie with red hair. There's Irish blood in the Watermans, too.' Nudging Charlotte with one fur elbow she said, 'There's a lot of it about,' and hacked out a laugh. 'Well, can't stay here all day chatting. Cheers.'

'Cheers,' Charlotte said.

She closed the door on the zebra stripes. The room was warmer now. Positioning herself carefully between the furniture, struggling out of her poncho, she thought of the red-headed seaman rocking across the ocean, blithely unaware of the genes he had left behind him, tucked under a fun-fur. Perhaps he was on his way to Sulanasia.

Smoothing down her hair, straightening her skirt, Charlotte went back to the waiting room.

She fortified herself with a couple of scotch and sodas in a pub draped from floor to ceiling in mortuary satin before her watch said two o'clock and she put out her cigarette and dodged the traffic to the glass corn-cob that reared up over the street. Somewhere within its fifteen storeys was the UK Headquarters of the World Campaign for Small, Healthy and Wealthy Families and since this was the organization that was funding her trip to Sulanasia, Charlotte had taken unusual care to look as suitable a recipient of their confidence as possible. Her hair was trapped at the back of her head in two combs whose teeth dug rather painfully into her scalp, she wore a charcoal dress with only one intransigent stain and well-polished stack-heel shoes that showed off her legs and slender ankles to advantage. The poncho had been discarded in favour of a sage-green anorak with many zips that Charlotte hoped added the proper globe-trotting touch to her otherwise urban outfit.

The uniformed doorman pointed her towards the lift and she rose in its vibrationless interior to the tenth floor and a jungle of potted plants. There she sat at a long table piled with SHWF publications, all of whose front covers depicted radiantly smiling young women and children of various non-white races, and waited for Mr G. Grant.

Fifteen minutes later, when she had flipped through most of the publications, read six articles on contraceptive activities in steamy parts of the world and was beginning to fear that she'd got the time wrong or the day or possibly both, the lift door slid back to reveal a short man in a natty green suit and tan shoes that matched his briefcase. He lifted a palm at Charlotte.

'Mrs Macanally? Ah. Glad I caught you. Come.'

17

She followed him to a nearby office where he slapped the briefcase down on a desk, tapped its top, clicked up its locks and said, 'Small, Healthy and Wealthy, UK Div., at your service.'

Charlotte blinked, half-expecting to be confronted with rows of condoms, diaphragms, vaginal sponges and other devices of his trade, but when he whipped it open, it contained only papers.

'By the by, I'm Gordon Grant. Far East Desk.'

They shook hands. Mr Grant took off his jacket, hung it at the back of his chair, rubbed his hands and said, 'Sulanasia, eh? Fascinating part of the world. You've been there before, of course.'

'Never,' Charlotte said.

'Funny. I thought . . .' He scratched a fleshy ear.

Long practice on Mrs Wren had made her adept at mind-reading.

'You're thinking of Pat Wilshaw. *She's* been. She was going to go. At the Cotterstock. But it's me now.'

'Fine, fine,' Gordon Grant said, looking politely mystified. 'Well, we'll fill you in, never fear. Have you met Stanton Koval yet? My boss.' He rolled up the sleeves of his shirt and turned. 'Ah, Stan, speak of the devil.'

Stanton Koval filled the doorway. He had a dark tan and his shirt was buttoned very low, its deep V edged by a thin gold chain.

'Hi,' he said, extending a powerful hand to Charlotte. It did not quite reach her so she got up to allow it to close over hers.

'Charlotte Macanally,' she said.

'Charlotte Macanally,' Stanton Koval repeated and nodded several times to confirm her in her choice of name. 'Right, Charlotte Macanally. Glad to have you aboard. We need all the help we can get.'

He released her hand and she edged to her chair again, relieved to be out of the forcefield of the Koval torso. Stanton waved towards Gordon Grant. 'You've got him, you don't need me. This man knows more about Sulanasia than the Sulanasians. Right, Gordon?'

Mr Grant in his turn moved obligingly doorwards to let Koval administer slaps to his back. That done, Koval pointed a finger at Grant. 'Over to you,' he said. His smile dazzled. 'See you, Charlotte Macanally.'

The door swung shut behind him and immediately opened again. 'I want you to know, Charlotte,' he said, 'that Sulanasia is the jewel in the SHWF crown. Our Koh-i-noor. I know you'll think so, too. Have a good trip.' The door closed again.

'Stanton', said Grant in the short pause that followed, 'is a great energizer.'

Charlotte gave what she hoped was an energized smile. Her hand, cradled in her lap, was already coming back to life.

A half hour later, the contents of Gordon Grant's briefcase were spread across the desk and over the floor and Charlotte's brain was engorged with statistics. Two secretaries tapped in and out, collecting key documents and returning them again with copies for Charlotte to keep. The secretaries were trim young women with glossy hair who were, Charlotte felt sure, most efficiently contracepted. As Gordon Grant talked, picking his way between papers, she made another effort to wedge her buttocks within the slim confines of the tube chair. Nothing in the colours and sheen of the Grant office furnishings nor in the warmth that breathed from the radiator at her back reminded her of Miss Cotterstock's bleak premises. This was a different world, a highly efficient one – she could hear the chatter of a telex nearby and telephones rang constantly, probably long-distance calls from busy and important people in places like New York and Tokyo and Rome. At the Cotterstock clinic you thought twice before you telephoned the nursing home in Redhill, where they did the abortions, but Small, Healthy and Wealthy Families was an international operation and had to be properly geared to cope with the grim realities of human suffering on the other side of the globe. It was suddenly exciting to realize that in however small a way she, Charlotte, was being given the chance to play some part in that global drama, and she was determined to be worthy of it. What were her own trepidations, her own *health*, when weighed in the balance with such a mission? Other people, many in these offices now, regularly gave their all in the service of the destitute of the earth and did they complain?

Gordon Grant said, 'Ugh. The coffee's foul,' and frowned at one of the trim secretaries who had come in with a tray. 'Can't we do better than this?'

'It's the new machine,' the girl said. 'It sort of rumbles when you . . .'

Charlotte sipped from her cup – a cup with a saucer and a spoon, not a stained and gritty Cotterstock mug – and thought the coffee delicious, though it did not seem tactful to say so. Instead, she beamed at the secretary. 'I think you're all doing a marvellous job here. I'm so impressed. Really.'

19

Grant said, 'That'll do, Bernice,' and the girl went out. He hooked up yet another chart on the wall. 'Now. This is the last lot of statistics I'm going to burden you with but these are our pride and joy.' He smoothed out its creases and stuck two pins at its corners.

The chart was headed CBR and r PROJECTIONS ACCORDING TO RESULT VARIANT OF PFP MEDIUM, HIGH AND LOW IN SULANASIA 1984/85–1990/1 and was criss-crossed by a lot of swooping lines with crosses and arrows on them that reminded Charlotte of a children's puzzle where you joined different points together with a pencil to make Mrs Tiggywinkle or Father Christmas. She had just begun to pick out the silhouette of a large bear or perhaps a kangaroo when Mr Grant coughed.

'As you can see,' he said, tapping the left paw of the bear or kangaroo, 'we have here a current user rate of 35 per cent. This is linked here' – and he traced down the bear's paw to where it curled across the belly – 'to a 12 per cent drop in childbirths since 1979. And here, the descending infant mortality rate, down by 10 per cent. But this is the really interesting graph.' He pointed at the bear's back. 'A rise in primary education for females of 70 per cent in the same time span. Which means Sulanasia now has *90 per cent* primary enrolment for both girls and boys. So that, projecting these figures into the next decade, we should have reduced birth rates to replacement levels and this in a country that ten years ago was one of the most populous in the world. We are very excited by this. Very.'

He spun round on his tan shoes and dropped in the chair beside Charlotte. 'You see, Charlotte – I can call you Charlotte? – this is our primary aim here at SHWF. To give our womenfolk in the LDCs, the Less Developed Countries, that most precious of human freedoms. Freedom of choice. Something that until a few years ago was completely lacking in the lives of women everywhere. Especially reproductive choice.' He leaned towards Charlotte, his face grave. 'Let me ask you a personal question, Charlotte. Do *you* have real, genuine reproductive choice in *your* life? Is your body your own, under your control, no strings attached? Tell me that.'

Charlotte wondered why she had not noticed before what nice eyes Mr Grant had, sincere and deeply caring. There were tiny threads of green in the brown irises that exactly matched his suit. Something melted inside her.

'Not really,' she said.

'You see? And you can say that. *You*. A highly educated, healthy and, yes, attractive woman from the affluent West with the best this world can offer at your feet.' His voice sank. 'Then how much more is choice lacking from the lives of the subjugated women of the Third World? Of Sulanasia? They struggle for survival at the bottom of the world's heap against' – he ticked them off on his fingers – 'poverty, hunger, continual childbearing, infant deaths, disease, religious domination, political domination.' Solemnly, he added, 'and they die at an average age of just over forty. Worn out.'

'Dreadful,' Charlotte said devoutly.

'Dreadful indeed.' He scraped back his chair, pulled out a drawer from the desk, took a paper roll and spread it in front of Charlotte. It was a large photograph of a dark-skinned Mater Dolorosa, a veil framing the skull of her face. In arms that were flesh-covered bones she cradled a stick-like infant who drooped at the empty lip of her breast, eyes sealed shut with crawling flies.

Charlotte sucked in her cheeks to prevent her eyes from watering. Grant lifted his hand and the photograph sprang back into a roll. 'That's what we're all about at SHWF, Charlotte. We're in business to wipe this sort of tragedy *off the face of the earth.*'

In illustration, he scythed a hand through the air. It grazed his discarded cup of coffee, toppling it to the floor. 'Shit,' he said and then, 'I *beg* your pardon.'

'Oh please,' Charlotte said, striving to convey the total irrelevance to her of a four-letter word compared with the grandeur of Mr Grant's undertaking.

At the door, he shouted and a young woman appeared. She wore a sari that showed her brown midriff. Together, she and Charlotte knelt and picked up the fragments of the broken cup and saucer, dumping them into a wastepaper basket. Then the Indian woman scrubbed at the dark patch on the carpet with some absorbent paper. When the carpet was clean, she smiled at Charlotte and went out. Gordon Grant stood up.

'I'll get you a copy of those last statistics from the library,' he said. 'Won't be a minute.'

'Thank you,' said Charlotte. She was still extremely moved. There was a general assumption among the women counsellors at the Cotterstock that men were at the periphery of life, that they were not involved, as women were, had to be, with central realities, the nitty gritty. Charlotte admitted to herself that she was as guilty of that assumption as any of her colleagues. Ursula, for instance,

21

frequently declared that all men were wankers, an opinion that seemed apt enough when voiced in the pervasive aroma of thawing semen. The work there was not conducive to a high estimation of men, dealing as it did with females paying a high price for the reproductive act while the males got off scot-free. Recently, Ursula had been particularly exercised by the controversy in the newspapers about surrogate motherhood.

'Typical,' she had snarled, holding up black headlines – 'I DID IT FOR THE MONEY SAYS RENT-A-WOMB JENNY' – at arm's length before scrunching the paper up. 'They scream blue murder when two or three women get paid for reproduction but look at all that' – and she waved angrily at the pot-bellied fridge squatting in the corner – 'semen doesn't come free. Men get *paid* for wanking. But is that disgusting? Is that heartless and money-grubbing? Not on your nellie. It's bloody public-spirited when it's men.'

But it was now clear to Charlotte that there were other kinds of men, men with whom the word 'wanker' could never be linked. Caring men like Gordon Grant and Stanton Koval. Indeed, the offices of Small, Healthy and Wealthy Families were full to bursting with caring men. She could see them through the open door, striding purposefully along the corridor, stopping to talk earnestly together with other men. She could hear them answering telephones all around her. The few women, the secretaries, seemed a frivolous bunch in comparison, unencumbered by the responsibilities so willingly shouldered by their bosses. They could go home at the end of the day without a care in the world. It was a different matter for the men. Small, Healthy and Wealthy was a cause, not a nine to five job.

As she thought these things over, Charlotte felt a curious tingling sensation at the base of her spine that she had experienced only once before, five years ago at Caxton Hall. The occasion was a Free Introductory Lecture by a woman guru, Mother Prayana from Uttar Pradesh, who promised spiritual regeneration to all those who followed The Prayana Path. Charlotte had read the ad in *Time Out* shortly after she had had the abortion, which had left her feeling hollow and tired and without direction. Perhaps The Prayana Path would provide one.

Reluctant to face a roomful of strangers alone, she had coaxed Bruce to come with her – much against his will, he did not like strangers, they set off his itch. The two of them had taken their seats in a large, dusty ante-chamber, along with another twenty or so dejected people, mostly women, and a dozen athletic-looking twenty-year-olds in white blouses and shirts who were evidently very excited.

Mother Prayana had eventually arrived, sailing majestically on to the platform – Charlotte noted with relief that her girth signified The Prayana Path was not a Spartan one – and sinking in a billow of snow-white robes into a carved chair of baronial proportions. Several silent minutes passed while the Mother scrutinized her rapt audience with dark and flashing eyes. She had then recounted the story of a man in a train.

'This man, like any one of you when you go on a journey, he is getting on the train. And, like any one of you, he is putting his baggage on his head and he is standing there. Then, *weee*' – she gave a loud shriek – 'the train begin to move and the train go. Puff puff. Varoom. It go along. Fast, fast. But the man with the baggage on his head, he is not moving. He is standing still. And his baggage on his head is standing still. But this' – she bent voluminously forward, fixing a hawkish gaze on the rows of upturned faces – 'is *illusion*. He think he is standing still but *he is moving too*. He is travelling because the train is travelling. He and his baggage – they *go*.'

She leaned back and fanned herself while the audience clapped. Bruce said grumpily, 'Can't remember the last time I put any baggage on my head.'

Mother Prayana leaned forward again. Her heavy brows, with the red caste mark over them, drew together. She put up a dimpled hand. 'Like that man on the train with his baggage, we are all moving. But in what direction? And under what power? What is carrying us along? Shall we be getting off the train or shall we be staying on?'

Charlotte was a little hazy about what Mother Prayana had said then, except that it was poetic and uplifting and Bruce had dozed off. But she remembered the awed shudder that had passed through the audience when the guru announced that she was about to try to raise the Kundalini in each and every person in the room, if they would give her their undivided attention. The Kundalini, she explained, was the Hindu name for the snake of life-giving energy that lay coiled at the root of the spine and must be lured from its nest, coaxed to uncoil and ascend the spine, if enlightenment and The Prayana Path were to be attained.

The audience bowed its head and closed its eyes. The athletic twenty-year-olds put out the lights.

In the darkness, the voice of the Mother swooped and soared. 'Feel it, feel your Kundalini. It is stirring. It is unwinding. Feel it, feel it. Please keep your eyes closed. Think, think of the Kundalini. Now it is raising its head. Now, now, it is beginning, slowly, slowly, moving up the spine . . . up and up. Let it go. Give it passage. *Fee . . . el* it.'

Charlotte, eyes squeezed shut, buttocks numb, focused all her thoughts on the words of the Mother and willed her Kundalini to uncoil. The young men and women, their white tops iridescent in the dim light, trotted down each line of bent figures, urging the various Kundalinis upward with sweeping motions of their hands.

'No . . . ow!' Mother howled. 'Up comes the Kundalini! Up! Up!'

An ecstatic cry sounded somewhere in the room. A middle-aged woman in a crocheted hat in front of Charlotte leapt to her feet, writhing. A bearded man on her row stretched up his arms and shouted. Pretty soon, the place was seething with erect Kundalinis. 'Up! *Up!*' yelled Mother.

The miracle had happened for Charlotte just as she was beginning to fear that spiritual enlightenment was not for her. There was a buzz in the environs of her coccyx, a squirming in her bowels as of a large reptile shifting about, nosing out The Prayana Path, and then the reptile reared. An insubstantial but pervasive heat shot up her discs, bending her bowed body back until she sat as straight as an arrow in her chair and then was lifted to her feet, abuzz from her heels to her head while Mother smiled from the platform upon her and the audience clapped and all the lights came on. Charlotte's Kundalini had risen.

It had been a miraculous, life-enhancing moment marred only – as she sank to her chair again burnished with blushes – by the sight of Bruce crouched beside her, mulishly rejecting Mother's selfless help. But Mother was too big a woman to reject him. With a snap of the fingers she sent five white-topped ones scurrying to his spine, stroking away in an all-out attempt to awaken his comatose Kundalini. From the platform, the guru directed their efforts, screaming, 'Up! Let it *up!*' at Bruce's bald spot, beating the arms of her chair with big brown fists. But Bruce skulked among his scarves and would not let his Kundalini budge.

In the end, with all eyes upon him, Bruce had walked out and Charlotte had had to stumble after him, scarlet with embarrassment

24

but supported in her hour of need by the loving sympathy she saw on every face. As they went through the door, Mother Prayana's boom followed them.

'That man is an Unascended. He is having no Universal Aura.'

In the bus home she had reproached Bruce for not trying, not desiring enlightenment, but he had only shrugged and started reading the paperback in his pocket, *The Deployment of Personal Space in Public Buildings*. It was impossible not to feel very slightly superior, however hard she tried. Though her Kundalini had become quiescent again she knew it was there now, hide though it might, and the knowledge gave her strength.

And today, in the Headquarters of Small, Healthy and Wealthy Families, UK Division, her Kundalini had stirred again, roused from its hibernation by the altruism of Gordon Grant and his colleagues whose lives were dedicated to the alleviation of Third World suffering. There was a moral there somewhere. The West giving material aid to the East. The East, in exchange, offering its spiritual riches. Charlotte thought that a very beautiful transaction.

Gordon Grant came back into the room carrying a file. 'This is the lot,' he said, giving it to Charlotte. 'Thought I'd include the stuff that's been written by other independent observers about our work in Sulanasia. Some of it is more than kind. Cheers us up, that sort of thing. Makes us proud. Foolish, but there it is. We're all human, eh?' He looked Charlotte square in the eyes. 'I hope, we all hope, here at Small Healthy and Wealthy, that you will enjoy your time in Sulanasia and judge our work in your report . . . worthwhile.'

'I know I will,' said Charlotte, overcome by his humility.

'Good, good, fine, fine,' said Gordon Grant, ushering her out to the lift. 'Don't hesitate to call us if you need any more information.'

As she zoomed down to the damp reaches of Threadneedle Street and walked out on to the crowded pavements and a light rain, she realized that she had left behind her on the tenth floor a group of men who came near to being latter-day saints. And one of them had called her 'attractive'. It was petty to recall it and not true, of course. But how thoughtful, how typically thoughtful.

'Hullo,' Charlotte said.

'Hullo, Char,' said Bruce.

25

'How are you?'

'All right. You?'

'All right, thanks.'

'Sit down.'

'Thanks.'

'Tea?'

'Thanks.'

She looked round the familiar sitting room. They had never moved to the new development in Esher. Charlotte had not become pregnant again so there had been no need. Another more fertile couple had doubtless taken the Macanallys' place in the neo-Georgian terrace, to breathe the fresh air, chat of an evening on the patio, cook tuna fish casserole in the wall oven and put their babies to bed in rooms wallpapered with bunnies and lambs. Charlotte and Bruce had remained in the flat in Kentish Town; it was quite big enough for two. When they had agreed to separate, Bruce had bought out Charlotte's half and stayed on. It had been his bachelor flat, so it seemed only fair. Bruce was always fair.

He came in with a tray. It had a cloth embroidered with daisies on it and two flowered cups and there were two biscuits on two matching flowered plates. His bald patch seemed larger and the fringe of brown hair around it made him look more than usually like a clerkish sort of monk. He was wearing the beige Marks and Sparks cardie and the pair of brown slippers lined with tartan wool that Mrs Wren and Charlotte had given him, respectively, two Christmases ago. There was a silvery sheen on his forehead.

'You keep the place nice and tidy,' Charlotte said.

'Yes,' Bruce said.

It hadn't been nice and tidy during Charlotte's time. She had tried her best, shaking Flash across the kitchenette tiles, Brilloing the oven, putting Javex down the loo, but she hadn't the knack. For all her efforts, things spilled or got lost or broken. Plates chipped, food boiled over and burned into black scabs on the cooker. Against onslaughts of Vim, the refrigerator clung grimly to its sour smell. Bread turned green in the breadbin, the toaster threw crumbs everywhere and sometimes breathed flames, dripping taps made sepia stains round plugholes and cupboards regularly voided their contents at Charlotte when she tried to find things.

She had accepted her fate philosophically, she had become resigned to mess. Bruce hadn't. His distress at his wife's lack of housewifely talents became his most powerful emotion. When he saw the sink full of unwashed dishes or the bed unmade, he began to scratch himself and went on, despite Charlotte's remonstrations, until his skin was a blizzard of flakes. He never raised his voice or lost his temper but when he found a dollop of marge on a chair or the ketchup bottle beside the loo or one of Charlotte's Silk Cuts ground out in the scrambled egg pan, a pink outline of eagle's wings flared up on his cheeks and he ground his teeth in the night. The next day he would go to the office swathed in scarves, with his black beret pulled as far down on his scaly forehead as it could be while retaining some vision.

Charlotte took this to be the reason for their splitting up, though Bruce had not said so. He had only said, one Tuesday evening three months ago that he thought they should get a divorce.

'You what?' Charlotte had called from the kitchen, unable to hear him distinctly over the crackle of frying that was spattering the counter with a fresh layer of fat.

He appeared at the door holding a hot water bottle – he was having an early night. 'A divorce,' he said, 'or at any rate a separation. For the time being. See how it goes. We haven't any kiddies so there's no one to mind.' He tore some sheets from a roll of household paper and laid them on the counter to soak up the fat.

'I suppose not,' Charlotte said.

'Well, we'll talk about it. I'm going to get my head down now. Goodnight.'

'Goodnight.'

They had not talked about it. There was nothing to say, only papers to sign and a few financial matters to settle. While these were going on, Charlotte had begun to eat rather more than she usually did, getting up in the night to make herself a bread and jam sandwich or spoon down half a jar of lemon curd. Standing in the kitchen in her nightdress, with the neon light overhead making popping sounds in the silence, she looked through the rain-streaked window at the puddles on the flat roof outside where, once, she had planned to put garden chairs and tubs of geraniums and trailing lobelias, and felt a humid melancholia invade her, not for the coming separation so much as those years in which nothing had happened, nothing had been planted and taken root and grown.

Their marriage, like most, had held an initial promise of

excitement, sputtering hopefully for a bit as if about to take off, emitting the random spark. But it had remained earthbound. Since that first pregnancy, terminated on a hospital table, Charlotte had had no confidence that she would become pregnant again. Their couplings, hers and Bruce's, were always polite and sometimes comforting, like wearing old clothes, but they lacked lift-off and the attention of the participants often wandered. The charging of her inner batteries required, Charlotte felt, rather more enthusiasm, a higher input of energy, than either of them seemed able to muster. Her husband's embrace made her feel she was enfolded in the tentacles of an octopus past its prime: the moist suckers of his kisses lacked adhesion, they merely raised small patches of her skin and let them go again. Nor did it help to know that she herself was not a succulent morsel but a large white mound on the bed, too unwieldy, too bulky for entirely spontaneous penetration. Feeling unappetizing gave her, perversely, an appetite. She kept a store of Mars Bars concealed behind a book by her bedside table and ate one each time the act of intercourse short-circuited on her. The day she left Bruce, she walked down the road and gave her last two waisted garments to Oxfam. From now on she would be a nomad and live in tents.

She put her cup of tea back in its saucer and looked pleasantly at a point just east of Bruce's left ear. 'How's the psoriasis doing?' she asked, for psoriasis was Bruce's plague, the leprosy of the Bible that had turned the Old Testament warrior Naaman white as snow before being cured by Elijah. It was the loose scales on the surface of the skin that gave the silvery effect. Bruce shed skin everywhere on bad days; he left a luminous trail.

'Better,' he said. 'The hands are clear. The forehead isn't too good today.' He brushed a strand of hair aside and one or two flakes took to the air. 'How's your stomach?'

Charlotte gave him a full and frank account of the doings of this, her own bête noire. Many dramas took place therein. For a while she had been convinced it harboured a thicket of lethal growths and the two short months of her pregnancy stood out as an oasis of calm. Since then she had given up ideas of malignancy and come to terms with the fact that her stomach held the patent on her emotions. It was unromantic but there it was. Other women's bodies were free-range; their knees might weaken with love, their nipples harden with lust, their eyes moisten with compassion or flash with pride, fear could blench their skins, anger flare their nostrils, grief wring their hands. She only got stomach ache.

'And what about the wheeze?' asked Bruce, updated on the stomach front.

Charlotte told him. When she had finished, their eyes met. Charlotte smiled, Bruce gave her a significant blink. This sharing of their fleshly ills warmed them towards each other. She thought of telling him about a particularly tenacious wart on one big toe but restrained herself. There was more pressing information to impart.

'I'm going to Sulanasia, Saturday,' she said.

'Oh. Why?'

Charlotte did not invent a South-East Asian swain nor give the impression that she was off on a mad-cap whim. Feminine mystique was not in her gift. She said, 'I got a grant. Or, rather, the clinic got a grant from Small, Healthy and Wealthy Families and I was the only one who could go. I'm to be an independent witness of the birth control programme they fund out there. Write a report on it to go to the World Bank and the IMF and so on. People do it every year. It's a sort of spot check.'

She took a cigarette out of her handbag, lit it and dropped the match in the dregs of her tea.

Bruce scratched the back of one hand. 'Still smoking, I see.'

'I'm a bit nervous about going,' Charlotte confided, inhaling deeply, 'but Sulanasia will be interesting, don't you think?'

'Very,' Bruce said in a voice from which all interest had drained. He watched a cylinder of cigarette ash drop on a cushion and scratched the back of his other hand.

'They've given me a lot of background stuff to read.' For Bruce's sake she added, 'I'm not even sure where Sulanasia *is*.' She knew how much he liked looking things up, it was his favourite activity, though he seemed oddly unresponsive to her prompting today. She leaned towards him, scattering biscuit crumbs to the carpet. 'Is it on the Equator, Bruce?'

'Yes.'

She blew out a last gust of smoke, twisted the stub of her cigarette into a handy pot plant and walked across the crumbs to the bookshelves that lined one wall of the small sitting room. But he was ahead of her, standing with his back to the shelves before she got there. This was more like the old Bruce. She smiled at him. Poor man, the psoriasis wasn't really better, he had said that so she wouldn't worry. There were the eagle's wings spread over his cheekbones, clear as anything.

'I've got all my books sorted out since you left,' he said.

'So I see.'

'*Don't* . . .'

The atlas had slipped from her hands to fall heavily on the floor. She bent to pick it up but Bruce forestalled her. Some flakes floated from his forehead as he scooped the atlas into his arms. Tenderly, he laid it on the flap of a writing desk and turned its large pages.

'There's Sulanasia.'

Charlotte peered across his arm. The island lay like a green leaf on the deep blue of the Sula Sea, its edges indented with tiny inlets, its surface veined with hundreds of looped fingerprint lines.

'What are those?' asked Charlotte, poking a finger towards the page. Bruce's elbow blocked her. 'Mountains,' he said. 'Volcanic, mostly. That's Bolimarra. Erupted ten years ago, killed 36,000 people. Will you be thereabouts?'

'No.'

'Pity,' said Bruce. He described the majestic scenery of Bolimarra at some length.

'There's Banabalu, up at the top, the capital. That's where I'm off to first but only for a day or two. Then I go into the field.' She laughed uncertainly. 'Field. Sounds very English, doesn't it? Grass, cows, dandelions, daisies.'

'It won't be like that.'

'No.'

Bruce closed the atlas and put it back in the space it had occupied. 'Where will you be staying in this field?' he asked.

'To be honest, I don't really know. They'll arrange something. There's a man coming with me most of the way. An interpreter. A Mr Premben something. I can't get the hang of his name.' She attempted another laugh.

'He'll cost you something,' Bruce said, rubbing along his hairline. 'Are you getting expenses?'

'Will he?' said Charlotte, disconcerted. 'No, I'm sure not. He's an official of the Sulanasian Family Planning, the KNNA. Dear, now I'm worried. Money's so difficult in other countries. When do you pay, when do you tip . . .'

'All the time,' Bruce said, 'in my happily limited experience.'

'I've never been abroad alone,' said Charlotte. 'Isn't that ridiculous, at my age?' She nipped the top leaf of the pot plant, pressing her nails into its rubbery surface.

'Char,' Bruce protested, scraping his chin.

'Sorry.'

'Talking of expenses,' Bruce said after a pause, 'there's an electricity bill. For the quarter before you went. Could you give me your half?'

Charlotte wrote out a cheque and Bruce tucked it into his cardigan pocket. There didn't seem much else to say and Charlotte got up to put her coat on.

'Right,' said Bruce. 'Well, bon voyage.'

At the door, Charlotte turned. 'Mother thought I ought to tell you I was going. Because you're my next-of-kin.'

They stood far apart in the dark corridor.

'Fine,' said Bruce. The wings of his eagle were fading. 'Very sensible.' In the flat, a telephone began to ring. 'I'd better get that. Cheers, Char.'

'Cheers,' said Charlotte.

She pressed the time switch in the hall and started down the stairs. Then she heard Bruce call.

'Char?'

'Yes?'

'Be sure they take out insurance on you. Important.'

'I will,' she called back.

With a click, the light went out.

'I'm going to Sulanasia.'

'Nice,' said the girl behind the counter. She held up a string of blue beads to her neck and craned round Charlotte to see the effect in a long mirror. The girl was small and electrically blonde and her nails were painted black.

'Not for a holiday,' Charlotte said. 'To work.' She did not want the girl to think she was the sort of person who went to Sulanasia for fun. The girl hooked a pair of perspex ear-rings in her lobes and moved her electric head from side to side. Charlotte turned round, saw in the mirror her own dishevelled hair and worried eyes. No one would take her for the sort of person who went to Sulanasia, or anywhere else, for fun.

'Lots of cottons back there.' The girl waved vaguely behind her. 'Half price. We're closing down.'

It was the large banner across the shop window – 'Bankrupt Sale! Everything Must Go!' – that had brought Charlotte in from the rain. Summer clothes were hard to find in London in winter and, two days before take-off, she had begun to panic. Last summer's dresses, forlorn after their long sojourn under her bed, no longer encompassed the outcome of her post-Bruce snacking. Besides, they exposed a lot of bosom, unacceptable to Third World people and far too acceptable to Third World mosquitoes. Charlotte was allergic to mosquito bites. Once in Viareggio – and again in Florence – mosquitoes the size of buzzards had homed in from miles around to picnic on her flesh.

'They're everywhere,' Ursula at the clinic had said of her time in Thailand. 'The moment it's dark, they come in clouds. Incredible.'

Anxiously, Charlotte quizzed her on precautions but Ursula had only mumbled something about burning coils 'which gave me instant lung cancer' and gone her way. No one, it seemed, could be restrained for a moment from listing in picturesque detail every unpleasant, hazardous, embarrassing and potentially lethal aspect of long-distance travel but all grew curiously vague when it came to preventative hints and tips. There was clearly a sort of trial-by-fire you had to undergo before you were accepted into their company, like tarring and feathering people the first time they crossed the Equator.

Elspeth had added her tuppence-worth to Charlotte's unease. 'They're Moslems in Sulanasia, aren't they? Bad,' she had said and would have left it at that if Charlotte hadn't cornered her. Afterwards, she wished she hadn't. Elspeth's descriptions of being spat at and stoned, though not quite to death, in various Islamic strongholds were vivid and remorseless. 'You can't show your hair,' she warned Charlotte, 'nor your arms nor your feet. They're not keen on the bits in between, either.' Charlotte had felt a passing stab of sympathy with Moslems then. She wasn't keen on the bits in between, herself, though it was unsettling to discover whole nations in agreement with her. 'And don't', Elspeth had advised, 'wear shoes you can't get in and out of easily. Moslems won't let you wear shoes indoors.' As a parting shot she had added, 'Best to buy patterned material, it hides the sweat.'

32

The task of finding garments that were cool enough and patterned enough and also covered her from top to toe against lustful mosquitoes and modest Moslems, in January in London (but not in Harrods Cruisewear Department, due to the price) was a daunting one. Thus it was in some desperation that she collected three cotton jump-suits from the rails and crammed herself into a curtained cubicle to face another daunting task. Over the years, Charlotte had perfected the technique of undressing without exposing more than an absolute minimum of flesh. The strictest Order of Enclosed Nuns could teach her nothing of this skill, though the nuns' aim was to avoid lewd thoughts and Charlotte's to protect those few she had left. At bedtime, a nifty manoeuvre rid her of whatever garment she wore above her waist, whereupon she dived into an ample male nightshirt (mail order from a shop in Oxford) that was already arranged for easy access and provided cover for the peeling off of the skirt or trousers beneath. Her baths were taken in the greatest privacy, the door locked against matrimonial or any other intrusion, and were concluded in the shortest time conducive to hygiene. She soaped her limbs as dispassionately as a fishmonger sluicing his slabs of an evening or a sailor swabbing his decks.

Even so, the glimpses she could not avoid of her large thighs or the promontory of her stomach mightily depressed her, so that washing was an effort of will not to be undertaken lightly. To the best of her knowledge, Bruce had never seen her completely naked in the six years of their married life. Nor had he ever indicated, during that time, that he found this an unsatisfactory state of affairs. The permissive society had come and was now receding without a ripple eddying the Macanally way.

Charlotte managed to divest herself of the necessary clothing in the confined space of the changing box and array herself in one of the jump-suits. It fitted. It more than fitted. It bagged from neck to ankle while being marvellously evasive about what lay in between. True, it made her look a little like a sheep but not a bad-looking sheep; woolly-bodied, yet with delicate extremities, a slim neck, a startled face and quite nice eyes.

'You all right in there?' the girl shouted.

Charlotte took a last glance at herself and thought, sadly, that the only role in which her disadvantages would seem perfectly accept-able was the one she would never now get: that of an expectant mother.

She bought all three garments, in rust, light green and turquoise. The bill came to £30, a bargain.

'Have a good time wherever,' the girl said, filing her black nails.
'Thanks,' Charlotte said.

On Friday, the day before her departure, she called in at the clinic to collect some hotel discount vouchers that Pat had ordered for her to use in Banabalu. She felt disembodied, as if she were already far away, but nobody noticed her ethereal state. Ursula, Jean, Elspeth, Isabel and Pat were all there, drinking their morning mugs of coffee and exchanging the usual client gossip before counselling began. A Ms Bishurst played the starring role today.

'She said she was dead scared of getting pregnant after the last time,' Ursula said, 'and wanted someone to check her cap. So I got Jean in and she feels about a bit, inside, and can't find anything. After a while, La Bishurst says I didn't put it up there, I put it up *here* – and she pats her bum. Her boyfriend likes it that way, it turns out. And can you believe it, she's stuck the cap up her anus?' Ursula rolled her eyes in amazement at the ignorance of the Bishursts of this world. 'Well, you know what the sphincter muscles are like. She'll have to have an operation to get it out. Wicked.'

Everyone laughed. Sotto voce, Charlotte thanked her stars that whatever sex with Bruce had entailed of discomfort, embarrassment and disappointment, he had never demanded any one of the eccentric sexual practices Miss Cotterstock's clients took for granted. She had a brief mental vision of the mechanics of anal intercourse and abruptly censored the treacherous thought that Bruce's erection might not have been sufficiently (and here she hovered over various adjectives and picked the most obvious) *erect* to travel that particular by-road. The unfairness of this struck her immediately and she added to her mental picture certain punitive details concerning the size of her own buttocks, for balance.

'By the way,' Elspeth said to Charlotte, 'there's someone in the waiting room who asked for you. I told her you wouldn't be in but she's still there.'

It was Mrs Waterman, beiger than before. She clutched her zebra around her and sidled with Charlotte through the door of the nearest cubicle. On the threshold she said with some truculence, 'I want you to get me an abortion.'

34

Caught off guard, Charlotte gave an unprofessional squawk of disappointment. Mrs Waterman said tartly she thought that was Charlotte's job, to get people abortions.

'Not necessarily,' said Charlotte. Then she said, 'I mean, if that's what a client genuinely wants. But I thought you . . . what happened?'

Mrs Waterman stuck her hands in the pockets of her coat and stared out of the window at the grimy chimneys of Clerkenwell. 'I don't want it. That's what's happened.'

'But you did. Only a week ago. What made you change your mind?'

'I opened my eyes, that's what.' She turned on Charlotte. 'I reckon you should have opened them for me.'

Charlotte sat down on a dwarf chair, for once leaving the client to loom over her. 'I thought . . .'

'You thought, I thought.' Mrs Waterman was almost hissing. 'But Trevor didn't. I wasn't going to tell him but he was that cocky it got on my tits. So I said the kid wasn't his and he give me this.' She jabbed a finger at one eye, where a dull yellow halo was discernible. 'He said I'd better get rid of it quick or I could bugger off and I was dead lucky he was giving me the choice because most men wouldn't. So that's that.'

Charlotte said, 'You couldn't manage by yourself?'

'No, I bleeding well couldn't.' Mrs Waterman's voice rose. 'I've got no training and there's no jobs. Tell you what, though, I could do yours. How much do they pay you?'

'Have you a family who might help you out?'

The sandy mouth opened on a loud cackle. 'My mum booted me out when I was sixteen. Haven't seen her since, the old slag.'

'We could try to get you temporary housing and with the allowances and . . .'

'Temporary housing. Don't make me laugh. If you think I'm going to sit in some pigsty eating cold baked beans and watching my belly blow up you've got another think coming.'

'Could you have another talk with your husband? He might come round.'

'Yeah. With a brickbat.'

'No chance of contacting the . . . father?'

Mrs Waterman made an unpleasant bubbling noise in the back of her throat. 'How do I do that? Phone up Navy headquarters and say you've got a sailor called Kev on one of your ships and he's put me in the club so send me his wage packet from now on? Do me a favour.'

'Look, Mrs Waterman, we . . .'

'Never mind look Mrs Waterman. *You* look. I want an abortion and I want it now. It's legal. It's my right.'

'Very well,' said Charlotte. She had to make an unusual effort to sound amiable. 'I'll get the appointments book.'

She went into Pat's office where the comings and goings at the hospital in Redhill were logged. The room was empty. She looked at the clock on the desk. There were so many last-minute things to do and at this rate it would be noon before she got home. She picked up the book and a leather picture frame near it fell over. She propped the frame in position again and stared at the photograph it contained, a coloured snap of Pat's son, spotty and solemn in a black gown and a mortar board perched skew-whiff on his head. He was married now, to a fellow graduate, they'd just had their first child, a boy they'd called Patrick, after Granny, Pat had told her, trying not to look pleased. Back in the cubicle, Charlotte said, 'Mrs Waterman . . .' and stopped. Persuasion, either for or against the continuation of a client's pregnancy, was strictly forbidden. The decision had to be made by the woman herself. The counsellor was only a sounding board for her client's feelings, allowed an occasional facilitating word but no more. Charlotte thought of Ernestine Cotterstock, campaigner for prevention but never for the sort of cure that had happened to Charlotte in that Denmark Hill Gynae Ward.

'I could do any day next week,' said Mrs Waterman.

Charlotte scraped her chair closer to her client's. Their knees touched.

'I shouldn't say this,' she whispered (could Pat Wilshaw be listening, huddled over earphones like a spy in the War?), 'but I had an abortion once and I can't tell you how much I regret it.'

Mrs Waterman's sandy lashes blinked. 'You mean, it wasn't your husband's?'

'Oh yes. Yes, it was.'

'Well then.'

'But the point is, what I'm trying to say. I wish I hadn't.' Acid fizzed in Charlotte's throat. 'I mean, I'm going away tomorrow, apart from anything else, and I might crash or get some horrible disease abroad and die. And who would care, Mrs Waterman? Who would care?'

'We go to Yarmouth,' said Mrs Waterman. 'Buy British, Trevor says.'

'It's terrible not to have anyone. A child of your own. You know, to pass on things.'

'I got no things,' Mrs Waterman said.

'But a *baby*,' pleaded Charlotte. 'A baby's something you've got, it goes on. It's life. You've passed on life. The torch. The flame.'

'Yes, well,' Mrs Waterman said, glancing uneasily at her watch.

Charlotte edged to the front of her chair and clasped her client's chapped hands. 'Give it a few more days, Mrs Waterman. Don't say no to life. Where there's a will there's always a way. You can win over any odds, if you have the courage. Give life a chance, Mrs Waterman.'

Overburdened by this last burst of eloquence the chair creaked ominously. Charlotte struggled to her feet, determined to carry on the crusade, and gazed down at the carrier of life. Passionately she said, 'You have a *choice*, Mrs Waterman.'

Mrs Waterman's eye in its yellow nimbus looked back. 'No I don't, love. But ta, all the same.'

Defeated, Charlotte reached for the appointments book. Mrs Waterman said, 'So you're going away, are you?'

'Yes. To Sulanasia.'

'Holiday, is it?'

'No. I'm going to study the birth control programme there. How about Tuesday the 4th?'

'That'll do nicely,' Mrs Waterman said. She picked up her bag. 'Good thing they're doing something to keep the blackies down. Ta ra.'

When Charlotte came downstairs she found Mrs Wren already up, standing in her dressing-gown at the kitchen window with one eye applied to a hole in the blind.

'That policeman's been there for the last ten minutes,' she announced. 'Mumbling into a little box. If those people next door had their wits about them, like Uncle Arthur, they'd give him something to do. That garden of theirs is a disgrace.'

'Hush, mother, he'll hear you.' Charlotte opened the fridge and poured herself a glass of orange juice. Her eyes were dry with lack of sleep. She wore the rust cotton jump suit under her poncho, blue woollen socks and slip-on sandals. Beside her stood a strapped suitcase on wheels and a bulging red nylon rucksack.

'He sent your Aunt Helen away for a holiday. To a very nice hotel your father and I used to stay in near Torbay. He had a bad knee and his strawberry plants were running amok. Charlotte, are you listening to me?'

The battery clock on the wall gave a dull rasp. It was coming up to a quarter to seven. 'Yes, mother,' Charlotte said.

'The neighbours talked. At the end of two weeks the police had dug over his whole garden for him. Then Aunt Helen came back. He won the dahlia award at the Royal Horticultural Show the next year. You should have seen those dahlias, Charlotte, they were . . .'

'I'd better be off,' Charlotte said. She bent and heaved up the rucksack, buckling the webbing round her.

Mrs Wren turned round. 'At this hour?' She peered in her daughter's direction. 'Where are you going?'

'To Sulanasia, mother.'

'It's *today*, is it?' Mrs Wren said with interest. 'Have you packed a bird book? I believe they have wonderful birds in that part of the world.'

In the hall, Charlotte bent and kissed her mother's soft cheek. 'Take care of yourself, ma. I'll send you a telegram when I've arrived.'

'I had a hat once, with feathers on it. Blue and green,' said Mrs Wren, watching her daughter struggle sideways out of the front door. 'Of course, they don't allow that sort of thing now.'

Walking backwards, Charlotte waved. 'Goodbye. Goodbye, ma.'

She bumped her suitcase over the cracked paving stones. An old black woman trundled past her, carrying a brown plastic bag, and then two black girls, at a run, the beads in their tiny plaits clicking. Ahead, some dustmen crossed and recrossed the road, chucking their loads into the roaring maw of a rubbish truck. At the underground a black man in an upright coffin glanced at her ticket. She got herself and her suitcase on to the escalator and shook with cold as the wind whipped up from its subterranean lair.

'Sulanasia, here I come,' she hummed to the empty stairs. It sounded like a dirge.

At Heathrow, she heaved her suitcase on to the runnels of the conveyor belt and thankfully watched it bounce away. Then she found a seat outside the departure lounge, wedged her rucksack between her knees and immediately became so engrossed in the farewell dramas taking place around her that the crackling of the loudspeaker only caught her attention after its third plea for Mrs Charlotte Macanally to come to the Messages Desk.

'It's Pat, ' said the tinny voice in the receiver. 'Tried to get you at home but you'd gone. They phoned up from SHWF and said you're being met at the other end by a Miss Gina Millichip of Global Family Funding. Got that?'

'Millichip,' repeated Charlotte.

'And, Charlotte, this is important. They said to tell you you're not her baby. She's taken you over *at very short notice* from someone else. So they said would you be extremely nice to her. Thank her a lot, make her feel good. Okay?'

'Okay.'

'Well, that's it. Are you all right?'

'Yes, thanks, Pat.' The rucksack belt was cutting painfully into her middle.

'The Third World's just the place for you at the moment. It'll take you out of yourself. The way things are there, your own worries will . . .'

A noisy band of youths clattered past. Charlotte pressed her ear to the receiver. 'My worries will *what*?'

'Fly away. Vanish,' Pat said. 'Must go. Via con Dios.'

Charlotte put the phone down, pulled out a notebook and wrote, 'Millichip, GFF. Make feel good.' She underlined the last three words, stuffed the notebook back in her pocket, heaved up her rucksack and trudged in the direction of Departures.

As she went, she thought how kind Pat was to be concerned with her welfare. It seemed possible, however, that the Third World might have more pressing priorities than helping one fat white woman snap out of a mild depression.

Part Two

'This is the bit I don't like,' said the girl at Charlotte's elbow in the compressed accents of South Africa.

In truth, this was the only bit Charlotte liked; the rush along the runway, the plane bunching up beneath her as if she were on the back of a stallion before it soared over Beecher's Brook. The usual pre-take-off tension was pulverized out of existence the moment the plane began to pick up speed. Some piece of elastic attached to her guts stretched to breaking point and then, as the wheels left the ground, snapped and set her free, rocketing into the sky, cut off from all connection with the world below, that shrunken world of toytown cars and houses and roads of no possible interest to the winged daughter of the gods that was herself; part woman, part bird. As the Boeing 747 levelled off and exhilaration faded, Charlotte recalled that a woman who was part bird was called a harpy.

The girl was called Bep – Charlotte never discovered her full name. But as the hours passed, she discovered everything else. Bep had come to England sixteen months ago to have a look at the Old Country, though why this chip off an Afrikaner block considered England her old country was not clear. She had settled at Earl's Court in a flat with a nomadic population of Australians, New Zealanders and Rhodesians; Bep confided that she couldn't get her tongue round *Zimbabwe* and the way she pronounced it made Charlotte feel this was just as well. Once installed, she had kicked up her heels at disco after disco, night after night, knocking back the booze – Bep was inordinately proud (without much cause, as it turned out) of her ability to knock back the booze.

Then, one night, she had done something so far out of her normal character that despite the excuse of drunkenness it remained, to Bep and Charlotte both, inexplicable. She had danced with a black man ('I don't know what *kind*,' she said in answer to Charlotte's question, 'just some kaffir') and in the small hours had gone home with him to his bed-sit and slept with him. She had become pregnant. Ignorant or unwilling to acknowledge her condition and search out such as the Cotterstock clinic, she had continued to dance ferociously every evening, hoping, when she thought about it at all, that sheer physical exertion would shake loose the foetus in which she could not bring herself to believe.

But the foetus proved tenacious. It dug itself into that healthy South African womb and hung on for dear life, blind to the hostile vibrations of its hostess, unaware that it was an alien transplant that ought, by all the laws of Afrikanerdom, to be rejected. Nine months later, it emerged on to a table in the Princess Beatrice Hospital, Fulham, SW10, with a howl of triumph and two tiny fists clenched in the Black Power salute.

'He was quite cute,' Bep allowed. 'I called him Piet. P.I.E.T.' Cute or not, the question of his mother keeping him did not arise. 'Mop and Pop would have died,' said Bep, giving a lively imitation of cardiac arrest. So Piet had been put up for adoption and his mother had had to cool her heels – 'Christ, it was boring' – until the many papers were signed that would sever her for good from baby Piet. In the second month of that three-month wait, Bep had met a suitably white and well set-up Australian and was on her way to meet his family and marry him. She flashed a diamond ring at Charlotte, symbol of happy endings.

Charlotte, bemused by this example of youthful savoir-faire, and with her stomach showing signs of a more Whitehousian reaction, congratulated Bep and drank two straight Scotches. Her insides sufficiently quelled, she ventured to ask if it had been very difficult for Bep to leave little Piet.

'Not really,' Bep said indistinctly through the two gold combs she held in her teeth. She was brushing her cropped corn-coloured hair while squinting into a mirror clamped between her knees. She stuck the combs back in place and added, 'Murray says he likes my hair this way, short. I don't know. I could sit on it when I met him. What do you reckon?' Murray was the Australian fiancé.

'Does Murray know about Piet?'

Bep gave Charlotte an incredulous sideways glance. 'Are you kidding? Nobody knows. Except the hospital people and you.'

'You couldn't . . . I mean, your parents . . . they wouldn't . . .?'

'Piet's *black*,' said Bep and shook her head, amused at Charlotte's evident inability to grasp the ways of the world.

A stewardess, lipsticked to match the red in the red, white and blue of her uniform, stopped her trolley beside them. 'Tomato salad?' she asked Bep.

'I'm game.'

'No thanks,' Charlotte said. She sat back, then, and watched Bep munch her way through the contents of the plastic tray, awed by the girl's strong even teeth, her muscular neck, her swimmer's shoulders and her silky hair that concealed, Charlotte imagined, a mind as round and rubbery and full of bounce as a tennis ball. Hundreds of miles behind and below, a small dark infant lay in a crib, abandoned forever by big young Bep now heading for a new life where her summers would be her son's winters, his nights her days. Soon his adopted parents would claim him and he would start a new life, too, never to know this mother who had already forgotten his father.

'I wonder if they'll call him Piet?' Charlotte mused.

Bep opened her mouth and pushed in a huge spoonful of peaches and cream. 'Naa,' she said. 'That was just my name for him. Oh, wow, you should try these peaches. They're all right.'

The clouds outside the window made a flat solid floor for the bowl of blue sky. Charlotte pressed her nose against the glass. She was the last repository for that little splinter of a name: Piet. Soon, perhaps, the only person in the world who would remember it. Her eyes crossed as she stared out and imagined meeting the child one day, years ahead, a tall graceful honey-tinted lad with a lost look in his face. She would take his hand and say, gently, 'Your name was Piet', and the lost look would disappear. And then, helped by Charlotte, he would insert advertisements in the Australian press. 'Piet is looking for his mother, Bep. Married to Murray. Please write'. Bep, an Australian housewife, those muscles gone to fat, with four more children and something unfulfilled about the eyes, would read the advertisement in her kitchen in the Outback – wherever that was – and the tears would come. That evening, under the glow of a paraffin lamp the ageing Bep would pen a letter and later

45

wait with a thumping heart in some airport – Sydney, Adelaide – until a tall dusky young man appeared from Arrivals. 'Mother!' he would cry, and 'Piet!' Bep would gasp, and they would enfold each other in a tearful but happy embrace. Reunited after a lifetime of regrets, they would heap blessings on her name. Dear Charlotte. *Aunt* Charlotte. Then Piet would go on to win the Nobel Prize.

At this juncture, Bep slapped her tray up, fixed it in place and gave Charlotte's arm a dig.

'What d'you say to that steward, eh? Nice hunk of he-man, isn't he? Wouldn't mind joining the mile-high club with him.'

'The mile-high club?'

Bep went into peals of innocent laughter. Her diamond ring winked merrily.

Shortly afterwards, with the aid of the whiskies and a Nitrozapam, Charlotte entered a kind of limbo that closely resembled her stay, five years ago, in the hospital on Denmark Hill. Efficient females came and went and occasionally stopped beside her, their mouths moving soundlessly. Piped music rose and fell, trays appeared and disappeared, trolleys rumbled up and down. A man on the wall who looked like Charlton Heston whipped two horses and a chariot into a silent frenzy. A blanket was tucked round her knees, a pillow wedged behind one ear. She dozed. At some point, prodded into half-consciousness by an arm prickling with pins and needles, a commanding voice urged her to alter her watch. Dutifully, she fiddled and little hands twirled. Bep's seat was empty – she must have gone to enrol in that club. Charlotte dreamed of an illuminated parchment unrolled by monks to the sound of angels singing and Bep, her corn-silk hair alight, scribbling a curly signature across it with a quill pen: Bep Vagina. Again, she rose from sleep to see dimmed lights above her and a cobweb of sequins far below through the misted glass of the window and Bep beside her, snoring musically close to her ear. Dazed, Charlotte peered in the semi-darkness at the incomprehensible face of her watch.

'How old is it now, in England?' she muttered at Bep and the girl's lids lifted for a second over glazed unseeing orbs and dropped again and Charlotte, after a vast yawn, joined her again in oblivion.

The next time her senses returned, cliffs of sand reared to the far horizon, their slopes pink with dawn. The plane landed and the doors swung open on a warm dry desert morning. Charlotte stood in the entrance with her face raised to the mild sun while men with scarves wrapped round their heads pushed silver containers in and out and heaped up rubbish into grey bags. There was no sign anywhere of a town or houses or even a road.

'Where am I?' she asked a supervising steward. 'I mean, where are we?'

'Muscat, madam.'

When the plane took off, Charlotte squeezed herself into the minuscule lavatory and was immediately confronted with the major drawback to her new cotton overalls. They had to be unbuttoned, struggled out of and rolled right down to the ankles before she was free to relieve herself. In that confined space, it was a task not unworthy of Houdini. Outside, the queue of passengers grew, their attention diverted from their own needs by the dull bumps and muffled groans within. Eyes met and withdrew hastily. A motherly woman in a pair of bedroom slippers prised her child away from a crack in the door and put her hand quickly over his opening mouth. When Charlotte finally emerged, cheeks flaming, no one looked at her and for some minutes no one took her place.

The day wore on. Meals became increasingly ambiguous, compounded of pineapple wedges and pressed ham and other ingredients that gave nothing away of time or of place. Bep stared into the middle distance, headphones clamped to her ears. Charlotte stared at a graph headed 'Number of Mobile Teams and Type of Vehicles Used in KNNA+Foreign Aid Clinics in Sulanasia.' Towards what was possibly afternoon, a great forest spread out below with rusty rivers lying upon it like the branches of fallen trees. Here and there at its edges a blue sea scalloped inwards to white sand and clusters of tiny brown huts.

'Look at that,' said Bep, craning across Charlotte. 'Wouldn't mind a dip in there. Some people have all the luck.'

Charlotte peered down at the Garden of Eden. 'Scenery's not everything,' she said. 'They could be starving in those villages.'

'What? With all those coconuts and bananas and things? Not them.'

The sea sparkled, the sun was glorious, the white sands shone. 'Malnourishment', said Charlotte, 'is not just a question of food. They could be deficient in vital proteins. Vitamins and so on.'

'They've got fish,' said Bep. 'More fish than you've had hot dinners.'

'It's an interesting fact,' Charlotte replied, 'and little known, that during the Irish potato famine millions of people died with fish all round them because fishing wasn't a part of their cultural experience. For all we know, those people down there may not . . .'

'Fishing boats,' said Bep, pointing.

Three black splinters tacked across an inch-wide bay, leaving white threads in their wake.

'Well,' said Charlotte, 'I certainly hope so.' She was not sure why she was so determined that Bep should see misery where none, apparently, existed. What a wet blanket she was.

'Typical of the Irish, that,' Bep said. 'Fancy not knowing how to fish. Have you heard the one about Paddy and the . . .'

It was getting warmer. Charlotte bent over and pulled off her socks. Leaning heavily against her shoulder like a friendly puppy, Bep shook with mirth.

'That's one of Murray's,' she chuckled. 'Man, what a sense of humour.'

As Charlotte was coming to terms with the fact that the pilot had overshot the edge of the world and would shortly land them all back at Heathrow, the plane began its descent over the Lego-packed peninsula of Singapore. In the cool vaults of the airport, full of plants and waterfalls, Bep – now clad in a remarkably short dress that exposed every inch of her good solid legs – receded from Charlotte on a moving pavement, waving absently, her mind already on Perth and humorous Murray. Charlotte, wilted and creased, beating at herself in panic over the whereabouts of passport, tickets, baggage checks and wallet, lugged her rucksack to a waiting room signposted 'Banabalu', where people of every race and variation of attire were gazing at a television screen upon which a man in a stetson was declaring that he was the toughest cowboy in town.

And then she was on the last half-hour's haul, in a smaller, shabbier plane whose hull enclosed drier, staler air. She sat zombie-like, too tired to care.

'Last year, we was in Nepal,' said the Frenchwoman in the next seat. 'There we buy amethyst and turquoise. *Very* sheep.' Her husband nodded across his wife in confirmation.

48

'In Sulanasia, also sheep. We buy there too.'

Charlotte, with a great effort, summoned up her meagre French vocabulary. '*Vraiment*,' she said.

'We have shop in Lyon,' the husband explained. 'We find many things in Sulanasia. Nice things, for *nothing*, 200 ratahs, maybe three. We make beeg profit. Then we can go next year to another place.' He smiled delightedly at Charlotte and patted his wife's hand.

'*Bon*,' said Charlotte.

'What you buy in Sulanasia?' asked the wife.

'Nothing,' said Charlotte. Then, afraid this might imply a critical attitude to French consumerism, added, 'I like, you know, to see the sights.'

'Why not?' the Frenchwoman said kindly. 'In Nepal we see a sight also. They have goddess there, a leetle girl. She is goddess until she has, how you say it? *Les règles*.'

'Periods,' Charlotte whispered.

'*Ah oui*. The periods,' the Frenchman said loudly. 'Then, she is finished. She cannot be goddess with the periods. Also she is very fat, too much good food. So she will not marry because no man can . . .' and he made a rubbing motion with his fingers.

'Afford her?' Charlotte said.

'*C'est exact*. She must live alone, bleeding, no husband, no children. It's very sad.'

'Very,' said Charlotte, trying not to brood on this melancholy fate.

'You are also alone?' asked the Frenchman. His wife cocked her head at Charlotte.

Fat, bleeding, husbandless, childless. 'No,' Charlotte said, 'I am with my husband.'

'*Alors*, where is he?'

Reckless with exhaustion, Charlotte said 'There.' She pointed up the aisle a goodish way. 'The man in . . . in that blue jacket.'

As she spoke, the man in the blue jacket rose, turned and began walking down the aisle towards her. The French couple monitored his approach with interest while Charlotte's jaw sagged. When he reached the row in front of her, she managed a smirk of the sort that might encourage friendly response from a stranger. It was of no avail.

'He is *très fatigué*,' Charlotte explained to the Frenchman. 'He is walking in his sleep.' She laughed brightly.

'*Ah oui*,' said the Frenchman without conviction.

Charlotte sought refuge from further encounters with Blue Jacket by pretending to fall asleep. Within a minute, the pretence had become reality and she awoke only as the plane was taxi-ing towards what appeared to be the flank of an ocean liner grounded among a grove of palms. The row of giant neon hieroglyphics across its top deck made a word so long that the letters toppled over at either end.

'Banabalu?' she said rather wildly, afraid that, like a passenger dozing on a bus, she had come too far and was in China. The Frenchman, on his feet now, reassured her.

'The name is of the airport,' he said, 'but I have not enough time to pronounce it.'

'*Non*,' said Charlotte. She wrestled her rucksack from beneath her feet and dug in her pockets to find her notebook. 'Millichip,' she mumbled as she shuffled to the door. 'Make feel good.' She felt terrible.

Though dusk was falling as the passengers trekked to the airport building, it had made no impact on the heat of the air. Already damp under breasts and arms, Charlotte forged through the hot soup in the wake of the French couple, determined not to lose sight of the only familiar figures in this alien sea.

'I'm being met by someone,' she panted at their rear. 'With a car. You could come with me into the city if you liked.'

'*Merci, Madame.*'

Upon which, Charlotte made her entry into Lilliput. At one moment she was a relatively average-sized woman, give or take the odd stone. At the next she was Gulliver's twin sister, a giantess of whale-like proportions around whose massive bulk schools of dark minnows swarmed, darting at her and receding in waves as she lumbered to the luggage bay. There, having retrieved a suitcase that had had several hundredweight of lead inserted into it since leaving London, she saw from her new vantage point above the seething multitudes another white face. The face began to swim towards her.

Watching its progress, Charlotte was immediately aware of the contrast between herself and it, a contrast that was to become ever more painfully obvious as time went on. Miss Millichip, for it was she, had a small shingled head and features so compact as occasionally to fade into invisibility before Charlotte's eyes. Her skin looked as if clothes pegs nipped it in at the back, taking up all unnecessary slack and, mysteriously, she seemed to advance within a capsule of frozen air that kept at bay the sticky heat that engulfed Charlotte. The pale green permanent pleats of her frock were as crisp as lettuce in an ice-box, and so little did she need to make concessions to the climate that her slim shanks were encased in stockings and her feet in shells of polished kid without a single vent.

'Mrs Macanally,' said the ice-box, consulting a clipboard.

'That's me. Hullo,' said Charlotte, smiling and nodding.

Miss Millichip neither smiled nor nodded. She extended two dry fingers into the air and clicked them. A shrimp of a boy with a thatch of black hair darted to her side and took hold of Charlotte's suitcase. His little muscles bulged.

'Oh dear,' Charlotte said to Miss Millichip. 'Are you sure he can . . .?'

'Follow me,' said Miss Millichip in clipped Bostonian.

As she turned away, Charlotte put a sweaty hand on that cool flesh. 'These are, er, friends of mine,' she said, indicating the Frenchman and his wife who stood at a polite distance. 'Could they come with us in the car? They need to get into Banabalu and I thought, if it was all right with you, that . . .'

Miss Millichip's trim lashes quivered and the faintest sigh escaped her lips. 'Certainly,' she said.

In the long air-conditioned limousine whose plush boot was now defaced with hitch-hiker luggage, Charlotte carried out her instructions. 'It was very good of you to meet me,' she said. 'I know how busy you must be.'

'Busy,' repeated Miss Millichip in the tones of one long used to absurd underestimation of effort. She rattled something at the driver and sat back in her seat, placing the clipboard on her pleated knee. The car zigzagged through shoals of bicyclers, little battered buses and large battered trucks and began to pick up speed as it reached the unlit highway. The French couple sat quiet as mice in the back.

Once they were on an even keel, Charlotte tried again. 'Do you have to meet visitors often?' she said. 'It must be difficult, fitting everything in.'

Miss Millichip ran two satin nails along the pleats of her dress. 'The point is,' she said, favouring Charlotte with a pinched smile, '*you* are not *my* responsibility. You belong to Irma. Irma Schultz?'

'Of course,' and Charlotte nodded to indicate that Irma Schultz was almost a household name in England. 'And you've kindly taken her place.'

Mollified by Charlotte's response, Miss Millichip became confiding. 'Two days ago,' she said. 'Just two days, and Irma Schultz suddenly announces she cannot cope and goes off to Sumino. Leaving this mug to take over as if I weren't up to my ears in work already.'

Charlotte tutted at the Schultz dereliction of duty.

'I said to Mr Sinoto, look, how do you expect me to manage? Some Englishwoman flies in at a moment's notice and I'm supposed to drop everything, cancel all my own appointments, turn up at the airport in the middle of the night and have ready a complete itinerary, meetings, bookings, all that, for this unknown person. I mean, *I* don't know what she wants to see. I mean, is it *fair*?'

'Absolutely not,' said Charlotte warmly. 'Most unfair.'

'It's not easy, you know,' Miss Millichip continued, tapping fretfully at her clipboard. 'How am I to guess what this person has in mind, coming out of the blue like this? They should know at SHWF how impossible it is to organize anything in this . . . place.' She waved a dainty hand at the rushing dark outside. 'And last-minute ministerial approaches lead so easily to *offence*. One has to be so careful.'

'Of *course* one does,' said Charlotte, indignant at the unexpected burden imposed on poor Miss Millichip. 'I can't *imagine* how this Englishwo . . .' She closed her eyes, feeling dizzy.

'We've had such a rush at the office lately, what with one thing and another. Yet they expect me to get heaven knows *what* sort of person the entrée to *everywhere*. Well, I told them. I said to them, "I'm sorry. If I can't do it, I can't do it. I'm *very* sorry."'

A lit-up Lucky Strike sign loomed over the car and vanished. On either side, high white buildings flashed past, their unfinished upper storeys poking steel rods at the dark sky as if alone God could deliver the necessary bricks and cement to finish the job. Piles of rusty earth lined the edges of the road while John Deare tractors butted at them under sulphurous lights. In the dim back seat of the car, the French couple whispered in French.

'It's too bad,' said Charlotte.

'You can say that again,' said Miss Millichip. She was sitting bolt upright now, crackly with energy, while Charlotte felt the life drain from her body. Miss Millichip's minuscule features blurred into a pale but animated disc. With an heroic effort, she managed to keep her eyelids more or less apart for the remaining eons of the drive, nodding occasionally as an accompaniment to the ceaseless Millichip lament. She longed more than anything in the world to stretch her bludgeoned body flat though it seemed increasingly unlikely that her bones, locked into an arthritic hunch, would ever straighten out again.

All at once, the car rocked to a halt. Charlotte, squinting out at what looked like a concrete hangar, thought for one dreadful moment that Miss Millichip had decided to dump the villainous Irma's burden back at the airport again.

'The Sulanasia Plaza,' Miss Millichip announced, and yawned.

Charlotte and the French couple disembarked in a scuffle of ornamental porters. Miss Millichip wound down a window.

'You will find,' she said, 'my extension number at Global Family Funding in your pigeonhole. Despite all obstacles, I have prepared a programme for you. Heaven knows how I did it. I will be in the lobby at eight am sharp on Monday. Driver? Home.'

Bedraggled and stained with particles of long-forgotten food, Charlotte watched the limousine glide away and peered at her French companions. 'Can you find your way from here?'

'*Si si,*' the Frenchman said, his face hidden behind a large map.

'Our hotel is near,' said his wife. 'Many thanks, Madame, for the car. *Merci, merci.*'

They shook hands and Charlotte stood as they walked down the slope that led to the street. As they turned the corner she called after them. 'Monsieur. Madame.'

The couple halted.

'That man in the plane. He was not my husband. *Il n'était pas mon mari.*'

'I am glad,' the voice of the Frenchman called back, 'because you leave him at the airport, *le pauvre.*'

Charlotte awoke. Above her head the air-conditioning hummed, across the room no light penetrated the thick brown folds of curtains and on the bedside table her travelling clock stood in sullen silence, its hands flung hopelessly apart at a quarter to three. She wondered what her mother was doing on the other side of the earth and was slightly cheered to realize that if her mother had been in the room with her, she would be wondering the same.

Except for a few tender points along her spine and some lumps of kapok stuffed into her skull, it was impossible to believe that she had come so far. The room gave no clue to its provenance, it could exist as well in Torquay or Paris as in this far east city of Banabalu. Carpets muffled sound, machines controlled climate. The tailored twin beds were simply twin beds, the bathroom – with a lavatory whose pedestal leaked water – was a bathroom anywhere. A television set stared morosely at her from a corner, there was an armchair, a table, a chest of drawers, a niche of sliding cupboards, two parchment-shaded lamps and a radio in the bedtable that emitted the muzak of the West. Only the notepaper, tucked into a leather case in a drawer, gave the game away with its engraved heading 'Hotel Sulanasia Plaza, Highway 6, Banabalu'. If it had not said that, Charlotte thought, if it had said 'Hotel Peking Plaza' or 'The Cross and Keys, Orpington', a crucial vein might have burst in her brain, leaving her forever a vegetable in some corner of a foreign field.

It was while she was preoccupied with this tragic fate that she came across a notice tucked in with the notepaper and stood for a moment, breathing heavily. The silent room was not as silent as it seemed. Indeed, though undetectable to human ears, it was ticking away frenziedly, gulping up dollars with every tick. In her particular room, that appeared to be sixty dollars a day, without breakfast, and Small, Healthy and Wealthy Families had given her exactly 1,000 dollars in travellers' cheques which would only last her, if she stayed Plaza-bound, about a fortnight without so much as a wet teabag for sustenance, or the shortest trip beyond its doors.

Moving at some speed, she emptied the contents of her suitcase across the bed, yanked out another cotton garment as creased as the last, but clean, made herself look as intercontinental as she could with the aid of a broken comb and a tube of Lypsyl, rooted out the hotel discount vouchers Pat Wilshaw had given her and headed for the lift.

It turned out to be seven o'clock in the morning, and the man at the reception desk had the heavy-lidded look of a night creature disturbed in its burrow.

'Ah yes,' he said, patting Charlotte's vouchers, 'we give you discount already. Of course, of course.'

54

'So I won't be paying sixty dollars a day?'

'Of course, of course,' he said. A well-manicured hand screened a yawn.

Charlotte tried again, speaking very clearly. 'Could you tell me how much discount I will get?'

The clerk ran his fingers up and down somewhere behind the desk. 'Thirteen per cent,' he said. 'Very good discount.'

'So I will pay sixty dollars a day minus 13 per cent?'

'My-nus?' He was halfway down his burrow again.

'Less,' Charlotte said. '*Away*. Sixty dollars and take *away*' – she yanked her hands apart as if she were extracting them from melting toffee – 'off, 13 per cent.'

The man stuck his index finger in the air and smiled brilliantly. 'Ah. I understand. But is not right. Sixty dollar a day *already* discount. Yes.'

'But,' Charlotte said, pushing hair out of her eyes, 'in my room it was printed. On card. Sixty dollars. Not discount.' Her English was fraying under the strain.

The clerk blinked sleepily, teetering back and forth on his fingertips. 'Very nice card,' he said, 'very good printing. Sixty dollar. You can see it fine.'

Tensely, Charlotte waited beside the counter until the clerk had found keys for three grey-haired Dutchmen holding burnished briefcases and a large Australian who clawed his way out of camera straps like a bear caught in a hunter's net. When they had gone, she edged up to the clerk again.

'Room 25,' she said. 'Just to inform you, I must check out tonight.'

The clerk looked hard at the bottom of his tie. Then he picked up a card. 'Room 25. Mrs Macally?'

'Yes.'

'You stay four nights,' he said agreeably. 'Maybe six.'

'No, no, no, no.' Charlotte shook her head. 'Tonight, I go.'

'Not possible,' the clerk said. 'Look. Here, you see? Minister for Internal Affairs. Is all here. You stay.'

The card he extended for her to see had a gold stamp on the top in the shape of a dyspeptic bird of prey, a lot of typing in Sulanasian and a mimeographed signature scrawled across the whole. It could say anything, Charlotte thought, and probably did.

She sighed helplessly at the clerk and sat down in the marble

55

lobby. The great glass doors a hundred yards away slid smoothly back and forth to the purposeful entry and departure of early-risen white and black and brown men and a few heel-tapping women. The effect was as muted and polished and well-rehearsed as the opening scene of a disaster movie.

She got up and walked over to the doors, which obediently parted to let her through. The air outside was already milky with heat and traffic fumes. At the end of the ramp where the cars turned in she could see a line of ramshackle barrows selling some kind of food. The men who stood around them wore flapping shorts and had legs like sticks of bamboo. She could not summon up the nerve to go over to them and point and scrabble with unknown coins, wordless, foolish.

She remembered a story of Ursula's; of how Ursula had bought a snakeskin belt in a bazaar in Cairo and afterwards walked to the Hilton for a swim in the pool. Later, sipping a drink, she had taken the belt out of its bag and an American matron, blue-rinsed, gold-bangled, had leant over to admire it. 'Where d'you get that, honey?' she'd asked and when Ursula had told her 'in the bazaar' she had sighed and shaken her marcelled head as if Ursula had said she had been on a shopping trip to Mars. It turned out that the American woman had spent the last three months in Cairo with her husband, an oil man, and had never, in all that time, left the Hilton premises. 'Can you *imagine*,' Ursula had said. Shamefully, Charlotte could, and that was no way to be. Miss Millichip would fix everything tomorrow, Miss Millichip would get her out of this place and off to the field. Meanwhile, she had a whole day before her in a luxury hotel and that could not be bad.

It was not bad. She ate her way through many shapes of noodle and three drinks crammed with fruit and midget umbrellas. She wandered by the bright blue waters of the pool – swimming, for one of her size, was out of the question – and was startled to see that some form of apartheid held sway: all the long white people lay sprawled out at one end and all the short brown people sat in deckchairs at the other. She had written a comment in her notebook upon this distasteful fact before she understood that the sun was a poolside ingredient required only by the whites. The antics of a pop-eyed lizard occupied her for a while as it darted among the gleaming tiles. Then she watched a skinny cat lying stretched in the heat like some woman's discarded neckpiece. Then she went up to her room, rubbed Anthisan on two suspicious bumps, twiddled unsuccessfully with the knobs of the television, took a shower and rubbed more Anthisan on the bumps that were now clearly insect bites. Eventually, after reading one more of Gordon Grant's files on The Projection of Sulanasian Female Population Marriage Percentage 15–44 in 1985 (with illustrative graphs), writing in her notebook about the noodles, the lizard, the cat and the clerk and wondering whether, if she were a man, she would by now have explored the whole of Banabalu, made several lifelong friends and be sitting with them getting uproariously drunk in some crowded nightspot, she realized, to her relief, that the day could be considered, without too much exaggeration, over. She repacked most of her suitcase, put on her nightdress, set her alarm clock, lay down on the bed and shut her eyes.

Five minutes later, the man whom Charlotte might have been if she had been a man, returned from the nightspot to the room next to hers. He had brought with him every one of his new lifelong friends, who were all uproariously drunk.

Miss Gina Millichip leaned with one elbow on the leatherette back of a lobby sofa. Her knees were together and her legs tapered sideways. She wore a white shirtwaister with short sleeves and a square pocket over her heart, out of which peeped a dark blue chiffon kerchief that echoed the dark blue of her high-heeled shoes. There was about her the sportive chic of the more exclusive mail-order catalogues. She angled her wrist and eyed a slim gold watch.

'I'm sorry, I'm *so* sorry,' panted Charlotte, who had the sportive chic of a tent in a Force 8 gale. 'There was a party in the room next to mine and it went on to all hours and I had to take two sleeping pills and my alarm clock didn't go off or, if it did, I didn't . . .'

But Miss Millichip was already clicking away over the marble floor to where, at the steps, the doorman stood holding the open door of a long car. She jack-knifed in and arranged herself tidily at the right-hand corner. Behind her, Charlotte bumped her head on the door frame as she heaved herself inside.

'It might have been better to wear a dress,' Miss Millichip said, surveying Charlotte's jumpsuit and sandals. She snapped open a pochette and patted her matt nose with pressed powder.

Charlotte felt her palms dampen. 'I'm sorry,' she said again. 'I wasn't . . . I didn't . . . I thought . . .'

'Government officials are very formal here.'

Dismally, Charlotte said, 'I didn't expect to meet any Government officials. I imagined I'd go straight from Banabalu to the countryside.'

Miss Millichip's laughter tinkled like ice cubes. 'Heavens,' she said, holding delicately on to a strap as the car bounced over potholes into the flow of traffic on an immensely wide highway. 'Whatever gave you that idea? No foreigner can go straight into the countryside in Sulanasia. Permits must be obtained, permissions granted, itineraries checked. Visitors must meet all the relevant Governmental bodies, the Ministers and so on. It would be considered extremely discourteous not to make yourself known in these quarters. Extremely.'

A tasselled and bedizened bus drew alongside the car, each porthole window framing grinning faces and waving hands. Charlotte could manage no more than a lopsided smile back. Her stomach, unoccupied by anything more demanding than a glucose sweet for breakfast, was registering its underemployment in low gurgles, though it offered no competition to the cacophony of hoots and squealing brakes outside. She sucked herself in and squared her shoulders. Miss Millichip did not strike her as the sort of person you could easily have things out with but she would have to try.

'The thing is,' she said, 'I can't stay in Banabalu. I've only got three weeks altogether in Sulanasia and I have to report on the birth control programme in the field. I'm sure the officials here are most interesting and I don't at all wish to give offence but I really think I must be on the train tonight to . . . Tungban, is it?'

'Mr Jenja Zakir, whom we're off to see now,' said Miss Millichip, 'is the Chairman of KNNA. He runs the Sulanasian programme. An admirable man and a very busy one.'

'And I haven't enough money to stay at the Plaza, anyway. It costs rather a lot, you see, and I'll run out if . . .'

Miss Millichip held a paper in front of Charlotte. 'This is a copy of the letter I wrote to Mr Zakir, requesting an interview for you. Perhaps you would read it.'

Charlotte read. The letter was couched in language so obsequious that it seemed impossible to have emanated from the brisk Miss M. Mr Zakir was severally implored, beseeched and begged for the favour of a few minutes of his time on Miss Millichip's guest's behalf, who would go in sorrow to her grave should this blessing be withheld. God Himself, Charlotte considered, would have had to bestir Himself on her account, had Miss Millichip sought an audience in the same terms. The letter went on to describe her (under the pseudonym 'Miss Carylot Manaly') as 'the Founder and Director of the widely influential and internationally renowned United Kingdom organization, the Cotterstuck Truss'.

'Oh dear,' said Charlotte. She turned anxiously to Miss Millichip. 'I'm not a director, you know. I'm just one of the counsellors. And the Cotterstock Trust is very small. Most people have never heard of us.'

Two wine-red nails tweaked the paper out of Charlotte's hands and replaced it with another. 'And this,' said Miss Millichip, 'is the letter you wrote thanking Mr Zakir for granting an interview.'

This time, all three Ls in her name had been jettisoned in the rush to express Miss Charotte Macanay's gratitude for a fleeting moment in Mr Zakir's presence. The letter ended with enough sentiments of obedience, devotion and fealty as to make Charlotte fear she was agreeing to enter the Zakir seraglio.

'Sign, please,' Miss Millichip said, extending a pen.

Charlotte signed.

The car drew up under a large tree in a courtyard and Miss Millichip got out. Charlotte struggled after her and stood plucking the damp cotton fabric away from her posterior. A waft of marvellous sweetness assailed her nostrils and she looked up. The green branches above her were incandescent with creamy flowers, each bloom a bouquet in itself. She breathed in deeply and exhaled with a groan of pleasure. 'How lovely they are,' she remarked to Miss Millichip. 'What are they called?'

'Come along,' said Miss M. 'We're running late.'

By the time Miss Millichip and Charlotte arrived at the door of Mr Zakir's office they had acquired a fantail of interested bureaucrats, all of whose hands had been thoroughly shaken by both women in the course of their progress through the KNNA building. Introductions in Sulanasia clearly contained a bonding ingredient unknown in Western corridors of power which, thought Charlotte, was rather jolly, though it involved a certain strain on the facial muscles. She noticed that Miss Millichip had put on a smile the instant she had stepped over the KNNA threshold and it was still on her face, steady, unflinching and perfectly adapted to talking Sulanasian through, which she did with awesome fluency. Charlotte had tried to say 'How do you do' in Sulanasian when the opportunity presented itself, but the word had many syllables and she had not yet managed to enunciate more than three before Miss Millichip swept her on.

Mr Zakir's abode consisted of a large outer room in which three women sat at typewriters and an inner sanctum that was larger and furnished, in defiance of the heat, with as many cosy layers of padding and upholstery and rug upon rug as could reasonably be stuffed into one room. The furnishings splendidly ignored the proportions of the average Sulanasian. At one end of the chamber a desk of Brobdingnagian bulk took up most of both corners, bearing on its glassy surface a vast leather blotter and several rock-size crystal objects that served as desk tidies, though there seemed very little to tidy. On the wall behind the desk hung two enormous gold-framed photographs of fat and faded men, each wearing the rounded black hat of Islam.

'The President,' whispered Miss Millichip through her smile, 'and his Deputy. We must sit down.'

They sat, along with their three most adhesive male escorts, on gold velvet sofas that made Charlotte feel like Thumbelina. Ahead of her, under three floor-to-ceiling windows, stood a table some 8 feet long surrounded by majestic mahogany chairs and along each wall were high glass-fronted cabinets, within which gleamed row upon row of gold cups and trophies, gold plates and gold-framed snaps of many men and women smiling. By the sofa, closer at hand, a carved table displayed tastefully fanned-out copies of a KNNA publication upon whose front covers Sulanasian women and Sulanasian infants beamed as joyously as their peers on the SHWF magazines in faraway Threadneedle Street.

Charlotte thought it all most impressive and looked around her with interest for some time. The wooden blades of the fans on the ceiling gyrated in the humid air. A woman came in and backed out again. The heat increased. Charlotte sat. Miss Millichip sat. The three Sulanasian men sat. Whenever they caught Charlotte's eye, they smiled so actively that their toes left the ground. After a while, cheeks aching, Charlotte kept her eyes on her hands in what she hoped was a modest but attentive pose and wished she had taken Elspeth's advice about sweat and patterned materials.

The same woman returned, this time carrying a tray of glasses filled with an amber fluid which she laid on the mahogany table. Charlotte raised her eyebrows at Miss Millichip, indicating a desire to drink. Miss Millichip's eyebrows drew forbiddingly together.

Silence fell again, broken only by hoots on the street outside and the rhythmic thump of the fans above. Charlotte sat as still as she could since every movement, however isometric, produced eruptions of sweat from parts of her body that had not, until now, owned up to possessing sweat glands. Admiration swelled in her for brave Alec Guiness on his River Kwai bridge, with his beaded, suffering brow, his wan but gallant face. What wonderful men.

There was a swift patter of footsteps, the door opened, crashing against the wall, and Mr Jenja Zakir erupted into the room. Though short of stature, he made up for it in exuberance. His arms flailed, his eyes behind the gold-rimmed specs shone with merriment, his moustache wriggled like a live thing on his lips. Miss Millichip shot to her feet, only to bow her head so low that Charlotte feared for her balance.

'Ah. Yes. So. Ah,' said Mr Zakir in machine-gun bursts. He shook everyone's hands vigorously while managing to rub his own hands together between every handshake as if to keep up his supply of personal magnetism. He wore a short-sleeved safari suit with an open-necked batik shirt beneath that gave him the air of a military man on a short furlough between battles. As he shook the last hand, another woman entered, set down plates of cellophane-wrapped snacks beside the rapidly cooling beakers of tea and ducked out backwards.

'Good, good, good, good,' barked Mr Zakir. 'Sit, sit, sit, sit.'
Everyone sat.

Miss Millichip then explained, at great length and with many graceful gestures, the purpose of Charlotte's visit to Sulanasia, frequently including Charlotte in her gestures as if she might have forgotten why she was there. Charlotte listened attentively, in case she had.

'. . . like many others, Mrs Macanally has heard of the great success of the KNNA in implementing and consolidating the birth control programme here, for which success you, sir, are to be congratulated.'

61

Mr Zakir nodded his head, beaming.

'. . . very aware of the ceaseless demands on your time and she is therefore most grateful that you have been so good as to put aside your valuable work for however short a period in order to give Mrs Macanally the benefit of your unique knowledge and experience in this field . . .'

Miss Millichip inclined her head at Charlotte. Mr Zakir regarded her alertly.

'*Extremely* grateful,' said Charlotte.

Everyone smiled and nodded at each other, pleased with the extremes of Charlotte's gratitude.

'Good. Good. Good. Good,' said Mr Zakir happily.

'And now,' said Miss Millichip, inclining her head at Charlotte, as at a child required to recite a poem, 'Mr Zakir will kindly answer your questions.'

Charlotte jumped. She had put herself into low gear, expecting a long speech from Mr Zakir, and was unprepared to interrogate him, particularly since Gordon Grant's briefings and his ample files of reading matter had already made her confident that she could, at a pinch, have reported every detail of the Sulanasian birth control programme without ever leaving NW5. She tried to think of some question left unanswered, some data still a trifle obscure, and could not. But five pairs of eyes were fixed on her and she did her duty.

'I wonder,' she said to Mr Zakir, 'if you could kindly tell me what circumstances led to the formation of the KNNA?'

The Chairman raised both hands and slapped them down on his well-pressed knees. 'Aha,' he said. 'Aha, aha.' The three camp followers leapt to their feet. One shot out of the room, another pulled out an immense drawer in a cabinet and the third magically produced four files from his hitherto empty hands.

'Now,' said Mr Zakir to Charlotte, 'you would like to take notes.' Instantly, a large white pad and two sharpened pencils appeared before her. He waited until Charlotte had taken them up.

'Good, good, good, good,' he said. He rose and began to pace the room, talking as he went. Within half a minute, Charlotte recognized the contents of the first entry in Gordon Grant's pamphlet 'Basic Information on Population and Family Planning in Sulanasia'. Mr Zakir, she noted, was very nearly word perfect. Perhaps he had written them in the first place.

'The National Population and Family Planning Programme in

Sulanasia,' recited Mr Zakir, 'is now entering its twelfth year and has reached new acceptors to the total of eight million active participants.' He arrived at the end of the room and turned, under the photograph of his President, to regard Charlotte. 'Eight million,' he repeated.

Dutifully, Charlotte scribbled.

'. . . after twelve years it is important to systematically compile all information about the operations that have been' – here, he paused considerately but not for long – 'carried out in order to document where the programme has been and to provide . . .'

Charlotte scribbled some more. Turning over a third page, she said to Miss Millichip under her breath, 'I know all this.'

Intent on Mr Zakir, Miss Millichip gave no sign of having heard.

'. . . Sulanasia, as a developing country, is facing the same problems as most developing nations . . .' intoned Mr Zakir, treading carefully down the centre of a red Afghan rug '. . . based on the population census of 1961, 1971 and 1980, Sulanasia's population was, respectively . . .'

Charlotte's hand begun to curve into a stiff hook.

'. . . in the year 2000, the population of Sulanasia will become three times the size of the population of 1961 . . .' inexorably recited the Chairman. He had reached the other end of the room and swivelled on his heels to peer at Charlotte, who had dropped her pencil and was massaging those ligaments that had gone into spasm. 'I will wait,' he said kindly.

He waited. The cramps eased. Charlotte took up her pencil again. Mr Zakir resumed his recitation.

One of the ceiling fans, not as conscientous as Charlotte, gave an agonized squeal and stopped. The temperature in the room doubled. The three KNNA officials, their files beside them, relaxed upon the gold moquette cushions, their eyes fixed on Charlotte's writing hand. Mr Zakir's step grew springier and with every step his fluency increased. Statistics poured from him, interwoven here and there with acronyms of increasing length and complexity. As the drama of his message gripped him, his voice took on an ever more compelling resonance.

'In the Outlines of State Policy brackets RDNP brackets Number 4 of the MAP TLP 1978 it is stated that . . .'

This, Charlotte thought, the pencil slipping in her wet fingers, is what hell may be like. A Dralon-upholstered oven wherein the sinner must forever copy down that which she knows by heart already without even the hope of gaining temporary relief by scribbling nonsense since Beelzebub's watchful handpersons would instantly detect the subterfuge. Charlotte could imagine them now, the three men and Miss Millichip, springing up in shrill denunciation: 'She scrawls mere poppycock, oh Satanic One! She has omitted all detail of Enclosure LVIII stroke 3, oh Lord of Sulanasian Flies . . .'

Suddenly, the voice of the Chairman halted in mid-flow. Charlotte arched her aching back and gazed upwards.

'So very sorry,' said Mr Zakir. He pulled back a cuff, scrutinized a large gold watch and fell back in amazement at the winged passage of Father Time. 'Now I have more appointments. Too busy. Busy, busy. Please excuse.'

Miss Millichip and the three Messieurs Recamier leapt up. Charlotte dragged herself to her feet. Miss Millichip offered up a collective prayer of thanks for the existence of Jenja Zakir, in which Charlotte joined, her broken hand hanging inert by her side. With a flourish of farewell, the chairman vanished through the open door, to be replaced by four underlings who took photographs of Charlotte with her hair pasted to her forehead and spread out several visitors' books in front of her, politely requesting written comments upon her audience. 'A most constructive meeting,' Charlotte wrote three times, the words drawn by sheer will-power from her injured mitt. The underlings snapped the books shut, picked up the glasses of tea and the plates of snacks and vanished.

'A wonderful man,' said Miss Millichip to the three followers, gathering her clipboard to her meagre bosom.

'Yes, yes, oh yes,' agreed the followers.

She tapped off down the corridor with Charlotte at her rear. As they reached the lobby, a door to one side opened and Charlotte saw, within, the figure of Mr Zakir reclining at full length on a sofa. As she watched, he reached out to a tray by his side and popped a snack into his mouth.

Outside in the parking lot, the sun had turned the air from simmering consommé to a thick brew of diesel fumes at full boil. Cars stood everywhere, their black rooves blazing, while their drivers squatted under the inadequate shade of the odd palm tree. Miss Millichip dodged expertly round the blistering bonnets until she found her own. It was empty.

'Oh *no*,' she said. 'He's too bad, that man. I told him to wait and he's gone to get his breakfast.'

Among her various twinges, Charlotte felt an extra and respectful one for any man who dared to put his breakfast before Miss Millichip.

'I shall have to do something about him. I cannot be left waiting about like this. It is most inconvenient.'

Charlotte attempted a sympathetic cluck but gave up, being out of spit. They stood together under the white sun, Miss Millichip erect and alert, Charlotte doing her best to keep her balance on feet that seemed to have become lumps of melting wax. To banish this worrying impression, she stuck one out. The straps of her sandal strained over a lump of melting wax; all normal indentations at the ankle bones had gone AWOL. She ran a hand beneath the hair on her neck and held the damp locks out for a second, waiting for a breeze. No breeze came.

'Gina,' she said, driven by heat to an unauthorized familiarity, 'I think it would be best to postpone any further meetings until after I get back from the countryside.'

'Postpone?' said Miss Millichip, giving each syllable its full value.

'You see, I already know the sort of . . . *documented* part of the programme. But once I've seen it in action, I'll have questions to ask on my return. Informed questions. Do you see what I mean?'

'Where is that man?' Miss Millichip's eyes raked the parking lot.

'Whereas now I am very much afraid that I'm . . .'

Darting forward, Miss Millichip exclaimed '*There* he is.'

'. . . wasting other people's valuable time,' explained Charlotte earnestly to a palm tree.

The driver, catching sight of Miss Millichip as he rounded the corner of the building, broke into a sprint, reached the car and wrenched open the door. Miss Millichip was not appeased. She assailed him with a barrage of Sulanasian though her expression, Charlotte observed, remained as cool as if she had left her face in the fridge. The driver, too, stood expressionless as the bullets whistled round him. He looked old and dented but not at all remorseful, merely closed, like a house with its shutters up for a storm. As Charlotte followed Miss Millichip into the car, she gave the man a small smile. The smile said 'we are not all so unsympathetic'. The driver's face stayed closed.

'As I was saying, aah, ooh,' said Charlotte, gasping as her bottom touched the molten seat, 'I don't want to waste people's time when they're all so busy.'

Miss Millichip uttered a sound like a broken concertina. 'I'm the one who's busy.'

'Your time,' added Charlotte, pressing the unexpected advantage. 'I don't want to waste *your* time.'

'Everyone else does. Why not you?' responded Miss Millichip and rapped on the window.

The car pulled away from its parking place with a banshee screech, causing one of the driver's colleagues to wrap himself lovingly round the trunk of a coconut tree. Pressed backwards into her scalding seat, Charlotte gave up all thoughts of the future in a concentrated attempt to survive the present. For the next eight minutes, she clung on to whatever of solidity presented itself as the car hurtled through a termite's nest of alleys and eventually, skidding sideways like a hard-pressed crab, reached the fast lane of a motorway. At the first traffic light Charlotte offered a shaking cigarette to the daemon of the wheel. She was aware of Miss Millichip's disapproving frown but it held no comparable imperative. The driver accepted her sacrificial offering and the car calmed down, chugging quite decorously onwards in a pall of diesel smoke that put to shame the old-fashioned London particular. At the edges of the smog phantom figures with scarved heads and faces featureless under gauze masks hung grimly on to road drills like so many Mr Rochesters embracing mad wives while, among the banks and ditches of red earth, the John Deares see-sawed aimlessly about. Somewhere out there, Charlotte thought, was the East in all its tropical splendour. But not here.

In a while, the car left the highway and began bouncing down unmade-up lanes between bungalows whose roofs were barely visible above the palisades topped with barbed wire that surrounded each one. It was hard to imagine what these suburban dwellings could contain to justify such Fort Knox security.

Asked this question, Miss Millichip shrugged. 'Trouble,' she said. 'There's always some trouble here.' She pointed ahead to where an ugly concrete block rose incongruously among the bungalows, its facade blackened, its gates charred. 'The Antanda Department Store. A bomb, last month.'

'A bomb? Who?'

Miss Millichip bugged her eyes in a meaningful way at the driver and Charlotte gaped, her own eyes bulging. Surely they were not being chauffeured by a man who, in off-duty hours, chucked bombs about? And, if so, was it not foolhardy of Miss Millichip to employ him and positively reckless to chastize him?

'The driver?' said Charlotte, employing only her breath and winced as Miss Millichip, apparently bent on suicide, jabbed her finger under the terrorist's nose.

'Upul,' she said to him. 'In there.'

The car slowed down between spiked gates and halted at a sentry box. Miss Millichip flattened a card against the window and the car was waved on.

'The headquarters of the Kartikis,' Miss Millichip said. 'Here,' and she handed Charlotte a large blue booklet upon whose cover two ultra-feminine hands cupped a sphere within which were drawn a tank, a fighter plane with guns artistically blazing, a cross-hatched battleship and a jumble of other weaponry. 'The Kartikis', she explained 'are a Sulanasian-wide organization of women in the armed forces. We've given them very short notice of this meeting so please let them know you are grateful.'

'But...' said Charlotte and said no more, since Miss Millichip was already halfway out of the car and obviously had no intention of providing details as to why her English visitor had been driven by an urban guerilla to meet a squad of female soldiers. Perhaps this was what was meant by the inscrutable East. She scrambled out after Miss Millichip but not before giving the driver something between a bob and a curtsey to show she was on his side. Whatever it was. The driver stared blankly at his feet.

Charlotte liked being with women better than men, on the whole. For one thing, they seemed to like being with her, whereas men tended to be noticeably less eager for her company. For another thing, women didn't have the disturbing effect on her internal organs that men did. If Miss Millichip had been male, Charlotte knew she would already have had recourse to her Ventolin and her Rennies. As it was, her chest and her stomach had behaved themselves rather well, all things considered, and though Miss Millichip could not as yet be described as a friend, she felt sure that intimacy was growing, if only of the bickering variety that occurred between sisters or women who had been at school together and hadn't much liked each other then or later. She accepted that Miss Millichip regarded her as a nuisance since, looked at from Miss Millichip's point of view, she *was* a nuisance. Occasionally, in

London, Charlotte had been required to shepherd about and generally inform foreign women visiting the Cotterstock Trust and though she had always carried out these duties to the best of her ability – and enjoyed them, if the truth were told – she could quite see that someone of a more volatile temperament than her own and weighed down with graver responsibilities, might find it a trial. And there was the heat, of course. Always the heat. That would more than account for the trace of fractiousness in Miss Millichip's dealings with her. It was important to remember, when Miss Millichip's voice took on a certain edge, that she was a female Gordon Grant, deeply involved in the great fight against famine and poverty that he had so movingly described. She was probably paid a pittance and went home, at the end of a long hard day, to a stuffy bed-sit where she tossed sleeplessly most of the night being stung by mosquitoes.

That others might consider this picture of Gina Millichip slightly at variance with the crisp limousine-accoutred person now tapping down corridor after corridor of the Kartiki building did not deter Charlotte. People could be less than kind, particularly about efficient and successful women who devoted themselves to helping others. They failed to see, as Charlotte did, the effort and even the moments of heartbreak that lay behind the efficient facade, that facade she herself found impossible to maintain and which constituted one of the reasons why she could only help a few people on a very small scale while Miss Millichip was able to benefit whole nations with her enterprise and knowledge.

Having settled the Millichip matter, Charlotte turned her mind to the Kartikis who were awaiting her. Admittedly, Miss Millichip's description of them as women of the armed forces had taken her aback. She considered her own sex to be naturally unaggressive, gentle, life-loving individuals far removed from the male domain of armaments, wars and the military, and though an occasional woman – Pat Wilshaw, say, in one of her moods, or Mrs Thatcher in most of hers – showed signs of refusing to conform to the general pattern, these few were neither here nor there and were not in the least comparable to, for instance, Hitler, whatever Ursula might say. Moreover, Charlotte reminded herself, beginning to pant with the effort of keeping White Rabbit Millichip in sight, this belief had its provenance in the comfortable West. The women of Sulanasia might well have to face, alongside their menfolk, a variety of alarums and

68

excursions the very idea of which would freeze the marrow in her bones. Here Charlotte was briefly side-tracked by the extreme desirability of having frozen bone marrows but forced her thoughts back to the subject in hand. It was not clear to her exactly what these alarums might concern – the phrase 'marauding tribes' suggested itself and was instantly censored as a colonial throwback. However, everyone knew that newly emerging nations like Sulanasia had many enemies intent on destabilizing them, and though she could afford a vague sort of pacifism due to her affluent background, Sulanasian women probably had no such choice. Therefore, if all the Kartikis were in full battle dress and armed to the gills with every weapon known to man, she would keep an open mind and remember that Judy O'Grady and the Colonel's Lady were sisters under the skin.

Thus conscientiously prepared, Charlotte was even more taken aback when Miss Millichip opened a door upon an aviary of cooing birds. The Women of the Armed Forces were a dozen or so dove-like matrons, their tresses drawn back in elegant chignons, their plump curves enclosed in the traditional Sulanasian dress – a heavily embroidered long-sleeved bodice and an ankle-length sarong so clinging that its occupant was hard put to walk, let alone execute any nimbler military manoeuvre.

They clustered around Charlotte, murmuring their welcome, their eyes milky, their plum-red mouths smiling. Quite overcome, Charlotte bowed deeply to right and to left, her hand engulfing the delicate brown fingers laid therein. Rather late, she noticed that her nails were crescented with grey and thereafter held her fingers in a masonic crook in her palm. She felt like a chunk of pumice among precious stones and was touched that these women had gone to so much trouble – their make-up alone was a work of art – in order to receive a damp and unimportant stranger. She could not for the life of her see the staff of the Cotterstock Trust thus arraying themselves for a Sulanasian visitor. Elspeth would not be prised out of her jeans if the Queen came to call and Ursula's wardrobe was such that any down-and-out with half a heart would have started a collection for her.

The lullaby of greetings over, Charlotte was led to a table the size of a small football pitch while the Kartikis, with many courteous after-you gestures to one another, took their perches opposite her. As they twittered away, she glanced nervously around and the glance did nothing to reassure her. The room had clearly been purpose-built for speech-making. It contained no other furniture than the table and chairs, it was lined with soundproof tiles, there was a lectern equipped with a microphone, and loudspeaker grids were set here and there in the walls. Perhaps this was the Control Room where the Armed Forcettes were briefed before battle, with a map laid out on the table and rakes to move counters about, as in *Battle of Britain* starring Richard Todd.

Into these ruminations the modulated voice of Miss Millichip intruded, offering Charlotte's gratitude, a sentiment that was received with gracious applause. The Kartikis smiled sweetly at Charlotte and Charlotte smiled back.

There was a pause. The cold steel of Miss Millichip's elbow pierced Charlotte's ribs.

'I would be most interested,' Charlotte said hastily, 'to hear of some of the activities with which your organization concerns itself.'

After a small flurry of consultation, a heavily powdered Kartiki of mature years – possibly a General, Charlotte thought – took her place at the microphone. As she cleared her throat and composed herself, Charlotte sat back, anticipating an interlude of open-eyed snoozing. However interesting it might turn out to be, this meeting could do without manual coverage. Neither Pat Wilshaw, a Greenham Camp follower, nor Gordon Grant, who must certainly be CND if not a full-blown pacifist, would require a report on what Sulanasia's enlisted females did when not on active service.

'You would like to take notes?'

It was the Kartiki Chairwoman who spoke, bending towards Charlotte.

'No,' said Charlotte, 'thank you. I have a very good memory.' She tapped her temple several times to show the Kartikis that her grey cells could take anything they cared to hand out.

'I think,' the Chairwoman said with maternal solicitude, 'it is better you take notes.'

A grim sensation of déjà vu enveloped Charlotte as she observed the entry, as if by ESP, of a secretary bearing paper and pencils.

'And now,' said the Chairwoman, 'Madame Sanari, please begin. But' – and she dimpled charmingly – 'do not go too fast or our poor Madame Macanally will be so-o . . . tired.' There was a ripple of amusement round the table as Charlotte closed her stiff fingers round the pencil. Are we sitting comfortably, she asked herself. Then let us begin.

Madame Sanari began. She continued. She continued to continue and she continued some more. As she showed signs of ceasing to continue and verged on the beginning of an ending, a bespectacled Kartiki with a martial bun edged up behind her and, like a runner in a relay race, caught up Madame Sanari's last words as they dropped from her lips and bore them triumphantly onward into the next lap until she, too, was relieved.

This marathon event imparted an attractive flush to the cheeks of each participant and an orgasmic glaze to their pretty eyes as they fondled, while they talked, the priapic microphone. Meanwhile, from Charlotte's beet-red face, large drops of perspiration fell to irrigate her scrawls. She made one bid for freedom with a surreptitious flash of her watch at Miss Millichip but the Chairwoman forestalled her with an encouraging 'We have *plenty* time' before settling cosily back in her chair again. An escape from Colditz must have been, Charlotte thought enviously, a piece of cake compared to Fort Kartiki from which no prisoner returned.

But at last even the Kartikis seemed to be running out of steam. No one edged up to the eighth woman at the microphone. Refreshments appeared. Seizing what might be her only opportunity to see the outside world again, Charlotte stood up and made a farewell speech that outdid by some lengths Miss Millichip's tribute to Mr Zakir. Her final peroration, she felt in all humility, would not have shamed Mr Churchill in his finest hour.

The Kartikis' applause was warm, warm enough to spur her into reaching out a hand towards a glass of tea. At that moment, the Chairwoman rapped lightly but authoritatively upon the table.

'Before we part,' she said, smiling at Charlotte and removing the glass of tea, 'I would like to give you a message for the women of the West, our sisters. We send them our greeting through you, dear Madame Macanally.' She raised a pair of perfectly plucked eyebrows. 'Please, you are ready?'

The sun was in retreat and all the young men of Banabalu were out on their motorbikes to chase the evening talent by the time Charlotte crawled up the steps of the Sulanasia Plaza. She carried a set of Kartiki pamphlets wherein was printed every word of every note she had taken, including the Chairwoman's emotional message to her Western sisters. She longed to lie immobile on her bed for the next thirteen hours but her stomach, made redundant since the same time the day before, had other ideas. Reluctantly, after a cold shower that did not deflect it from its aim nor soothe her throbbing fingers, she gave up the unequal struggle and went down to the lobby again, where she took the penultimate chair at a small table in the crowded Plaza Coffee Lounge and picked up the menu, hoping it would contain something high in bulk and low in price.

'Mind if I join you?' said a male voice in an unmistakable drawl.

Charlotte looked up. 'Not at all,' she said, removing her handbag so that Adonis could sit down.

'You alone here?'

'Yes.' She had glimpsed him before, fighting his way out of camera straps at the reception desk – could it be only yesterday? He had a camera bag with him still, which he unhooked from god-like shoulders and put down beside him.

'Hey,' he said, swinging round to look directly at Charlotte. 'You wouldn't, by any wild chance, be Nina Kowalski of the *Sydney Herald*?'

'I'm afraid not.' She shook her head, barely able to conceal her sorrow that she was merely Charlotte of the Cotterstock Trust. A vision of Nina Kowalski rose vividly in her mind, complete to the white T-shirt, under which semi-transparent garment the Kowalski breasts, low-slung and uninhibited by anything so suburban as a bra, swung free as she loped towards whatever glamorous assignment the *Sydney Herald* had seen fit to give her.

'Christ knows where that sheila's got to,' said the god. He extended a huge paw. 'The name's Kelly. How you going?'

Charlotte's hand was swamped. But the paw gripped hard and she cried out.

He loosened his grasp immediately and regarded her hand. 'You got trouble brewing there,' he said. 'Look at that.'

Charlotte looked. The throbbing she had dismissed in her tiredness as the consequence of too much stenography, had a more alarming source. Her ankles had swelled but so had her fingers and the one that was encircled by her wedding ring ballooned from the confines of its gold band, hyacinth blue.

'You want to get that seen to,' the Australian said. 'Been taking salt tabs?'

'No.'

'No. Well, start taking them. That's why it's swollen. You sweat, you lose salt, you got to replace it. Didn't anyone tell you?'

No one had told her, no one had bothered. No one had fed her or let her drink a cup of tea or asked her anything, however minor, about herself. And now here was this Olympian stranger showing concern, acting as if he cared whether an anonymous fat-fingered woman lived or died. The accumulated stresses and strains of the last few days, unacknowledged until now, caught up and, among the tinkling coffee spoons and forks and knives, Charlotte became for a moment unhinged.

The god, all-seeing, saw. 'Come on,' he said, 'let's get you out of here. We'll go to a beaut Chinese place I know and if that finger isn't better after a few schooners of rice wine we'll get it axed. That suit you?'

Swallowing hard, smiling blearily, Charlotte said it did.

They caught one of the bedizened buses and rattled at break-neck speed through the neon lights of the town, Kelly bent nearly double under the hot tin roof, Charlotte squashed among a band of piratical Sulanasian youths, their foreheads brilliantly banded, their denims steel-studded. She breathed in lungfuls of toxic fumes that magically cleared her muzzy head. The pot-holes bashed at the floor of the bus, sending her reeling between warm body walls and unhitching her hair so that it fell down her back. When she got out, running with sweat and half-crushed, she was laughing.

The restaurant was a cavern hewed out of a pock-marked wall. It contained a number of empty tables, a silted-up fan on the ceiling, a stretch of rush matting on the floor richly embroidered with Chinese meals past and a dozen Chinese waiters who stood in attitudes of terminal boredom, hands folded, staring out at the neon-lit passersby. Flies boomeranged off every surface. Altogether, Charlotte thought happily, a little bit of Paradise.

'A change from the Plaza,' she said, looking up at Kelly. It was a change to look up, too.

'Well, they do better tucker here,' he said, folding his long legs under the table. 'Cheaper, too. What d'you fancy?'

'You choose.'

The array of dishes was splendid, the intermingling aromas

seductive but Charlotte, taking up her chopsticks, paused on the brink. 'It's no good, I'll have to have a fork,' she said apologetically. 'My finger.'

A fork was brought but again she paused.

'It's all right, is it? The food, I mean. You know, because of . . .' She could not bring herself to go into detail.

'I've survived,' he said.

'But you look as if you could survive anything,' she said and flushed rosy red. It was the most personal remark she had made to a man since her wedding and carried, to her sensitive ears, distinctly adulterous overtones.

'I burn out the bugs with alcohol,' Kelly said, batting around him. 'And you don't want to worry about the flies. They don't eat much.'

Giggling, Charlotte took a mouthful of potentially lethal germs and washed it down with the first of many swigs of rice wine. When every dish was clean and the bottles empty, the Australian leaned dangerously back in his chair and said, 'So. What's a nice girl like you doing in a place like this?'

Charlotte told him. It didn't take long. 'And what about you?' she asked.

'Freelance,' he said. 'Photographer. Have Brownie, will travel. They commissioned me in Sydney to do some stuff on women out here. Paddy fields, village life, oriental beauties washing their undies by the well, you know the sort of thing.'

'And Nina Kowalski?' In spite of the rice wine, which was corroding her synapses in the most delightful way, Charlotte had no difficulty remembering the name.

Kelly shrugged. 'She didn't show. Maybe she had a headache. So I'm just about to call it a day and bugger off back to Sydney. I'll shoot a couple of reels around Balu tomorrow morning and then . . .'

'Why?' Charlotte interrupted rather sharply.

'Why what?'

Charlotte felt a stupid question coming on and hoped Kelly would spare her the obvious answer. 'Why do you need Nina Kowalski?' She waited.

'She's a woman.'

He hadn't. She looked intently at a nearby waiter. He fidgeted uneasily under her stare and began to edge backwards to the safety of the kitchen.

'You'll learn, if you haven't already,' Kelly said, 'that you can't move about in this flaming place as if it were Disneyland. It's a military dictatorship. You gotta have permits, passes, the lot, if you want to get off the tourist beat. It's a Moslem country, too, and they aren't that keen on their women standing about saying cheese to a strange bloke. You need contacts and a female to smooth the way. Can you see me butting into a village unannounced? The women'd have the screaming abdabs. This Nina – she's a journo – I've never met her but she's been here lots before. She'd have got me in and she even spoke a bit of the lingo. No Nina and I'm up shit creek.'

At the end of this speech, Charlotte smiled so radiantly at the waiter that he tripped on a loose piece of matting and disappeared head-first through an archway of tinkling beads.

'If you wanted,' she said, 'you could come with me.'

She spent the hour of midnight on her second evening in Sulanasia sitting on a three-legged stool beside a rickety roadside stall. On its wooden counter were tidily arranged some rusting tools of the jewellers' trade. Kelly held her wrist down firmly on another stool as an infinitely wrinkled old man monitored by a small crowd of absorbed spectators sawed her wedding ring in two.

For her part, Charlotte could hardly sit still for laughing.

The drawn curtains held diamonds of sun caught in the loose yarn. Her finger was better but her head was very bad. For two pins, she thought, staggering out of bed, I'd pay that old man to saw it off. In the blue light of the bathroom her mirrored face caused a blanket of depression to descend, extinguishing the last of yesterday night's euphoria. A hideous morning-after clarity took its place. She had drunk too much, she had made a spectacle of herself and she had entered into an agreement that she couldn't keep. That she didn't want to keep. She saw herself for a bitter moment through Kelly's eyes, her hair in a frizz, her face fixed in a lunatic grin, cavorting about on the streets of a strange city like the worst sort of tourist let loose from England's shores. She couldn't bear to contemplate what Pat Wilshaw would have thought if she'd seen her, or Gordon Grant. And Kelly had. But then, Kelly had been a dissonance from the beginning, a warp in the woof. Men like Bruce were one thing,

Kelly quite another. Men like Kelly did not have bald patches and dry coughs and skin conditions, the luminous trail they left was not composed of silvery psoriatic scales and they were not in their natural element alongside buffoons of women their age or more. Fleetingly, Charlotte envisaged the sort of women who would inhabit Kelly's natural element and a bone in her neck cracked with grief.

She dressed very slowly, partly out of weariness and also to allow her stomach the time it needed to decide it had had enough. Nothing happened. In twenty minutes she stood befrocked and beheeled and still her stomach lay doggo. It was too bad. In all fairness, she should be convulsed by now, in the rigid embrace of a really severe attack of foreign bugs, too sick to meet Miss Millichip or the Kartikis or Kelly again, so sick that the Plaza would have no alternative but to call in the men in white jackets and get her shipped home. Instead, the disloyal organ was merely complaining under its breath as always, muttering its usual wolf, wolf.

Meanwhile, the day would have to be faced and, since that was the case, it was her duty to face it efficiently. Jet-lag was no longer an excuse, she had a job to do. Today's appointment must be kept but, after that, it was farewell Millichip and hullo field. No more dithering about in Banabalu, spending money she couldn't afford, meeting people who weren't relevant and taking down speeches that had already been made, printed, circulated, pulped and reprinted before she had ever heard of Banabalu. Of course Miss Millichip meant well, so did they all, of that she was sure, but the time for formalities was over and the time for action had begun.

With a hand as firm as will-power could make it, Charlotte dispensed from her medicaments bag two aspirin, two salt tablets, a multi-purpose vitamin capsule and a sweetie for luck. She washed them all down with a draught of sterilized water and, sucking the sweetie, left the room.

'*Much* better,' Miss Millichip said in the lobby, surveying Charlotte. Nevertheless she was still far outpaced. Miss Millichip, this morning, had moved from the Sportswear Section of the mail-order catalogue into Formal Attire. She wore a pale green chiffon number prettily draped at the neck, pearl studs in her ears, and her hair was a sleek cap scalloped over her temples and at her cheeks. Her bijou features were almost non-existent, so matt her powder, so discreet her lipshine.

'Where are we off to today?' Charlotte asked cheerily as they walked to the car.

'I did phone you,' Miss Millichip said. 'Last night, to tell you. But you were out.'

'Yes,' said Charlotte less cheerily. 'Sightseeing.'

'The museum closes at 5 p.m. Such a shame, I always think.'

Charlotte made an expansive gesture, shaving a Japanese businessman. 'I like to wander,' she said. 'The streets, the people.'

'Ah,' said Miss Millichip.

The driver looked older and more impacted. They got into the car.

'What did you mean, yesterday?' Charlotte whispered, watching the driver move round the windscreen. 'About him throwing bombs?'

'Who?' said Miss Millichip but it was too late. The bomb-thrower was at the wheel.

'Now,' she said, shifting to face Charlotte. 'By a small miracle, I have managed to persuade Madame Surnano, Minister for Women's Affairs, to see you for a minute or two. Where Irma Schulz failed, I have succeeded.'

'Hurray,' said Charlotte. In case this sounded flippant she added, '*Thank* you.'

'And I have also,' Miss Millichip added, 'persuaded the Minister to attend a small luncheon after our audience. Where' – and she paused for Charlotte's full attention – 'you will meet the Kartiki women again.'

At this good fortune, Charlotte was rendered speechless. After a pause she said, 'How perfectly lovely.' The irony was lost on Miss Millichip and on Charlotte, too, for that matter. She was unfamiliar with irony.

'Madame Surnano is a most interesting woman,' Miss Millichip said. She said no more. The two women sat in silence, swaying in the car. Miss Millichip's chiffon remained bouffant in the heat. Charlotte's frock wilted.

The Ministerial building was missing a top floor but otherwise rose majestically from a garden of fronds that licked like green flames at its bottom storey.

'There is time to freshen up,' Miss Millichip said pointedly, holding open the door of a women's toilet in the lobby. To Charlotte's relief, she did not attempt to enter. Peeing with Millichip, Charlotte thought, would be all wrong. In some people, bladders were a natural part of the human equipment. In others, they were not.

Inside, she splashed water on her face, mildly surprised that the drops did not hiss on her steaming cheeks. Her head, thanks to the aspirin, was quiet. Only her finger, wrinkled and pale where the ring had been, caused her anxiety. It was near normal size again and had lost its hyacinth hue but it still gave pained stabs when she moved it.

Emerging, Charlotte said with unusual firmness to Miss Millichip waiting outside, 'I'm afraid I can't take notes today, Gina. I've had trouble with my finger.'

'Very well,' Miss Millichip said, cool as *crème de menthe frappé* in her green chiffon, 'take this.' She handed Charlotte a slim leather object. 'My tape recorder. I'm surprised you don't have one.'

The fragile tendrils of a new emotion uncurled in the region of Charlotte's heart, unpleasant and, for an instant, quite powerful. 'I wish you'd offered *before*,' she said and immediately regretted expressing herself in so peremptory a way. 'But, of course, you didn't realize. It's my own fault. I'm not myself this morning.'

Miss Millichip's eyebrows joined the scallops of her hairline.

'Thank you for the tape recorder,' said Charlotte meekly.

'You're welcome,' said Miss Millichip.

In the ante-room of the offices of the Minister for Women's Affairs a party of Sulanasians was waiting upon Her Excellency. Its members were clearly looking forward to the coming audience with the keenest anticipation and chattered excitedly amongst themselves, bowing now and again as if to make certain their spines were at peak flexibility for the occasion. The six men wore identical brown shirts patterned with pear-shaped delineations which, Charlotte thought, might signify an association of fruit-growers, though what fruit-growers had to do with the Minister for Women's Affairs escaped her for the present. The three women were in full festive plumage, their sarongs so skin-tight that one highly-rouged lady confided to Miss Millichip, who confided it to Charlotte, that she could not obey any call of nature, however urgent, while thus clad. This sobering fact, which Charlotte knew would have precluded her, were she Sulanasian, from taking part in any sort of ceremony, appeared to amuse the lady greatly, prompting in Charlotte a desire to warn her of the risks inherent in incontinent laughter.

At the end of the ante-room, a heavy door emblazoned with the gold Sulanasian seal opened and shut regularly as officials shuttled in and out carrying papers and briefcases. Watching them, Charlotte soon became aware that the speed of their progress was seriously impeded by the depths of the obeisances executed within, which they did not unfold from until the door was safely shut behind them. They also emerged backwards, which gave them the doubled-up appearance of persons who had just received a hefty boot in the breadbasket. She grew a trifle apprehensive.

After some time, a woman in a navy-blue skirt and white blouse came out of the office and when she had recovered sufficiently to stand upright, beckoned to Charlotte, in whom apprehension had by now conjured up a gargantuan female with a baseball bat sited just behind the door, where she could biff her visitors in maximum privacy. At this summons, a shiver of excitement passed through the Sulanasian party that was, to Charlotte, disquietingly free of the normal irritation at her queue-jumping. Could whatever was about to be enacted within be a favourite Sulanasian blood sport?

The two women were ushered into an immense, high-ceilinged and, to Charlotte's relief, empty room and took their seats upon a banquette of padded chairs two sizes larger and more regally golden than those that had graced Mr Zakir's suite. The table at their knees bore upon its carved legs an inch-thick slab of onyx whose variegations resembled a snap of the planet taken from outer space. The door closed behind them with a discreet click and in the ensuing silence, Charlotte detected a mouse-like scratching that seemed to emanate from a far corner. Peering into that dim reach, she discerned the outlines of a desk and, at its other side, shadowy as the moon in eclipse, the dark crown of a bent head. Her Excellency was writing. Presently, the scratching ceased, a chair was pushed back and there came the light tap of approaching heels.

As the Minister stepped into the pool of sunlight beneath the windows, Charlotte's jaw sank. Madame Surnano was exquisite. She was also exquisitely young, a girl, a child. Charlotte's grasp of haute couture was feeble in the extreme but even she could see that what Her Excellency wore, despite its bows and ribbons, its artless posies at neck and hem, was very haute indeed. Ditto her footwear. Ditto ditto her jewels.

Madame Surnano's astonishing youth, however, in no way impaired the ageless tranquillity of her fair face, except for that moment during which she gazed upwards in wonder as Charlotte rose to her full height. After shaking hands – could it be said that one shook hands with a petal? – the Minister seated herself on the only hard chair, straightened her back, tucked her gauzy knees together, arranged her hands in her silken lap and looked with sweet gentility in Charlotte's general direction.

'Most grateful . . . Your Excellency's time . . . great kindness . . . valuable experience,' Charlotte gabbled, as familiar by now with the necessary patter as if she had learned it at her mother's knees.

The Minister inclined her head with grace.

Miss Millichip echoed the formula. The Minister acknowledged her with equal grace.

'Perhaps I should explain my purpose in coming to your country?' Charlotte said and waited for the restraining wave of a woman well-briefed by her numerous staff.

No wave came.

Charlotte explained. In her efforts to make herself comprehensible, her English was evolving into a curiously condensed version of the real thing in which all tenses but the present were fast disappearing, along with many prepositions and adjectives and almost every adverb. She filled this grammatical vacuum with animated gestures of the hands.

'. . . and so it is very useful to me,' she continued, 'if Your Excellency can tell me what is the function of the Ministry for Women's Affairs? What does it do?'

There was a pause, which the Minister showed no inclination to fill.

'Let me put it another way,' Charlotte said. 'What does your . . .' She hesitated. The word 'job' seemed vulgar, almost blasphemous, when applied to this lovely lily of the field. 'What does your *brief* entail?'

The serene countenance did not alter. No words fell from the enchanting lips.

Charlotte racked her brains for simpler expressions. 'What work is it you do? As the Minister. For Women's Affairs. Your Excellency.'

Madame Surnano remained tongue-tied. Indeed, she appeared to have fallen into a light doze.

Charlotte cast an imploring glance at Miss Millichip but could not arouse her from the close attention she was paying to her right foot.

Distractedly, she hunted for the magic turn of phrase that would waken Sleeping Beauty but none came to mind. 'Your work,' she repeated hopelessly. 'What do you do?'

At this, there came a quickening of the velvet lids. The lustrous lashes rose, as did the silken bosom. The Minister's voice, when it finally made itself heard, was tuneful. 'Ah, *tea*,' it crooned.

Tea it was, borne by an underling. When the glasses had been set out on the table, Madame Surnano took up her own and, sipping, gestured at Charlotte to follow suit. Startled by this rare impetuosity, which she ascribed to the Minister's tender years, Charlotte removed the metal lid from her glass and took her first draught of the national drink. Too late, she realized what she had hitherto been spared and fought to control her features as the perfumed liquid trickled down her throat.

'Jasmine,' cooed the Minister, 'you like?'

'Delicious,' Charlotte managed to get out.

Another pause followed. It seemed rude to interrupt Her Excellency's obvious enjoyment of her cuppa but time was passing and Charlotte feared an imminent invasion of fruit-growers maddened by their long wait. The hiss of Miss Millichip's tape recorder, recording nothing, reproached her. Something must be extracted from this perfect little person but how, oh Lord, how?

'You like my ring?' asked Madame Surnano suddenly. She waggled a tiny finger at Charlotte. Upon it, the rock flashed lighthouse rays.

'It's beautiful,' said Charlotte, grateful for small mercies.

'My husband give me. So *good* husband.' She gave a trill of soft laughter and Charlotte smiled at the engaging child. Her Excellency might not be the predictable figure of a politician one took for granted in the West but, perhaps, in developing countries, people were expected to learn on the job. And it was heartening to see such opportunity given to one so young and so . . . *female*.

'You have no ring,' the Minister said with compassion.

'Er . . . no.'

'Why? You have no husband?'

In the background, Miss Millichip made several small grating noises reminiscent of a bucket being hauled up a well. But the Ministerial dam had been breeched and Charlotte was not about to staunch it. Rapidly eliminating unnecessary detail, she affirmed that she was married.

'And you have babies.'

'No. No babies.'

The Minister gave a sigh of sympathy. 'So pity. I will have many babies,' she said. 'Many, many. I like very much.' She stroked the air maternally, conjuring up orderly rows of toddlers.

Charlotte said, 'I, too, like babies very much. But sometimes, you know, they do not come. I try, but . . .'

The voice of Miss Millichip sliced across these intimacies. 'We must not take up very much more,' she said, 'of Her Excellency's valuable time.'

'No, of course,' Charlotte said hastily. 'Um. What programmes involving women are you working on now, Minister?'

Madame Surnano raised her hands briefly from her beribboned lap and let them drift downwards again. 'So many programmes,' she said, her raven tresses wafting from side to side. 'So *many* programmes.'

Miss Millichip said loudly, 'There is the programme for equal partnership in development between men and women.'

'That is one,' said the Minister.

'And the programme for bringing nutritional advice to village women.'

'That is another.'

'Also, the programme for women's income-generation.'

'Also.' Madame Surnano gave Charlotte a sideways smile, as if assuring her that it would not be long before they could return to the more interesting subject of babies and rings.

'And of course,' said Miss Millichip to the tape recorder, 'the project that most concerns myself and my colleagues at Global Family Funding. The programme of family planning. Perhaps – and her voice compressed – 'you would say a few words about that, Your Excellency.'

Her Excellency sat up straight and took a deep breath. 'The programme of family planning,' she recited, 'is in the forefront of the endeavours of the Sulanasian people and of the selfless wishes of our beloved President in Sulanasia we say a small family is healthy and wealthy and two children are enough we teach our mothers this we teach our children in school also and our grandmothers so that they do not ask for grandchildren our women are eager to do their duty in this great programme for the sake of our country that it may become also healthy and wealthy this our President asks us and our God also.'

When the Minister had regained her breath, Charlotte said, 'But you say you would *like* many babies?' Almost immediately, she regretted her words, seeing in them an unintended criticism.

Miss Millichip coughed.

'Maybe not so *very* many,' said Madame Surnano quickly. She regarded the ceiling, two pearly teeth indenting her bottom lip. 'Maybe fine for me but not good for village women. They too poor. They not know how to do nutrition. They not know many *many* things.'

Her eyes came to rest on Miss Millichip. 'And now,' the Minister said, her tranquillity recovered, 'I think it time to eat. No?'

The little luncheon arranged by Miss Millichip was, in fact, rather large; Charlotte counted fifteen platters of delicious-smelling foodstuffs on the damask table in the room next to the Minister's office. The Kartikis were there in full force and greeted Charlotte with charming little cries, so that she forgot at once her ordeal of the day before. There were also a number of the Minister's staff, now fully upright and tucking in with a will, and all nine of the deputation of fruit-growers whose patience, Charlotte was glad to see, was receiving its just reward.

'I like to speak English,' said a fruit-grower at Charlotte's elbow.

This was her chance. 'Oh good,' she said. 'Then do tell me what organization you represent? I noticed the drawings on your shirts when I was outside and I thought, though I expect I'm wrong, that you might have something to do with growing or harvesting fruit?'

'Froot,' the man said, nodding assent.

'I was *right*,' Charlotte said, incorporating soundless applause into her repertoire of gestures. 'And have you come to see the Minister for Women's Affairs because it is women who grow fruit in Sulanasia and you represent the interests of these women?'

'Wimmin,' said the man, staring up at Charlotte.

'Well,' Charlotte said gaily. 'I think that's quite clever of me, don't you? I mean, to have guessed that. It was the pear on your shirt, you see. This pear?'

'Pare,' said the man, 'bye bye.' And he vanished into the crowd. Though a little put out at this abrupt curtailing of what promised to be an interesting conversation, Charlotte was pleased that she had gleaned this much information from what otherwise had to be described as an unproductive morning.

A Kartiki with a refined Edwardian hair-do took the man's place and, speaking with skill through a mouthful of noodles, said, 'I come special to see you again.'

'How kind,' said Charlotte warmly. She had not yet found time to sample the food.

'It was not easy. So many troubles I have.'

'Oh *dear*.'

'My cook, she very difficult girl. Always she cry. Cry, cry, cry. Also my maid. She come new from the mountains. She not go to school, she know nothing. I must teach her *all*.'

Though surprised at this insight into the home life of Sulanasia's female soldiers, Charlotte soon rallied. 'You teach her reading, do you?' she asked. 'Writing?'

'*Dusting*,' said the Kartiki. 'Cleaning. Sweeping the yard. Much trouble, servants.' She swallowed the last of the noodles and pattered off for a refill.

A photographer appeared, crouching at Charlotte's feet, and Miss Millichip came to stand beside her, slipping one hand affectionately through Charlotte's arm. Pleased at this confirmation of a deepening relationship, Charlotte took the opportunity to whisper in her ear, 'How *old* can Madame Surnano be?'

'Thirty,' answered Miss Millichip, gazing pleasantly into the middle distance.

Charlotte's face lengthened with shock. 'Thirty? Good heavens. But she looks so much younger.'

The photographer moved away. 'They all do,' said Miss Millichip and added, mysteriously, 'It's the oil,' before she, too, moved on, leaving Charlotte to peer through the throng for another glimpse of the political prodigy. But the Minister had gone.

Shortly afterwards the guests, too, took their leave, offering copious thanks to their hostess, Miss Millichip. As the last of them hovered in the doorway, Charlotte took a plate and advanced to the table, where she stuck a spoon into the remnants of a dish of prawns speckled with some mouth-watering spice.

'My pleasure, not at all, goodbye, goodbye,' said Miss Millichip at the door. She wheeled round, then, and called to Charlotte, 'Come, we must go. I do not like to keep the driver waiting.'

Hurrying past the Minister's office, Miss Millichip well ahead, Charlotte peeked for a second through the Ministerial door. Sitting well back among the cushions was an elderly but well-groomed man and on his knee, perched for all the world like a pretty bird, sat the Minister for Women's Affairs. As Charlotte watched, hypnotized, the Minister took a sweetmeat from an enamelled bowl by her side and popped it ever so delicately into the man's mouth.

The doors of the lobby swung open on a heat sufficient to glaze clay. Even the immunized Miss Millichip formed her lips into a silent O as she got into the car and Charlotte suffered third degree burns as her rear met the upholstery. It was clear that the driver, fresh out of bombs, had improvised by leaving his car in the full blaze of the sun, determined at least to char his employer.

'I must have a drink,' she said, adding as Miss Millichip looked at her with alarm, 'I'm just so thirsty.' It went against the grain to be demanding but her throat had nearly closed and some liquid was vital to forestall an emergency tracheotomy.

Miss Millichip said something to the driver, who got out and went over to where a boy in a peaked denim cap stood on one heron leg beside a box on wheels. He came back with an open bottle of Coca Cola and a straw, which he handed through the window to Charlotte. She thanked him profusely, took it and paused.

'Is there something else you want?' asked Miss Millichip in tones that suggested Charlotte's needs might at any moment escalate to Dom Perignon.

'It's just . . . I expect it's stupid but I was warned not to drink anything from stalls and places. I meant to fill up my water bottle this morning but I didn't have time.'

'Oh, Coke's all right,' Miss Millichip said airily. 'It's sealed. Sterile.'

Abashed, Charlotte said, 'Of course it is.' She stuck the straw into the liquid and siphoned steadily until the bottle was empty. As she drank, the trees around grew green again and the noises of the street lost their discordancy.

'Of course, they do say,' Miss Millichip observed, watching her, 'that these stall-holders take the tops off the Coke and water it down.'

Charlotte said, 'Oh,' and stared at the empty bottle, seeing in its misted glass a ghostly image of her future: ravaging, squalid and extremely short.

'No more appointments for you today,' Miss Millichip told her as the car trundled up to the sentry box and was waved through the barrier. 'I must soldier on but you can take it easy until the morning. Swim, have your hair done, whatever you like.' She waved at the traffic-choked street to indicate the Epicurean delights about to overtake Charlotte. 'Tomorrow, we have a very full day. Here is the list of appointments I've managed to make.'

Charlotte scanned it through half-closed eyes to protect herself from the names of those she was determined never to meet. She had planned to telephone Miss Millichip that evening from the hotel, before she boarded the train to Tanjung, but that was the coward's way. The decent thing was to tell her now, minimize the damage and take the flak on the chin. She clutched the handbag and opened her mouth.

'It is interesting,' Miss Millichip mused, 'how every individual visitor here is regarded as an ambassador for his or her country. I always put that down to the situation.'

'The situation,' said Charlotte gruffly.

'The troubles here. They tend, shall we say, to complicate normal diplomatic intercourse, leaving the ordinary traveller to bear a greater share of that task. I have often noticed this. In Banabalu, for instance, they regard me as Miss America, for good or for ill.'

'For good, I'm sure,' said Charlotte, plucking distractedly at her hair.

'Do you think so? I'm glad. God knows, I try, but I do so depend on the cooperation of such as yourself. My work here, though I do not complain, is not easy.'

Gordon Grant did not complain, either. Those who toiled in the name of Small, Healthy and Wealthy, like Mr Grant, and Global Family Funding, like Gina Millichip, were used to putting their own petty anxieties aside for the greater good. It became crystal clear to Charlotte that she had sullied the word 'duty' by pretending it was this that made her so intent on leaving Banabalu when it was in sad reality her own discomfort and misgivings about what lay ahead. One day was all Miss Millichip required. One extra day of support and solidarity. In her mind's eye, she could see Gina, rhinestone tiara crowning shingled head, advancing to the forefront of a vast stage while an audience of brown folk sang 'Isn't She Lovely' and cheered her to the echo. Tears sparkled on the exiguous Millichip cheeks.

Charlotte handed the list back. 'I look forward to meeting them all,' she said. 'And I'll get my hair done, too.'

She got her hair done, though it cost a great deal and provided, because the air-conditioning in the salon had broken down, some insights into the inner chambers of hell. On her way down to cash her second 100-dollar traveller's cheque, she bumped into Kelly. He had on nothing but a pair of blue trunks and a towel draped over his shoulder and Charlotte recoiled from the sight, trying hard not to visualize him meeting the Minister for Women's Affairs.

'I'm off for a swim,' he said. 'You wanna join me?'

She replied in the negative.

'Just had your hair done, don't want it messed up.' He shook his golden head, grinning. 'Women. Come and sit there, anyway. We can have a chin-wag about the trip.'

Charlotte had meant to leave a note in his pigeonhole telling him of her change of mind, to be found after she'd gone. Underhand, sly. Besides, it was nice of him to pretend it was her hair that prevented her from swimming. A sudden hope flared that he had not noticed her body. It expired as suddenly. The point about her body was how much you noticed it.

'All right,' she said. 'I'll be there in a tick.'

The pool glinted in the sun like an advertisement. Charlotte, aware that whoever was buying wouldn't buy it with her there, withdrew to the shade on the Sulanasian side and attempted to look casual in an uncompromisingly upright plastic chair. She watched Kelly arrowing up and down at daunting speeds and flinched as he roared out of the water beside her, spluttering and laughing, in a whirl of silver drops. Life, she thought, was so crassly unfair that someone ought to take it to the Hague.

'Why', she asked of no one in particular, 'do Englishmen have big noses and no chins and Australians no noses and big chins?'

'Is that so?' asked Kelly, towelling himself. 'I've never been to the Land of the Great Unwashed.'

She twitched. 'What do you mean, the Great Unwashed?'

He sat down beside her. 'Had a bad day?'

The husbandly remark touched her. Bruce sometimes said that to her. Other times he said 'Had a good day?'. You never knew, with

Bruce. She wondered what he'd say if someone told him she'd cut her wedding ring off and she wondered why she was thinking of him. Perhaps because Bruce never swam, either. He had once told her that he ought to go to the Dead Sea, where they ran a clinic for psoriasis sufferers. Something in the water, Char, he said and had gone to look it up, leaving her imagining all the flaky people floating about, scratching. What if two of them fell in love? It would have to be more than skin-deep or it wouldn't be there in the morning.

'Penny for them,' Kelly said.

'I'm thinking unkind thoughts,' she said. 'I don't know why.'

'It's this place. It stinks.'

A young Sulanasian stood on the diving board, as brown and perfect in miniature as Kelly was, writ large. A girl with a flower in her dark hair skipped past, holding out her hands to a toddling brown cherub. A waiter walked down between the tables carrying tall glasses of pink ice-cream. Soft music drifted across the crimped blue waves and birds hopped, twittering, among the leaves of the potted plants.

'How can you *say* that?' Charlotte said.

'I just open my mouth and out it comes. Listen, you eaten?'

She shook her head.

'Why not? Were they all too busy controlling births to feed you?'

'No.' Charlotte was indignant. 'They put on a very elaborate meal. I just didn't get round to eating.' She told him, then, about the Minister, about her surprising youth, her extraordinary beauty. 'The odd thing was, everyone else I met talked a great deal but Madame Surnano hardly talked at all. I expect she was tired.'

'Shagged out, I'd say,' Kelly stretched out his arms behind him, gave a huge yawn and slumped again. 'Oh, she's a corker, all right, I'll give her that. Miss Sulanasia, my first trip here. Ten years ago, that'd be.'

'Look,' Charlotte said patiently, after she'd taken this in, 'that's impossible. You must have the wrong woman. I mean, I know you get a prize when you're a beauty queen but I don't *think* they'd go so far as to give you a Cabinet post.' She laughed softly at her little joke.

Kelly screwed up his eyes. 'That's right, I remember now,' he said. 'She got herself hitched to old Surnano, the Minister for Internal Affairs.' He gave a low whistle. 'You've got to hand it to her. She's done all right.'

'That's absurd,' said Charlotte. She bounced in her chair at the absurdity of it.

'Why? You against opportunities for women or something?' Kelly's eyes were as blue as gas flames.

Charlotte snorted. A small boy took up a position close to her, stuck his thumb in his mouth and stared. She stared back vacantly. 'Naturally, I'm for women's equality, opportunities and everything else but I cannot feel' – the boy commenced an assiduous picking of his nose and Charlotte turned to survey the pool – 'I really cannot feel that a woman should or would be given an important position like that just because she's someone's . . . well, some man's . . .'

'Floozie?' Kelly suggested. 'But I told you, she's married. You want to be a woman in Government here, you gotta be a respectable wedded wife. They don't hand out whole Ministries to floozies, you know. Christ, no. They got standards in Sulanasia.'

Charlotte felt she was paddling in unexpectedly muddied waters and she did not at all care for Kelly's tone. 'I take these things rather seriously,' she said. 'I see you don't.'

'You wanna be serious,' Kelly said. 'Let's eat.'

They ate by the pool, a plateful each of tiny round soft-centred cheese-balls and a salad tasting deliciously of peanuts. Charlotte, preoccupied, drank three glasses of a rather expensive red wine and smoked two cigarettes from her last Heathrow carton while Kelly expounded on the art of taking photographs in strong sunlight. She listened only intermittently.

'What about the Kartikis, then? I don't suppose you know about them.'

'The Kartikis?' Kelly reined himself up from a longish description of the effects of heat on film. 'What about them?'

'Now, there's real equality of opportunity. Not that I approve, in one way,' she hastened to add, 'but it's nice to know that if a Sulanasian woman wants to join the Armed Forces, she can. I've met them. They're a very interesting group and, I may say, they haven't given up one iota of their femininity. There they are, high-ranking officers in the Army or the Air Force or the Navy, yet to meet them you'd think they were just a bunch of housewives.'

'They are,' Kelly said.

Charlotte gave a pained smile at a cat that was attempting to eat her cigarette stub.

'You got something against housewives as well as floozies, eh?'

Kelly said. 'You're just one prejudice on legs, Mrs Mac. Shame, when you look such a nice lady.'

The cat successfully ingested the cigarette stub.

'Perverse little bugger,' Kelly said. 'Think I'll have another dip.'

'You've just had a meal. You'll get cramps and drown.'

He stood above her, blocking out the sun. 'I've had more swims after hot dinners than you've had hot dinners,' he said and, turning, sliced into the water without causing a ripple. At the shallow end, his face emerged among the splashing children. 'Thanks anyway for caring, Mum,' he bellowed.

Mortified, she examined her nails. As always, they were none too clean.

When he came back, shaking himself, he said, 'Well, when are we off to Tanjung? Tonight?'

Handsome men were often so at the expense of a certain sensitivity in their characters, Charlotte had observed this many times. They seemed to think that they could trample on women's finer feelings and then, offering the placatory gift of their looks, be immediately forgiven. She remembered with sadness a boy called John, a neighbourhood friend when they had both been ten, or thereabouts. John had had a lot of streaky blonde hair and eyelashes as long as a girl's. Another girl's, not Charlotte's, hers were stubby and kept falling out. She had said to John one day, attempting a serious experiment in thought transference, 'I've got a secret.' Responding satisfactorily, John had asked what her secret was. 'I'm going to think of it very hard,' Charlotte had replied. 'I'm going to close my eyes and really *think* and you'll have to close your eyes, too, and make your mind all empty. Now.' She had squeezed her eyes tightly and concentrated with all her might for quite a long time, until her mother's voice had said, 'Charlotte, why are you sitting on that damp grass with your eyes shut? John's already having his tea. Do come along.' Charlotte had been hurt and, more to the point, disappointed in John, whom she'd thought an intelligent boy until then, as well as handsome. In the kitchen, John had said, 'I'll tell you *my* secret, shall I? I've eaten all the cakes,' and laughed in a way that made the length of his lashes irrelevant. Since then, Charlotte had steered clear of good-looking men, though she had to admit to herself, rather glumly, that they had not exactly plagued her in their turn. She had known Bruce would be trustworthy from the moment she laid eyes on him, and the way he cleared his throat – drily, with a pause between the two sounds – confirmed it. She suspected Kelly was the type of man who never cleared his throat at all.

'What did you mean, about the Kartikis?' she said, looking at him with the severity of a woman armoured by bitter experience against bronzed male chests and the macho smell of chlorine.

Kelly said, 'You won't like this, Mrs Mac, but the Kartikis aren't women in the armed forces. They're the wives of *men* in the armed forces.' Seeing Charlotte's incredulity, he explained further. 'All the women in Sulanasia – well, the ones who count – belong to women's groups based on the jobs of their husbands. So if your old man's in the army, you belong to the Kartikis. If he's a boring old fart in the civil service, you join the women's civil service group. And so on. If you were married to me, you'd have to join the merry band of women photographers.'

The revelation of this mirror world confounded Charlotte. 'You mean, if I was the wife of a General, I'd be . . .'

'Madame General in the Kartikis. You got it.'

'But that's ridiculous.'

'What d'you expect?' Kelly gave a rich, watery sniff. 'Sulanasians aren't like you and me, are they?'

'I don't care for that remark,' Charlotte said coolly. He was making it a good deal easier for her to tell him the trip was off.

Kelly remained uncooled. 'There's nothing remotely resembling the Kartiki set-up in the good old U of K, right? Nor a trace of it back in Oz. I tell you, it makes you proud to be white.'

Charlotte cleared her throat drily, with a short pause between the sounds. 'I meant to tell you earlier,' she said, 'but I'm afraid you can't come with me. On the trip. It's simply too difficult.' He was looking at her but she couldn't see his expression, a hand shaded his eyes. 'I'm a guest here myself. It would be discourteous to invite someone else along. I should have known better than to offer in the first place. I'm sorry.' She added hoarsely, 'I was a bit drunk at the time.'

'I'd never have guessed,' Kelly said. He scraped both hands across his jaw. 'No, it's okay. No sweat. Forget it.'

At this point Charlotte's stomach struck up the Funeral March from Saul.

'Excuse me,' she said, getting abruptly to her feet, 'I have to make a phone call.'

'An internal one, I presume,' Kelly called after her.

Really, Charlotte thought, he was very coarse. Handsome is as handsome does and he wasn't doing well.

She wished she had the build for a dignified exit.

The third and last day of the Millichip regime was the most gruelling. Hour after hour, under the laser effect of a heat that left flesh unmarked but cooked to a turn the offal beneath, she trudged from car to building and back again, having pressed more palms and smiled more smiles than a visiting Royal. Miss Millichip expressed regret at attending only one in three of these rendezvous but *someone*, as she pointed out, had to keep the good ship Global Funding afloat, no matter what other diversions were on offer.

On these occasions, she instructed Charlotte beforehand as to the name and address of her interviewee and waved her and the driver off, leaving Charlotte to pray he would not try to gain publicity for his rebel cause by blowing them both up on the way. Once, en route to meet yet another civil servant thought to be crucial to Charlotte's grasp of Sulanasian family planning – he turned out to be in charge of the nationwide People's Jogging Campaign – they passed a horribly scorched and gutted building. As they did so, Charlotte kept the nape of the driver's neck under close surveillance, on the assumption that if he were the perpetrator he would give himself away with a smug glance at the ruin. The nape remained immobile. Indeed, the only break in the monotony came as they stopped at some traffic lights beside a luxurious complex of ranch-style bungalows less thoroughly barricaded than others of their type. Glancing idly through one gate, Charlotte perceived a woman – poised at that instant to dive into a turquoise pool – who closely resembled Miss Millichip in a bikini. Chance, Charlotte thought, envious on poor Gina's behalf, would be a fine thing.

She was, however, accompanied by Miss Millichip to the final appointment. By this time, the mosquitoes had emerged for their evening meal and Charlotte, limp as a wet mop, became acutely unsure of her ability to pack, pay her hotel bill, find her way to the station and catch the 11.00 pm train to Tanjung.

'I really must opt out of this one,' she told Miss Millichip with as much firmness as she could muster. 'I know you've been working as hard as me' (this was difficult to believe, Miss Millichip looked as dewy as a recently rained-upon frangipani) 'but I am exhausted and

92

I have to do a lot before I go off to Tanjung. So, if you don't mind, I'll say goodbye for the time being . . .' and, resolutely, she got out of the car.

The skin of her arm was nipped by fingers whose slimness belied their iron strength. 'But Deborah Doody is waiting,' Miss Millichip said, as one invoking Jahweh's name. 'Mrs Doody is American and a key figure to all of us at Global Family Funding. She *must* be *met*.'

Awkward but unswerving, Charlotte stood her ground. 'I do apologize,' she said. 'I'll write to Mrs Doody myself to explain. I'll tell her . . . how upset you were at my discourtesy. But, Gina' – and now she appealed as one traveller to another – 'you know how it is. One has to be organized if one wants to do a decent job of reporting in the field.'

'I *don't* know,' Miss Millichip snapped. 'Personally, I have never seen any point in leaving Banabalu. The pulse of the programme is right here.' Nevertheless, forced by Charlotte's intransigence, she left the car to stand by her charge in the dusty alley-way. Bringing her head close to Charlotte's ear and glancing around as if for eavesdroppers, she said, 'I would not advise this, Charlotte.'

It was the first time Miss Millichip had used her Christian name. Charlotte prepared herself for a showdown.

'How do you mean?' she asked.

'You intend to arrive in Tanjung tomorrow morning?'

Charlotte indicated that this was so.

'And you are being met there by our Mr Premendongerum?'

Charlotte nodded.

'Who will afford you, while you are there and wherever you wish to go later, the full facilities, including transport, of the KNNA organization plus Mr Premendongerum's own services, gratis, as interpreter, so that you may have access to the village women, without which you could not prepare your report?'

Charlotte confirmed this, adding a few words to express her appreciation of these facilities and her mounting anxiety to partake of them.

'Then,' hissed Miss Millichip, her diminutive features contracting further with the import of what she was about to say, 'I have to warn you that unless you keep this appointment with Deborah Doody, there is every reason to believe these facilities will be withdrawn.'

'I don't understand,' Charlotte said, though it was limpidly clear.

Helpfully, Miss Millichip repeated her statement and, before she had time to weigh her reply, Charlotte found herself saying, 'That's blackmail.'

'Heavens to Betsy,' Miss Millichip said and laughed twice through her nose. 'Blackmail! What an idea!'

'You're saying that if I don't meet Mrs Doody, I can forget the rest of my trip.'

'Regrettably, the matter is not in my hands,' Miss Millichip answered, lifting up her hands to display their emptiness. 'I am simply passing on to you what I have learned, from long experience, is the usual outcome of this sort of behaviour. You and I understand each other. But *they* do not so easily understand us. *They*, I fear, will not forgive.'

They found Mrs Deborah Doody ensconced in Room 1004 of the Banabalu Park Hotel, along with a television cameraman, a sound technician, a lighting man, the director, the director's assistant and a gofer. Everyone present was American except for the gofer, who was indigenous. Mrs Doody, Charlotte noticed, was a good deal podgier than she was herself. She wore an ethnic robe and her grey hair was coiled in plaits over each ear.

'I have brought these dear women friends of mine,' Mrs Doody informed Charlotte, gesturing towards the bathroom where her dear friends, to judge by the noise, were turning on and off all available taps while interminably flushing the lavatory, 'all the way. From Pilatan. One thousand and fifty kilometres east of here. In a chartered helicopter. It is the first time. Any of them. Have left their village. The first time. They have ever flown. The first time they have ever been. In a building with more than one storey.'

'Goodness,' Charlotte said. There was something tantalizingly familiar about Mrs Doody.

'But I am glad to say. These wonderful women. Trust me.' Mrs Doody spoke in small slices, as if endeavouring to share her words fairly among a crowd of greedy children. 'I am honoured. To be counted. As their true friend.'

'Triffic,' said Charlotte childishly.

Mrs Doody raised a commanding arm towards the director. 'I believe we may now. Begin.'

The room became flooded with an eerie light. A boom waggled above a group of chairs. The camera was shunted into place in front of the chairs.

'Now,' Mrs Doody declared, 'I will call. My ladies. In.' She rose with something of a struggle from her chair and advanced to the bathroom, whence she emerged a minute or so later with her arms spread like St Francis of Assisi over six bird-like Sulanasian women, their dark eyes agog. These she settled, with many soothing sounds in Sulanasian, upon the chairs.

'Long-term acceptors,' Miss Millichip mouthed at Charlotte, jerking her head at the women.

Charlotte, aware from her burrowing among Gordon Grant's files that 'acceptor' was the trade word for a contraceptive user, nodded back and as she did so, recalled in a flash Mrs Doody's doppelganger. It was Mother Prayana of Caxton Hall, possessor of the very same hypnotic eyes and regal bearing. She hoped her quiescent Kundalini would not confuse the two and arise at an unseemly moment to seek The Prayana Path.

Mother Doody took her place before the awed village women, adjusted about her ample person her ethnic folds, drove an erring hair pin into one coiled plait and nodded at the director. The filming began.

It developed to a formal pattern. First, Mrs Doody addressed her ladies in measured Sulanasian while her plump hands moved steadily up and down in the air as if milking a cosmic udder. Then she listened to the women's answers with grave attention, one finger poised beneath her chins and at last, turning majestically around, she explained to the camera, in English, the gist of what had passed between them.

'I asked. My friends from Pilatan. Why they had chosen to use. The intra-uterine device. They tell me a woman may forget. The Pill. Husbands do not like. The condom. And the injection must be given. Every three months. Therefore the IUD is the most popular. Choice.'

'Who is the film for?' whispered Charlotte to Miss Millichip while Mrs Doody talked again to her women.

'TV.' Miss Millichip mouthed back.

Charlotte scribbled on a piece of paper IUD UNUSUAL CHOICE?, underlined CHOICE and passed it across to Miss Millichip, who glanced at it and put a finger on her lips, indicating that Mrs Doody was about to speak English again.

'The women say the IUD. Has helped them improve in. Body and soul. They say that with only two children. They have time to make their houses more attractive. Also themselves.'

It occurred to Charlotte to wonder why having no children at all had not noticeably improved her in body or soul, nor helped make her house more attractive. Was it remotely possible that her failure in the housewife and personal grooming departments had acted on Bruce as a contraceptive or even a kind of abortifacient? Unconsciously, of course. Perhaps Bruce had come home one evening in her first weeks of pregnancy, gauged the detritus around him, doubled it, metaphorically speaking, taken away the number he first thought of and booked her into Denmark Hill.

But these were deep waters, into which one was well advised to wade only in wellies (metaphysical wellies, of course) and, besides, Mrs Doody was in full flight again, summarizing the extraordinary changes the IUD had wrought in the lives of her simple Pilatanians. These included, among many health benefits to mothers and babies, the ineffable bonus of an harmonious family life.

'Before the IUD,' she intoned, her eyes sombre as she looked back upon the stygian darkness of uncontracepted times, 'the women say there were too many children. So the husbands became. Bad-tempered. They were not nice. To the children. And sometimes they would' – here her voice sank to Old Man River depths – 'leave the house and *wander*.'

Bruce had never wandered. Sometimes, when he coughed and scratched while imparting to her from his books more little-known facts than usual on a wet weekend, say, or a bank holiday, she had asked him why he didn't go for a nice walk in the fresh air, whereupon he would read out to her the latest statistics on lead pollution levels or the effects of acid rain. Nor, in truth, could she easily visualize him, alone in beret and scarf, roaming the streets of Kentish Town. Perhaps, if they'd had a child, he would have walked with it. Perhaps too, the sort of scenery available to the wandering men of Sulanasia – palm trees, lagoons, dusky maidens with flowers in their hair – might have encouraged him. It dawned on Charlotte then that what Mrs Doody meant to imply had to do with sexual rather than shank's pony excursions. Here, all connection with Bruce broke down.

'The women say,' continued Mrs Doody, twinkling humorously over her shoulder at the ladies, 'that their husbands are in favour. Of family planning. They are responsible men. Also. Before the IUD the women sometimes had to refuse. Their husbands' demands. Now when he wants. They say they are always. Ready.' She shared with the camera her joy at this outcome and turned back to the group, leaving Charlotte pink-skinned at the untoward revelation. Happily, the women did not seem to share her embarrassment. They looked a little tense, certainly, but then who would not, if scooped up of a sudden by Doody-copter while chatting at the village well and deposited ten floors above sea level to have one's sex life vivisected? Her own recent journey had had a disorienting effect upon her nerves. If Deborah Doody had then commenced to probe into her marital habits, she could not have answered for the consequences.

DO THEY KNOW WHAT'S GOING ON? DO THEY UNDERSTAND ABOUT TV? she wrote on another piece of paper. Miss Millichip nodded. DO THEY EVER SEE IT? scribbled Charlotte. Miss Millichip, a trifle impatiently, shook her head.

At this point Mrs Doody was to be heard confiding to the camera that in her opinion there was one word not sufficiently used in the context of family planning and that word was 'Love'. She rolled love around in her mouth like a large boiled sweet before releasing it, partly chewed, for the easier ingestion of future viewers. She then consulted her women, who were equally enthusiastic about the emotion.

'Oh yes, they say. Love is a very. Wonderful. Result of the IUD. They say now. We can devote more love. To our husbands. And children. Because we have only two children and so. More time on our hands.'

What a good thing, Charlotte thought, at this pleasing sentiment. All too often she had witnessed Cotterstock clients slapping their offspring heartily in the waiting room of the clinic, a sight that invariably distressed her, though she put it down to the tiredness of mothers who often had a babe-in-arms to cope with as well as a toddler. It was curious that they did not seem to have time on their hands. She imagined Mrs Watkins; sharp-featured, hard-handed Gloria Watkins, a difficult client, always cuffing her two kids while explaining to any interested party what rotten little bleeders they were. How would she take to Mother Doody's theories concerning her leisure hours? Shutting her eyes, Charlotte could hear her reaction all too clearly. 'Sod off, scumbag,' Gloria Watkins opined.

She returned from Clerkenwell to discover with relief that the filming session was drawing to a close. At Deborah Doody's maternal prompting one of the Sulanasian women, older than the rest, whose deep-set eyes jumped from the camera as from a sleeping but dangerous beast, made a long statement. Mrs Doody, her voice more vibrant than ever, translated, ending with an assurance that her dear friend. Wanted every viewer to know. That she had become an acceptor of IUD. Not from fear. Not because people chased her. But because she was aware of the social and economic benefits. Her wise Leader. Had promised. Would ensue.

At this, the camera ceased rolling and Mrs Doody enfolded most of the women in a capacious embrace. Shortly afterwards the women were hustled out. Mrs Doody lay down on a sofa to fan herself, and Charlotte and Miss Millichip, after reverential farewells, tiptoed away.

'A dedicated human being,' Miss Millichip said, on the steps of the Plaza. 'She has a way with peasant women.'

'She does,' said Charlotte.

'Now, as to your plans. I will telephone Mr Premendongerum in ten minutes to tell him you will be arriving in Tanjung at . . . ?'

'6.30 tomorrow morning.'

'6.30 am. Very well. You have plenty of time. It is now exactly . . . 10 pm.'

At this stressful news, Charlotte shot up the steps. Miss Millichip accompanied her as speedily. The glass doors slid open. Miss Millichip inserted herself between them and handed Charlotte two pieces of paper. 'If you would,' she said, 'settle these before you leave. Have a good journey. We'll meet again on your return.' She tapped briskly back to the car.

In her room, Charlotte picked up armfuls of scattered clothes and papers and crammed everything, higgledy piggledy, into her suitcase and rucksack. As she staggered with them out of the door, the mirror in the little hallway framed a full-length portrait of a more than usually demented bag-lady. There had been no time to put to cosmetic purposes.

At the reception desk, she quailed at the astronomical bill and cashed yet another travellers' cheque, seeing bankruptcy just round the corner. Then she remembered Miss Millichip's papers and extracted them from her pocket. They were both invoices, made out to her. One said: 'To Luncheon for Madame Surnano – $100.00.' The other said: 'To use of Global Family Funding transport plus chauffeur, 20 hrs – $220.00.' At the bottom of each bill was neatly printed 'if receipt required, please return to Ms G. Millichip, GFF Building, P.O. Box 468, Banabalu'.

'Thought I'd find you here,' said Kelly's voice behind her. 'I wanted to . . .'

She swung round, holding the bills out to him wordlessly. She was afraid that if she parted her lips, loud screams might emerge.

Kelly scanned the two bills and looked at Charlotte. He gave a whoop of laughter, smacked the newspaper he was carrying against his thigh and said, 'Oh, man. Isn't that great? What a rip-off.'

In the face of this innocent delight in another's adversity, Charlotte had no option but to diagnose psychopathy. The surface charm, the rather brutal good looks, the callousness – it all fitted. How sad, she thought, how very sad. With dignity, she turned from this damaged human being and walked over to the cashiers, where she took her place in the money-changing queue for the second time. The train would be missed. Mr Whatsisname in Tanjung would await her in vain, her project lay in ruins along with any reputation for efficiency or a proper frugality she might once have had, but, as Pat Wilshaw so often and so rightly said, que sera, sera. As for certain inhabitants of an erstwhile penal colony, the less said the better.

The penal colonist was right behind her. 'What time's your train?'

'What train?' asked Charlotte and read her name on her passport several times with great interest.

'Oh, don't be so bloody stupid,' he said, taking her arm. 'It's the 11 pm to Tanjung, right? You haven't got time to hang about in queues. Here' – and he shovelled at her a wad of dollar bills – 'pay me back when you're next in Sydney. Come on.'

He took up her luggage as if it contained no more than eider down and swung with it towards the hotel entrance, hailing the doorman as he went. Charlotte stuffed Kelly's dollars into an envelope, scribbled Miss Millichip's name on it, flung it at the Head Porter and ran after him. Within seconds Kelly had stowed both her and her luggage in a cab.

She looked at him standing on the steps. 'Would it be too much,' she said, trying to keep out the note of apology that kept trying to get in, 'to ask if you'd come to the station with me?'

By the time she had bought her ticket and Kelly had ferried her luggage across a cataract of people, all of whom seemed to have too many children entirely to please Mother Doody, the Tanjung train was emitting bursts of steam from its many gussets and clanking its carriages impatiently together preparatory to take-off. Charlotte pulled herself aboard and wedged her arms on a grimy window-sill.

'Kelly,' she said formally, as one addressing a small but deserving congregation, 'I would just like to say that, if you still wished, I can now see no reason why you shouldn't come to Tanjung. Say, the day after tomorrow, so that I can clear it with them. I feel strongly that Gina Millichip owes me something and it might as well be you.' Since this sounded a mite indelicate, she attached a phrase or two concerning solidarity between working folk. The train underwent a metallic convulsion and began to pull away.

Kelly loped alongside. 'Great,' he said and put up his thumb. 'Where do I get you?'

'Mr Pre . . .' Hastily she gave up on that one and said, loudly now, 'The KNNA offices. Everyone will know.'

'Hey,' he shouted. 'I wasn't going to show you this but I reckon you'll see the joke now.' The train picked up speed but he managed to thump his newspaper into her outstretched hand.

When she had given the dwindling Kelly a stiff-handed salute that indicated cordial appreciation of help received without yielding an inch to the low melodrama in her stomach, which was fluttering about as if it was Olivia de Havilland waving Ashley off to the war, she lurched into the adjacent carriage and found a seat. On impulse, she had treated herself to a first-class ticket, rationalizing this unprincipled luxury on the grounds that it cost not much more than a bus fare at home.

Justifiably, it did not buy much more either. The seat looked as if it had been requisitioned from some bankrupt airline or salvaged after a not-too-bad plane crash. But these were quibbles, entirely inappropriate in a Less Developed Country where the comforts of the West would have seemed decadent, even corrupt. Suppressing an unaccustomed nostalgia for British Rail, Charlotte sat down and was grateful for the relative comfort of the seat, its ability to recline two whole degrees from bolt upright and the airline tray it proffered, attached to the back of the seat ahead. She unclipped this from its stud, found it was not in fact attached to the seat ahead, and massaged one temporarily numbed big toe. There was also a form of air-conditioning. To judge by its heavy breathing, it had entered a terminal stage of metal fatigue, but it had succeeded in reducing the temperature in the carriage to the perfectly bearable level of an English heatwave.

The seats were in pairs and the young Sulanasian man who had nodded politely to her when she appeared, took up little room at her side. Making a mental note to cease assuming that all Sulanasians not actually in coffins were necessarily ten years old because they were nearer ground level than her own race, more delicately built and a good deal more wrinkle-resistant, she sat back and, for one severely rationed moment, allowed herself to think that she would see Kelly again in two days' time. That over, she went on to contemplate the joys of Millichiplessness, the fast-increasing miles between herself and Banabalu and the ever-shortening distance to the real Sulanasia, the grassroots where she could at last begin properly to work.

The newspaper that Kelly had given her lay on her lap. She unfolded it and saw that it was the English-language *Sulanasian Star*. Idly, she flipped through its pages, reading an article here and there under vaguely familiar by-lines. Obviously, the paper culled much of its content from English and American sources and was presumably subscribed to by Western multi-national executives based in Banabalu, since financial news and stock-market dealings figured largely. On the back page, she discovered a crossword and, while trying to work out the first clue, stared absently at a large photograph above.

Slowly she brought the faces therein into focus. The most prominent among them belonged to Miss Millichip, smiling pleasantly and with a nice concern at the happy throng about her. Beside her, however, was a tragic figure, a sadly retarded European female from whose facial deformities and lumpy body she was not unnaturally looking away. The caption below provided details of the occasion: a luncheon party given the day before in honour of Madame Surnano, Minister for Women's Affairs, by Miss Gina Elizabeth Millichip of Global Family Funding, the well-known and popular member of Sulanasian-American society, an indefatigable worker in the cause of closer relationships between these two great countries and a gracious hostess whose generosity was much appreciated by her many Banabalusian friends.

The names of these friends were recorded. The name of the deformed one was omitted, presumably on compassionate grounds.

Part Three

The overnight journey lasted through several dark ages. Whenever Charlotte closed her eyes for a few seconds the train would roar in and out of a tunnel or thump itself fractiously about on its wheels. When, once, she dozed for a short period, she dreamt of asphyxiation by Adult Wheeze and awoke in fright to discover that the air-conditioning unit had encountered a frog in its works and was slowly but noisily choking to death.

Upon its eventual demise with a horrid rattle, the heat in the carriage solidified into a cloying ointment in which she was the fly. The sepia bulb overhead, though useless for reading, was purpose-built for the shedding of a funereal light over the sleeping passengers that was highly conducive to speculations of a cosmic nature. Charlotte wrestled for some time with the problems of good versus evil and the ultimate meaning of life but came to no very satisfactory conclusions other than the conviction that enlightenment would be nearer if only she had a child. As always, this merely depressed her. Not only was a child unlikely but to believe giving birth would solve anything was, as she well knew, a retrogressive illusion common to the more inadequate of Cotterstock clients. Nothing much suggested itself as an alternative except a belief in God. She decided that if He existed, she would happily put her affairs in His hands. If not, however, would it be better to deposit the capital from the sale of her half of the flat in a building society or a unit trust?

She fell asleep half an hour before the train, with a lot of attention-grabbing clamour, drew into Tanjung and an early morning monsoon. The rain, of sufficient volume to warrant the launching of an ark, crashed on to the iron station roof and poured in torrents down the supporting pillars, but its wet warmth unglued Charlotte's eyes and revived her enough to drag herself to the station's entrance, where she was set upon by a horde of men with wastepaper baskets on their heads who proceeded to fight for some time over her luggage, oblivious to the weak protests of its owner. The eventual victor, bearing the scars of previous battles on his face and neck, gripped his prize between granite calves and regarded his new employer for the first time.

'Where to?' he enquired.

Charlotte, who had slumped to the station steps during the opening bout of the match, shook her head, slapping herself lightly on either cheek with soaking ropes of hair. 'Nowhere,' she said apologetically. Poor man, her suitcase was a Pyrrhic trophy. 'Someone meet me. KNNA.'

'Tanjung Grand?' he suggested.

'No. So sorry.'

'Central Hotel?'

'No. Thank you all the same.'

He did a quick down-market slide. 'Student hostel? Very clean.'

'No. Sorry.'

He frowned, perplexed at this unanchored female, and squatted down beside her on the wastepaper basket removed from his head. 'What your name?' he asked.

Charlotte told him.

'How old you?'

Charlotte told him. Then, afraid that such one-way confidences might seem unfriendly, she elicited the same information from him. She also gave him her last packet of Heathrow cigarettes as recompense for his trouble. He lit one. They gazed resignedly at each other until he lost interest and wandered off to join his erstwhile sparring partners, though keeping a wary eye on Charlotte in case she sneakily leapt up and bestowed her custom on a rival.

The wet street that led out of the station was empty of anything but the individualistic transport of Sulanasia – a large front-facing twin pushchair behind which the driver pedalled more or less blindly, unable for the most part to see over its hood – and a number of cars of uncertain age and abilities. None among them was the KNNA van that Miss Millichip had assured her would be there on her arrival. Nor did there appear to be anyone of the military mien she had come to expect of Sulanasia's bureaucracy.

Charlotte looked at her watch. For all its histrionics, the train had come in on time and ten more minutes had now passed. The station had emptied of its last Banabalusian passengers and the troop of drivers – her own with a last hopeful backward glance – drifted off to pastures new. She sat washed up on strange banks, an orphan of the storm. A telephone call was out of the question – the KNNA offices, even in Sulanasia, would not open for another two hours. But moving on was also out of the question. Righteous indignation, inertia and a fear of missing for ever the essential Mr Whatsit combined to keep her pinned to her step. The rain ceased and the sun took over, domineering even at that hour. She watched the street and steamed with it. Finally, she stretched out on the stone floor, wedged her head on her rucksack and resigned herself to the impossibility of closing an eye.

He stood before her, beaming. His jacket was a miracle of repressage, his shirt crackled with starch, his shoes shone, his clipped hair coruscated, his gold-rimmed glasses – evidently Government issue – put the sun to shame.

'Please. I think you are Mrs Macanally,' the vision said.

Charlotte sat up. The discs of her spine clunked heavily down to her coccyx and there cohered. Wet cotton clung lover-like to her loins, her skin smarted with sunburn, and something tragic had happened to her left nostril. 'Hullo,' she said thickly. 'Is it Mr Prem . . . ?'

He held up a laundered palm. 'No need for apology,' he said. 'I will hear not one in the world.' He swivelled expertly on his polished heels to demonstrate how little the world required an apology.

Charlotte hauled herself to her bare feet – her sandals seemed to have given her up and removed themselves to a distance. 'I'm so sorry,' she said, 'I went to sleep. I was here at 6.30 but I don't know what . . .'

A second palm joined the first. 'Is of no consequence,' he said, his smile extending so far across his face that his ears retreated. 'I forgive you. Complete. With my heart.' One hand smacked across this forgiving muscle, concealed beneath a pocket punctuated with pens. 'And now, we say no more on this sad question. You agree with me, dear guest Mrs Macanally?'

'But, really, it wasn't my . . .'

'I insist. No apology. You agree?'

Charlotte agreed.

'Then, please, follow me.'

Arriving at the van, he slid the door open and faced Charlotte again. 'Now we understand each other, I think. I make no more problem for this very late coming. I say no one word more.' He slipped a dry brown hand within hers. 'I am Hariyono Premendongerum, your most glad host.'

Charlotte said she was Charlotte Macanally and she was very pleased to meet him.

Hariyono Premendongerum twinkled at her, placing a finger on the side of his nose. 'I think my name very hard for English visitors. I am right?'

'A little,' Charlotte admitted.

'So,' he said and gave her a bow from the waist, 'please feel yourself very free to call me Harry.'

Relieved to have this obstacle so tactfully removed, Charlotte smiled her gratitude. 'And I'm Charlotte.'

'Welcome to Tanjung, Miss Harlot,' said Mr Premendongerum.

'Thank you, Harry,' Charlotte said.

Just before he clambered into the van ahead of her, he beamed at Charlotte once again and tapped her lightly on the upper arm. 'If you not mind,' he said, 'please call me *Mister* Harry.'

Mr Harry's place of work was a rambling many-roofed building skirted by wide lawns that kept at a proper distance the shanty-town at its hems. Here and there under fragrant trees, men sat cross-legged on the grass in mushroom rings.

'Learning,' Mr Harry said, waving at them. 'All learning.' Charlotte enquired what they were learning but her guide, trotting across the lawn, was already beckoning her to an imposing pillared entrance.

Once on the first floor, they progressed at intervals through inner vestibules towards the suite of the man Mr Harry described – flicking nervously at his lapels – as 'My Big Boss'. His nervousness was contagious and Charlotte did what she could to refurbish her appearance until a confrontation with her feet, duck-webbed with grime, forced fatalism upon her.

When eventually they were received into the sanctum, Charlotte was surprised to observe that the Big Boss was at least a decade younger than his employee; for Mr Harry, despite his sprightly exterior, was not a young man. In contrast to Mr Harry, too, the Boss (Charlotte never quite caught his name) had physical as well as official gravitas. He sat opposite his visitor with a Buddha's impassivity while Mr Harry sprang between, talking volubly first in Sulanasian and then, to Charlotte, in English.

'I explain to my Boss how you very very late coming from Banabalu and how I wait so long for you but he agree with me, we say no more on this subject. He think like me that is necessary we two – is this correct in English? – forgive and forget?'

Charlotte confirmed its correctness.

'My Boss say, like me, we both very love our God and our God – that is Moslem, you know – God tell us many many times, is not nice to remember things done against you. But is good to forgive and forget. You agree?'

Charlotte registered a degree of weariness at being quite so thoroughly forgiven but she said she agreed, whereupon Mr Harry extended both arms as one crucified for the sins of others and beamed alternately at her and his Boss. The Boss bowed his head gravely at Charlotte, she bowed gravely back and, at this evidence of reconciliation, Mr Harry regarded the ceiling for an instant, thanking his God for favours received.

'And now,' he said, 'my Big Boss have many many works to do. Therefore we must go.' He gave Charlotte a moue of sympathy for having to remove her so precipitately from the presence and, with many more bows, did so.

Outside, he took a spanking white hanky from a pocket and dabbed at the beads of perspiration on his brow. 'My Big Boss very happy I so good at English,' he confided. 'He not speak one word and I very useful to him many times with visitors as yourself.'

'He never learnt English?' Charlotte asked.

'Ah, *no.*' By his emphasis, she understood that a Big Boss had no time for such frivolities. 'Now come. I will explain to you our Tanjung Family Planning Programme. It is most good. You will see.'

Accessorizing himself with a large map, a box of coloured pins and a pointer, Mr Harry explained: profusely, repetitively and con brio. Most of it Charlotte already knew. The President, Mr Harry's Father and Leader, had decided six years ago, in his all-embracing wisdom, that poverty, undernourishment and what Mr Harry called 'underemployment' were as nothing compared to the evils of over-population. No other projects, no other endeavours – of which, Mr Harry assured her, the President had many up his sleeve – could be expected for a moment to succeed until the fecund wombs of Sulanasia's females had been efficiently and accountably stopped up. To this end, a new branch had been grafted on to the already massive trunk of the civil service and given a status greater than any other by virtue of the personal backing of the President himself. This branch was the KNNA, to which Mr Harry belonged and in which he looked, as he invoked his President, most personally backed.

The policies, the planning, the methods, these emanated from Banabalu and spiralled downwards from there across the island along a hierarchical chain of Regents and Governors, Regent-Governors and Governor-Regents, District Heads and Sub-District Heads of Village Headmen and Sub-Village Headmen until, at the lowest point of all, they were vigorously enacted upon the peasant women, by whose collective submission to the target statistics each member of the hierarchy rose or fell. It was, as Mr Harry told it, an epic tale of derring do, of Herculean obstacles overcome, of Augean stables sluiced and cleansed and of humble Goose Girls uplifted by the love of Princes. Charlotte was duly uplifted. The Sulanasian Family Planning Programme, as Stanton Koval had told her in Threadneedle Street, was indeed a jewel and shone with a crusading evangelism here at the grassroots.

After a while, she said, 'Is everyone who administers the programme a man?'

Mr Harry whipped round from his map. 'No, *no*,' he protested. 'Many, many women.'

'It's just that I don't see them. I mean, there . . .' and she pointed to the map, where each link in the chain was marked by a male silhouette of the kind more usually found on public lavatories.

Bewildered, Mr Harry peered at the object of Charlotte's index finger. His face cleared. 'That is only *drawing*,' he explained and gave a tolerant chuckle. He sat down beside Charlotte. 'You know,' he said, 'we have programme here. It is called Programme for Equal Partnership In Development Between Men and Women. And' – he paused impressively – 'that programme come, not from our President, but from our Minister for Women's Affairs. Who is *woman*!' He added, simply, 'That is my answer to you.'

'Ah,' Charlotte said. A cameo of said Minister came to her mind, complete with fluorescent diamond ring. But that was Banabalu. In the field, things would be down-to-earth, practical, plain-spoken, straightforward and it was premature to nag Mr Harry further. He looked so delighted by his conjuring of Madame Surnano out of a top hat and, besides, she was plumbing new depths of fatigue, no condition in which to ask pertinent questions.

Mr Harry jumped up and clapped his hands. 'So. We will go now and visit many women, Miss Harlot. Then you will see.'

Seizing her chance, Charlotte made urgent representations to her host concerning her sleepless night on the train, her dishevelled and unclean state and her urgent need to retire for a while to a cheap hotel in order to rectify these things before embarking on excursions, however illuminating. Mr Harry nodded energetically between each of her sentences. When she had come to the last of them, he gave her a dazzling smile.

'Is all true, what you say. You very dirty, I see that. Your hair most terrible. But I not mind. It not important. Because we now have' – and again he pulled out a struggling white rabbit – 'a Happy People Party!'

Charlotte gaped.

'Yes, yes, you see? I do good job for you. Happy People Party is in village now. You can visit. You can write many writings. You my very lucky guest.'

Lumbering out of Tanjung in the springless KNNA van, Charlotte remained immersed in various bodily discomforts – the mercilessly itching left nostril, the varnish of sweat on her flesh, her stomach's imitation of a starving cat – until the road dwindled to a dusty track and the last town buildings disappeared. Then, without fanfare, the star of the show made her entrance – primordial Sulanasia in all her opulent glory. Her curves rose to fill every window of the van, turning each one into an emerald cabachon. Charlotte rose, too, out of despondency into a spellbound delight that lasted until they reached the outskirts of a village surrounded by rice fields, encircled with high palms and set within a mauve bowl of mountains, each with a coolie hat of cloud tilted becomingly on its peak. The venue of the Happy People Party itself was humdrum enough: a cement bungalow flapping with banners, some youths propped up against motorbikes, several yellow dogs nosing in the dirt and four khaki-clad soldiers with handcuffs and holsters at their

111

hips, surveying the scene. The presence of these military men was unexpected as was their eerie resemblance to dolls of the Action Man type and Charlotte dodged past them with diffidence, afraid that the unexpected sight of a female who was clearly able to knock them sideways with one flick of a trunk-like finger, might cause them to lose confidence in their vocation. However, they showed no immediate inclination to turn in their badges, merely gazing up at her with amiable grins.

On the wide verandah that skirted the bungalow, some old men in black hats sat cross-legged between lines of gongs and xylophones, tapping on their instruments with padded sticks and chanting. Charlotte told Mr Harry as she threaded her way through them how glad she was to see that such music was still a living tradition and how enlightened it was of the Government to preserve the cultural heritage of the Sulanasian people, so ancient and so rich. Mr Harry received her compliments graciously and explained that the men were singing from a new Government issue of family planning melodies.

Inside the bungalow, rows of chairs faced a row of tables nicely furbished with stitched cloths and plastic vases of orchids. The chairs were occupied by forty or so village women in blouses and sarongs who sat with their babies slung at their sides, motionless and staring. The focus of their absorbed attention were the tables ahead, at which numbers of substantial males in safari suits were taking their places with much cheerful greeting of one another.

'All VIPs,' Mr Harry whispered as he ushered Charlotte to a seat at a side table. 'Some big KNNA bosses. Some have shops and factories. He and also he is religious leader. That man is village head.'

'And her?' asked Charlotte, indicating the only woman present, a winsome female in a tight plum bodice, long diamante ear-rings and many other shiny ornaments poked into her pancake bun.

'She headman's wife,' said Mr Harry. 'She first user of IUD in village. She use IUD for five year.'

Not for the first time in Sulanasia, Charlotte found this unabashed reference by a man to the inner furnishings of a woman's womb unsettling and distracted herself by examining the silky jaws of her orchid while Mr Harry kept up his running whisper on the outstanding personal achievements of each VIP. She ached to smoke as all the men were smoking but her last English cigarette was gone

112

and the sweet clove taste of the Sulanasian cigarette Mr Harry had offered her was still on her lower lip, purveying an odour of dentistry that panicked rather than calmed.

Nobody seemed to be in any hurry to start the proceedings. The women sat still in the still heat, their cinnamon faces entranced. Alongside them, all down the walls, young men in flared trousers lounged and chatted. The heat intensified. Charlotte perspired and watched, over her swollen nostril, a fly gyrate above her orchid. Mr Harry bowed assiduously around him but did not cease from whispering. Her ear lobe grew pink from his ministrations.

Eventually, a man with a wispy moustache took possession of a microphone and, turning his back on the women, talked at some length to the top tables, flashing his teeth now and again into the flash of a camera. He introduced the village headman, whereupon the headman's wife lifted two graceful hands towards the female audience and led its applause. Her husband then waxed marvellously garrulous, speaking for many minutes without a note and without Charlotte's comprehension since Mr Harry's translative talents dried up on the spot in deference to the speaker.

When the headman showed signs of tiring he was relieved of the microphone by another gentleman whose gold watch and rings gleamed with the vivacity of his gestures. More men came after him, abrim with words, awash with smiles. Charlotte watched the headman's wife who, unmoved by the oratory around her, pouted glossy lips into a compact, dabbed her nose with powder, spent several intent minutes disciplining her bun and, when thoroughly satisfied with her various parts, started to gossip with the soldier sitting beside her. The young men along the walls gossiped too, blowing out clouds of scented smoke at each other and grinding out the stubs under the stacked heels of their shoes. Here and there in the audience, women fumbled at their bodices and eased out pale breasts for their infants, managing to do so without even taking their eyes from the speakers. After a while, Charlotte began to doubt that such enthrallment could result from the mundane details of family planning. Perhaps the subject had been changed. Perhaps she was missing a fascinating digression into village scandal, a thrilling titbit on the life-style of some Banabulusian filmstar or a blow by blow account, for those without benefit of television, of the latest happenings in 'Dallas'.

'What does he talk about?' she mouthed at Mr Harry.

'IUD,' mouthed Mr Harry back.

Charlotte thought how delighted Ernestine Cotterstock would be, could she see this audience of women half across the world so captivated by the message she had spent her life delivering. It was peculiar. Worthy, of course, but peculiar. She tried to imagine what anyone could say about the intra-uterine device that would take quite so long, apart from listing the names of every woman in the country equipped with one. Given the national outspokenness on gynaecological matters, this was always possible. It was also possible that a speaker might suddenly turn and ask her to expatiate on her own internal decoration, forcing her to reveal her uncontracepted state to shock, horror and sensation all round.

There was a round of applause from the floor. Three women, older than the rest, were shuffling from their seats to be given large gold plaques by the village headman. They bobbed their heads low in thanks and one, overcome by such exposure, grinned madly with fright.

'They long-term acceptors,' Mr Harry said. 'They get prize. Maybe some time they meet our President. Maybe even they get money to go to Mecca, if they use IUD ten years. Then they are Hadj. Very high in Islam.'

'Per IUD ad astra.'

'Esactly,' Mr Harry said. 'And now it will be fashion show.' In anticipation of this new divertissement, he clasped his hands. In the audience, the women grew slack-jawed with amazement as the first model sidled in.

There were five models altogether, each vibrating with nerves. The first, in a cling-film sarong, inched across the floor like a clockwork mummy. The second was so swaddled by Islam that nothing could be seen of her but two startled eyes. The third, more sartorially liberated, wore the unexciting white blouse and navy skirt of an office clerk and the last two were decked out in daringly short striped frocks. But whatever they wore, trad or trendy, did not appear to dissipate their terror. Each paused for no more than a pulse-beat in front of the eager spectators before diving for the exit, backs bent, arms swinging, like miners making for the coal face. Unsurprisingly, the event lasted just under four minutes. As the last model ducked out, the men clapped kindly, Charlotte loudly and the village women not at all, too stunned by the spectacle to find their hands in time.

Charlotte was feeling relief at not having to compose a wardrobe from such subliminal glimpses when Mr Harry nudged her.

'And now, you,' he said, making disturbing gestures at the microphone.

She eyed him in alarm over the arc of her nostril. 'Me?' she croaked.

'To tell your impressions. To say some words. Please.' His hand was on her arm, urging her forward.

Huge, damp and nasally deformed, Charlotte got to her feet and tramped across the boards, giving a wonky smile at the rows of women. Silver teeth glinted as they smiled back. For the first time, silence fell upon the bungalow.

Charlotte cleared her throat and began. 'I would like to thank you all . . .'

There was a scurry at her side and a beaming Mr Harry popped up. He touched his lips to Charlotte and at her obedient pause, addressed the women, his translative juices once more flowing.

'For allowing me to participate,' she continued.

Mr Harry interpreted.

'In this interesting and . . .'

Mr Harry interpreted.

'. . . worthwhile event which . . .'

Mr Harry interpreted.

'I . . .' said Charlotte after a while. Later, she added, 'very much' and 'appreciate' and was glad no one seemed to be listening to her any more, since she had rather lost the thread of her original thought. Luckily, it seemed Mr Harry had not. Moreover, whatever polite banalities she managed occasionally to interject thereafter were not so much translated for her as quite transformed. That much was obvious, despite her inability to understand one word of those many that cascaded from his lips. Nothing that emanated from her could reasonably have been expected to evoke an audience reaction of the kind she saw before her. The women's eyes hoovered Mr Harry in, they smiled, they laughed, they grew grave at his direction. Deftly he spun responses from them, sinuously his hands wove circles in the air, hypnotically his voice rose, teetered at the edge of the highest tenor and spiralled downwards to basso profundo, with his eyebrows following suit. Every now and then he held out an indulgent hand to Charlotte and paused to let her feed in a line or two.

'The ability of women to control . . .' she said.

'. . . freedom from . . .' she said.

And Mr Harry whisked the phrases from her and whirled them around and threw them up and caught them again, juggling and spinning them as the women sighed and rolled their eyes in wonder. Charlotte, erect beside him like a snake forgotten by its charmer, would have forgotten herself too except for the itchy buzz of her nostril which, occasionally, she was compelled to scratch.

The applause, when it came, was ecstatic. Mr Harry bowed in every direction, his eyes modestly lowered. Charlotte bowed too, puzzled but pleased. The cameras flashed and everyone rose.

'Whatever did you *say* to them?' she asked as she followed Mr Harry out.

He turned, causing her to enclose his face momentarily in her cleavage. 'I tell only what you say, dear Miss Harlot,' he said earnestly, extricating himself. 'I just translator. You VIP. I humbly translate your every fine word.'

'Well. Thank you. You did it awfully well.'

'It is to me a pleasure. What, please, is that thing there?'

Shielding her nose from his pointing finger, Charlotte said awkwardly, 'I . . . I don't know.'

'Poor lady.' Mr Harry's face creased with compassion. 'You must think, always, God not care. God not care *what* you look.'

'No, no, you don't understand,' Charlotte said hastily. 'It's a bite. It's not always there.'

Mr Harry gave her a benevolent smile. 'And I not care, either, like my God. I not think at all about that big thing. Now we will see the Happy People. Come, come.'

The old men and their gongs had been swept off the verandah and replaced by a throng of overalled females who clustered round the village women as they emerged blinking into the sun and bustled them hither and thither, disposing them at various pamphlet-laden tables and newly-erected stalls or shooing them into the bungalow's side entrance.

'Why, there are the fruit-growers,' said Charlotte, surprised.

'What is that?' Mr Harry asked.

'Those women in the overalls with the drawings on them. I saw them at Madame Surnano's office. The Minister for Women's Affairs. The ones with the pears on their clothes.'

116

'You meet the Minister for Women's Affairs?' Mr Harry said, squinting at Charlotte.

'Yes, and they were . . .'

He blew vigorously through his moustache. 'You very lucky person.' He added, 'I not meet Minister for Women's Affairs. I not meet any Minister. I not meet any *any*one.' His face was woebegone.

This confession of deprivation touched Charlotte and she had already opened her mouth to tell him how unrewarding these encounters had been and how little he had missed when she realized that such assurances might offend. As an outsider, it was easy to underestimate the charisma of another country's bigwigs in the eyes of their subjects.

'When I get home,' she said, instead, 'I will write to Madame Surnano and tell her how well you speak English.'

Mr Harry's arms were pinned to his sides by the crush around him but his shoulders jumped appreciatively. 'You most kind,' he said. 'That help me very much. You not forget?'

'I won't,' Charlotte assured him.

'I think you are beautiful woman inside.'

Charlotte made a flattered noise.

'Your look outside is no importance.'

She made a less flattered noise. Tact was not one of Mr Harry's most obvious virtues. To avert further comment on her physical shortcomings, she switched the conversation back to the pear question.

Amused, Mr Harry said, 'Those drawings not pears. They wombs.' He pronounced it like 'bombs'. 'That is symbol of family planning. All KNNA field-workers have wombs.'

'I see,' Charlotte said, wishing she had left the pears alone. A certain queasiness assailed her and she wondered for a moment how well she would continue to cope with constant references to the female reproductive organs. In the nature of things, they were part of everyday parlance at the Cotterstock Clinic but at least everyone there, counsellors and counselled alike, possessed wombs and all adjacent apparatus and shared a tacit understanding of the problems and pleasures thereof. Here in Sulanasia, the approach was relentlessly unisexual as in unisexual hairdressers, establishments that Charlotte had always avoided. There was something disturbing about the reproductive terminology that rolled so fluently off the

117

lips of Sulanasian males. It was as if women were the inmates of some terribly progressive loony bin or open prison where kind and understanding male warders were trained to say 'we' when they clearly meant 'you'. It made her feel exposed, like a nude in the company of pin-striped men or a three-dimensional medical dummy exhibiting its privates to students. She had to repress a desire to say 'penis' or 'scrotum' aloud and often, just to even things up. Could it be the lack of cigarettes that was making her so tetchy?

Mr Harry had halted in front of a Heath Robinson contraption from which an iron hook protruded. Charlotte stopped beside him and watched a pear-ornamented woman relieve a young mother of the sling containing her baby, which useful conveyance she attached to the hook.

'Baby-weighing project,' Mr Harry announced. 'Very important in nutrition programme.'

The infant within its sling swung slowly backwards and forwards, regarding Charlotte solemnly from the folds of fabric. It was without the plumpness of a European infant, it possessed no fat bracelets of flesh at wrists and ankles. It had wide-set and sombre eyes and there was a curiously adult gravity about it as it hung and swung. Charlotte thought it adorable and watched wistfully as the mother took it back. She, too, had the same grave air, young as she was. The field-workers, often of the same age as their clients, were the Happy People at this Party, full of giggles and chatter, much given to patting arms and stroking backs, but the village women, focus of their attention, did not manifest the same *joie de vivre* but gazed wonderingly around them and held their babies close, as if for mutual protection.

Some of them were, at that moment, being hustled towards the side door. 'What's happening in there?' Charlotte asked Mr Harry.

'Aha!' he replied. 'In there, injections. Also IUD insertions. Come, you will see.'

Reluctantly, Charlotte followed as he butted through the crowd, reminding herself that she was here to report on such things however deeply her intestines disapproved.

The room was large and its walls bare but for the usual photograph of the President who gazed paternally down upon a clutter of wooden screens that zigzagged across the concrete floor. Mr Harry advanced upon one of the screens and to Charlotte's consternation, flipped it aside to reveal the young woman within.

She lay on her belly on a trestle table, her sarong folded back to expose her buttocks, at which a field-worker in black-rimmed specs was aiming a long syringe. Before Charlotte could avert her eyes, the needle punctured the brown flesh, the woman bit her lips and Mr Harry, carolling happily 'All over! Whee-hoo!' bustled onwards through the maze of screens.

'Was that Depo-Provera?' she panted behind him.

'Yes, yes. Very good. No come back for three month.'

'But . . .'

'And now,' he said, well into his role as master of ceremonies, 'here is IUD insertion!' and, ignoring Charlotte's protests, he whipped aside another screen. She tried to turn away but still glimpsed thin legs sagging apart and bony feet with the toes clenched, one on either side of an overalled back.

'She get IUD in. Whee-hoo!' said Mr Harry.

'So everyone can see,' Charlotte said weakly. The weakness, which had set in motion worms of sweat under her breasts, came less from squeamishness than from her own unforgivable intrusion.

'Esactly,' smiled Mr Harry. Then he saw her face. 'It not *hurt*, Miss Harlot. It is nothing. All finish . . . bam bam . . . one minute. Then the mother *so* happy.'

Having thus reassured her, he turned to greet a colleague. While he chatted, Charlotte saw the owner of the scrunched-up feet leave the cubicle. With her hair in a jaunty pony-tail, she looked no more than a schoolgirl, but there were beads of moisture on her temples and her skin was the colour of clay. She moved as if she walked on nails, her thin arms wrapped around her against the buffets of the crowd. Charlotte chewed her cheeks and kept the girl anxiously in sight as she negotiated the steps from the verandah. She sank down on the last one, folded her arms on her knees and laid her head on them. The pony-tail stuck up incongruously.

Charlotte interrupted her guide's conversation with a yank at his sleeve. 'Look,' she said, 'that girl's not well. Do something.'

Mr Harry gave an accommodating cough and disappeared behind another screen, emerging with a stout field-worker who made her way to the crouched figure and laid a plump arm across the girl's shoulders.

'She soon all right,' said Mr Harry, back from his errand of mercy. 'She fine. She okay.'

'She shouldn't be on her feet so quickly after an IUD,' Charlotte said with unusual sharpness. 'It can be painful, you know.' Gloria Watkins at the Cotterstock expanded frequently upon the ordeal of her insertion. 'Bad as bleeding labour,' she'd told Charlotte. 'Thought any moment the doctor'd say oh look, you've just given birth to two lovely little kidneys.' Gloria was nothing if not vivid in her accounts of the female experience.

'Anyway,' Charlotte added, 'the IUD can be dangerous for women. Bad for their health, you know?'

He shook his head, his eyes as round with disbelief as if she had informed him that Santa Claus was a child molester. Or in his case, Charlotte thought, adjusting her metaphor, Allah. 'No, no. Not bad. IUD *good*,' he protested. 'No trouble for the mothers. Just one time and . . .'

Charlotte saw that he was becoming enthusiastic and decided it would be as well to cut him short before he assured her that women positively enjoyed having the IUD inserted, looked forward to it, begged for it as a birthday treat.

'The fact is,' she said in her governess's voice, 'IUDs can cause many troubles. Take ectopic pregnancies, for instance.'

'E . . to . . pi? Please, I not understand.'

She expanded on the possibility of a fertilized ovum embedding itself in the fallopian tube. She waxed eloquent on the agonizing pain that resulted as this narrow channel split, the sudden and severe haemorrhaging that could, if not diagnosed immediately and as swiftly operated upon, prove fatal. She put it to Mr Harry: could he, in all honesty, say that the back-up services of the KNNA were sufficient to cope with this hazard? Would, for example, a woman from one of these villages have much chance of reaching a hospital before she bled to death?

During this bout of oratory, Mr Harry's eyes had jellified and as it came to an end he took two steps back, bumped against a stall, picked up something and held it out to Charlotte, saying with an uncertain smile, 'You like? Then please accept my gift to you.'

The object was a crochet square in an evil shade of pink, decorated with puce bows and containing a bar of green kitchen soap. Charlotte felt quite strongly that she could live nine lives without it.

'It's very nice,' she said. 'But you mustn't . . .'

The orbs of Mr Harry lost their film. 'Of course. I wish. You take, it is yours. And now, I think you see enough of Happy People. We go.'

He aimed his brilliantined head at the bungalow's exit and dived towards it, leaving Charlotte clutching his gift. She looked at the stall, upon which were arranged a collection of bottles filled with liquid, some sweetmeats wrapped up in banana leaves and other mysterious crocheted merchandise. The stall-holder, a gaunt grey-haired woman holding a balloon in one hand and a placid infant in the other, smiled purposefully at a bowl of coins. Scrabbling in her pockets, Charlotte gathered another six and put them all in, to the woman's salaams.

Then she beetled after Mr Harry.

The Hotel Puri, at whose entrance she was finally deposited after an afternoon wading through rice fields asking astonished women workers, upon Mr Harry's instructions, if they used contraceptives and learning, upon his translation, that they all did, was highly modernistic, having a facade of bathroom tiles scribbled with magenta neon lettering and an octagonal lobby crammed with Japanese tourists and their handsome luggage.

Charlotte dropped her own shabby trappings by the reception desk and, against the impassioned pleas of the hotel clerk, took the cheapest room on the price card. The journey to it, in the company of a small boy who lost his way twice, was a journey back in time. Room 101 appeared to have been uninhabited almost long enough to qualify as an archeological dig but it had its own bathroom, kitted out with sanitary ware of the sort that went down with the *Titanic* and, besides the bed, contained a three-piece suite with clam-shell arms and a wireless that could have been Signor Marconi's own, all clearly visible beneath a substratum of dust.

Her travelling clock told her it was 8 o'clock, too early to go to bed. On the other hand, she was too far gone to do anything else, in spite of a renewed outburst of spoon-banging from her stomach, which had received no nourishment for forty-eight hours other than the sop of a snatched peanut biscuit. Unwrapping two glucose tablets, she dispatched them to the mutineer. Then she lathered herself from a basin of rusty water, washed one cotton jump suit and hung it up, smeared Anthisan on her swollen nostril and extended herself on the bed, whose mattress felt as if it were stuffed with

121

corpses. Within seconds and without the aid of Nitropazam, she fell heavily asleep.

Awaking nine hours later, Charlotte lay for some time in a state of self-congratulation at her unexpected ability to feel so well under such bizarre conditions. Nothing ached, nothing much itched, nothing rumbled or wheezed. An inspection in the bathroom mirror informed her that her nose had shrunk to its British proportions and though her ankles were covered in scratches, mementos of the bristly rice plants, and carried the marks of some bug attention in the night, Autan had fended off the worst. Moreover, there was a becoming flush of sun on her skin and, marvel of marvels, she had lost some weight. She felt thinner, she looked thinner and a quick test with a belt proved she was thinner.

This fact, combined with the heat that had not noticeably diminished even at this early hour, so encouraged her that, against long custom, she stepped out of her nightdress and stood boldly mother-naked. The sight of herself no longer distressed her and experiment showed that by sucking in her stomach she could produce a passing simulation of one of the earthier Roman goddesses. Heartened, she left the mirror and humming a cheerful tune, leant over to release the blind that covered the window.

It shot up with a crash to disclose, inches from the glass, the profiles of two men outside, engaged in conversation. Wonderingly, they turned to face her and their eyes – now directly upon Charlotte's nipples – rounded to the owlish dimensions of an infant watching breakfast approach.

For one appalling second Charlotte stood paralysed, nipples poking at the men's engrossed pupils. Then she lunged for the cord, slammed the blind down and leapt for her bed, where she dragged the sheet up to her chin and stared up at the insect-ridden ceiling. How awful, she told herself wildly, how perfectly, dreadfully awful. It would be impossible ever to emerge from her room. Like an equatorial Miss Haversham she must now become a recluse, to be discovered cocooned in tarantula webs by the second explorer intrepid enough to hack a path to Room 101. She felt her chest begin to quake. Shortly after, the room resounded to hysterical peals.

*

An hour later she made her way cautiously through several abandoned halls and deserted courtyards until she found the lobby again. It was empty except for a man in a coolie hat hosing down the steps, as was the echoing chamber where the Hotel Puri dispensed its breakfasts. Beside a heap of fallen music stands she ate a plate of pineapple cubes and some slices of a strange fruit that smelt like a dustbin and tasted like nectar. The coffee set up the inevitable craving and she lit her second clove cigarette, only to grind it out after two puffs, defeated. As she sat keeping an eye out for Mr Harry a young man entered the room. He carried a briefcase out of which he took the carved figure of a dancer, holding it out to Charlotte.

'No, thank you very much,' she said politely.

He put the dancer back in his case and sat down beside her. He was wafer-thin, with the soft, sad-eyed look of a baby deer that had mislaid its mother.

'You are English,' he said.

'Yes. Yes, I am,' said Charlotte, managing to sound as if this was news to her.

'Do you like Chinese porcelain? I can find this for you.'

As it happened, Charlotte did. Her mother owned two large and beautiful Chinese vases that she had loved ever since she could remember and that had somehow and miraculously survived Mrs Wren's random ambushes with a duster. However, she had no currency to spare. 'No, if you don't mind,' she said.

He did not pursue the matter. Instead, he enquired as to Charlotte's business in Sulanasia. She explained.

'Ah. Our President likes very much this programme.' He regarded his intertwined fingers, yawned discreetly and added, 'Two children are enough.'

The phrase appeared to depress him. Charlotte said, 'You speak English very well.'

'I study at Tanjung University.'

'How nice,' she said inanely and asked him some questions about his studies which he answered in an absent-minded way, frowning at the tablecloth as if he were patiently waiting for her to stop. She stopped.

'What do you think of my country?' he asked then.

Charlotte said a few enthusiastic words in praise of the mountains and the scenery in general.

'Oh yes,' he said cheerlessly, 'the scenery. Very beautiful.' His collar-bones showed under his white shirt as he slouched further in his chair. She sought for something to arouse him from his curious lethargy. 'What do you think of the birth control programme here?'

'It is efficient,' he said.

'And do you agree with it? Do you think it's a good thing?'

His sloping eyes were concealed from her. He was examining her plate. 'Did you enjoy your breakfast?'

'Very much.'

A silence fell between them while Charlotte thought, for some reason, of the box of Kleenex in a Cotterstock cubicle. He yawned again and stood up, giving her a little bow.

'I work here, in the evenings. Perhaps we shall have more conversation?'

'I should like that,' Charlotte said.

He walked away, looking, in his thinness, as if his clothes hung from a coat hanger, leaving Charlotte vaguely disturbed. If this was his idea of conversation she couldn't see why he should want more. Besides, yawns were a bad sign. Cotterstock clients often yawned before telling her things she would have preferred not to know. But perhaps he was merely bored – he had wanted to sell a foreigner something, hadn't succeeded and had been too courteous simply to take himself off. She turned her thoughts to the probable arrival of Kelly some time during the day and forgot the student.

In the van on the way to what Mr Harry called 'an income-generating village', she settled down contentedly to watch the Sulanasian world go by. Mr Harry, however, was not interested in the scenery.

'I very glad to practise my English with you.'

'Mmm,' she said.

An old man jogged along the road outside, a bamboo pole across his shoulders that carried two panniers crammed with blinking hens.

'I not get chance very much.'

A pony drew up beside the van at a traffic light. Its mane was tied back with yellow bows and the shafts of the trap it drew were brightly painted. Charlotte craned her neck to watch it as they passed. 'What a dear little thing,' she said.

'You see, I not go to university.'

They were coming to a market square crowded with stalls and people. At one corner, on high poles, hung wicker birdcages of intricate design. Inside, grey doves fluttered. 'Look,' Charlotte sighed, 'how pretty they are.'

Mr Harry gave a much louder sigh. 'Oh, my poor, *poor* father,' he exclaimed.

Charlotte, fearing some incident involving Mr Harry Senior, said, 'Where?' and looked round nervously.

'Dead,' said Mr Harry, brightening, 'My poor father want me so much to go to university. But I say to him no, my father, I cannot go.' He paused, eyeing Charlotte. 'You ask me why?'

Giving up all hope of a sightseeing interlude, Charlotte turned away from the window and asked him why.

'Because –' and the wattage of his smile increased dramatically – 'I have very low IQ.'

'Oh, surely not,' she said, flustered by this frank admission.

'You think no. But it is true. I know this. I tell it to my father. I say, father, oh my father, I too low IQ for go to university. And you cannot pay, my father, you too old. But he say, my son, you must go. I order you. So I go because, Miss Harlot, in Sulanasia a son obey his father, my God tell me this.' Mr Harry tapped a finger on the metal above as if his God were strapped to the roof rack.

'So what happened?' asked Charlotte. 'You went and . . .'

'I went, yes. But for one year only. Maybe less, I not remember. Then my father come to me. He say, ah my poor son, please you forgive me.' Mr Harry crossed his chest and swayed slightly to illustrate paternal remorse. 'I wrong, you right. I too old, I cannot pay more. You must leave from the university.'

'Oh dear,' Charlotte said. 'How sad.'

The expression on Mr Harry's face was St Theresian. 'Yes, sad. But I not down-hearted. I say to my father, by Jove' – he pronounced this to rhyme with love – 'I will go to the English Club in Tanjung and work. There I will learn English good.'

'Which you certainly did,' Charlotte said. 'And then?'

'Then?'

'What did you do after that?'

Mr Harry did not answer immediately and she looked at him. For a moment she had the fleeting impression that another face altogether lay under the smiling one, like the flat face of a stone just below the surface of a babbling brook. Then it was gone, if it had ever been.

'I get job with KNNA. I very happy with this good job. My wife and children also most happy.'

'But what did you do before?'

'Please?' He had lost interest.

'I mean, between working at the English Club and joining the KNNA. Because that only started six years ago, isn't that right?'

'Right, right. See how nice the mountain.'

'So you were always in the civil service?'

'Right, right.' He waved his hand at the window. 'See. Very beautiful scenery. Volcano, water, trees. Everything.'

Everything was indeed beautiful. It also imposed a heavy strain on Charlotte's nerves. They were climbing on a narrow shelf of road that splayed out from the mountain's flank without any visible underpinnings and the van grunted like a buffalo as it edged up alongside a wall of rocks the size of houses, kept from toppling by luck alone. On the other side of the road, the land fell away in tier after rounded tier of paddy fields to the depths of the valley and swooped up again in the distance on a switchback of hills as if some stage-struck Titan had carved out an amphitheatre, complete with a thousand loges for the use of his giant guests. The hills wore a mantle more royally green than the most royal of botanical gardens, made up of great broad-leaf trees whorled at every level with the tossing heads of palms and embroidered with the sequins of the watery fields. Far away, the grey bitten head of a volcano – extinct, Charlotte devoutly hoped, remembering Bruce's death-dealing statistics – reared from a rusty river bed with a hundred silver waterfalls cataracting from its shoulders.

She took no photographs, having long given up the illusion that they would evoke anything from the home audience but witty sallies or, in her mother's case, more than usual confusion: once, armed with a drawing Charlotte had made of the male reproductive tract, Mrs Wren had endeavoured to find her way to Brighton. This landscape, above any other Charlotte had seen, was grand beyond hope of capture on film and besides, her hands had developed an inconvenient shake. Horizontals on this scale were not her forte, particularly when all that appeared to lie between her and a foreign grave were four rubber tyres that could not have bribed their way through an MOT.

Instead, she imprinted the picture onto her memory cells and when her insides began to mimic the switchback hills, removed her eyes and focused on Mr Harry's profile. It was, for once, immobile, and after a second or two she realized with a small jolt of surprise that, although not in the Kelly league, his features were in their more modest way fine and even handsome. His smile, that constant presence, unbalanced and obscured. It was a decent enough smile and the teeth it revealed were a credit to him, but it pulled his nose and chin askew, giving his face a clownishness it did not possess in repose. She found herself wondering about his wife and children.

'How many children do you have, Mr Harry?' she asked, relaxing now that they had reached the brow of the hill and were driving on the flat, among the domestic vegetation of umbrella peanut plants and neat rows of cassava.

'Two children only, Miss Harlot.' The smile was back in place. 'Two children is enough, I think. Is that not right?' and he winked twice rather clumsily, like a man weakened by a stroke.

'Boys? Girls?'

'Two girls only. I sad for that. I very like a little boy. But . . .' He shrugged.

'So your wife is an acceptor?' It was not the sort of query she would have dreamed of making to a relative stranger in England, but in Sulanasia such intimate details were common currency, if not actually compulsory.

'Of course, *of course*. She first acceptor in my village because she KNNA wife.'

The first houses appeared along the road, some thatched with rattan, some long and sway-backed with tiles. Three boys played football in a clearing, kicking the ball into a bamboo goal. Another boy limped along behind them on a bent and wasted leg, his eyes under a thicket of curls straining ahead.

Watching him, Charlotte said, 'She decided herself, did she, that she wanted to use contraception?'

'Of *course*,' Mr Harry repeated. 'My wife very emancipated woman. We discuss together. Then, when it is time for child, I take from her the IUD.'

'I see,' Charlotte said, shying from the image of this unilateral action. The van, wheezing badly from its long uphill run, groaned to a halt and nosed in under the urbane leaves of an acacia tree.

'We here,' proclaimed Mr Harry and slid the van door open with a flourish for Charlotte to descend. But they were not there. This stop was a courtesy visit: the income-generating village was still what Mr Harry called 'just a little round corner', waving around at the trees. It had been foolish of her to think she would progress directly from A to B in this country awash with jasmine tea and underemployed officials.

True to form, this official, a robust pock-marked man of a powerfully hospitable nature, provided Charlotte with pints of tea – in the field, one was compelled to drink it – while explaining at length, through Mr Harry, the successes of high-altitude family planning. He had sixteen gold trophies in his glass-fronted cabinet to prove his assertions and praised to the heavens the wonders of contraception that, according to him, would at some time that afternoon or possibly earlier, enrich the poor, provide jobs for the unemployed, erect schools and houses in their millions and purge from every part of Sulanasia the evils of illiteracy, infant mortality, disease and, if strictly administered, death itself. His faith in these miracles was appropriately religious in expression, provoking frequent uplifted glances and hands placed parallel in prayer. The only English phrase he knew was 'baby boom' and he interjected it whenever words failed him which was, Charlotte reflected, mopping her brow, not often enough.

Though she tried to avoid asking questions which, in this company, too nearly resembled throwing oil on a forest fire, a lecture on the campaign to raise the marriage age, another way of stemming 'baby boom', made her ask how this fitted in with the polygamy of Islam.

'Polygamy?' said Mr Harry, stumped.

'When a man has more than one wife. That is permitted to Moslems, isn't it? And that must lead to more children.'

The two men consulted in rapid Sulanasian. Mr Harry squared his shoulders. 'It is permitted to Moslems to marry more wifes, that is true. But our God not like it. In the Ko'ran' – he said this with an intervening hiccup, in the Arab way – 'it say is possible, if you must. But God not at all like it.'

'And divorce? Islam permits divorce to the man, doesn't it? That must also affect the birth statistics.'

Again the two men consulted, their faces anxious. Carefully, Mr Harry phrased his answer. 'God does permit. That is true also. But' – and his voice cracked with emotion – 'God hate divorce. God simply *hate* it.' There was a hushed pause then, possibly to allow God a confirming thunderbolt. Nothing happened. Mr Harry stood up and clapped his hands, indicating that question-time was at an end.

'We go see income-generating village now. Good, Miss Harlot? Very good.'

There was a short but thorough downpour on the next lap of the journey so that by the time the van had reached a gap in the wall of trees and parked, every item in the landscape was drenched and Charlotte's ears rang with the rattle of rain on the roof.

'The village,' Mr Harry cried and, jumping from the vehicle, filtered his guest between the trees whose leaves, parting above her, emptied their contents over her head with an efficiency that put most English bathroom showers to shame.

There was no village at the other side, only a slimy ribbon of mud that vanished into the steaming vegetation. For the next twenty minutes Charlotte plodded and slithered along it, collecting thick hooves of clay around her sandals, while Mr Harry leapt nimbly from boulder to boulder in a useful pair of rubber bootees with which he had stealthily equipped himself within the van.

'You will see new tofu-maker in this place,' he said, adding, in the interests of clarity, 'to make tofu. You know what is tofu, Miss Harlot? Oh, *poor* Miss Harlot.'

To a greedy sucking sound, Charlotte peeled herself off the path, where she had fallen for the fourth time. A fresh layer of mud adhered to one hip and encircled her bottom, which ached quite badly from its frequent contact with the Sulanasian countryside. 'Tofu,' she panted. 'Bean curds, we say.'

'Esactly,' Mr Harry buzzed about her, as did a cloud of gnats. 'Our women in this village very happy now. The new tofu-maker help them make snacks, quick quick. They make many many and they sell snack, many many. So, they have income.'

Charlotte extracted strands of hair from her eyes and peered ahead, wondering whether some chrome-and-formica kitchen could exist at the end of this Flanders trench.

'Who do they sell them to?' she grunted through fissured lips, but there was no response. The green had closed behind Mr Harry, its components snapping painfully at Charlotte's cheeks in the process, causing the moisture all around to reproduce itself in her eyes. Puffing, she bent her head against the entanglements and when she raised it again to wrench more hair from a passing vine she saw before her a dappled clearing in which stood Mr Harry and three other nattily dressed men, nodding a welcome. She lurched towards them, sadly aware of the grisly sight she must present and hoping only that the heat of the sun would not bake her within her clay shell like a chicken in a Habitat briquette.

But she was in a village at last, her first genuine Sulanasian village, and walking with the men, still breathing rather heavily, she marvelled at it. Each house appeared to grow from the land, at once a living part of the forest around and yet separate, fashioned, ordered. The struts of bamboo that formed the walls – no new-fangled concrete here – gave to its residents shade and air and privacy, and the palm-thatched rooves melted unobtrusively into the canopy of the palms above. Here and there, tied to the eaves, grey doves in wicker cages cooed and at each dim doorway women stood with children on their hips and at their skirts, timid, goggling and, when Charlotte caught their eyes, shyly smiling. The scene was an idyllic one, so much so that she found herself speculating for an instant on the possibility that it had been run up like a stage set for her visit and would be dismantled as she headed for the town again.

'And here is the tofu-maker,' announced Mr Harry. Proudly he patted a type of outboard motor that jutted from an assemblage of iron and cement. The whole lay in the shelter of a rattan outhouse at the back of the village meeting hall, a bamboo building of delicate proportions in whose dark interior women huddled while the men gathered outside, around the motor. 'It is given to the women by the organization Global Family Funding,' he said.

'Ah,' said Charlotte.

'Before the engine come, the men must grind the soya beans. Look. Here are the old grind-stones. Very difficult work. The men very tired. But now, whee-hoo! So quick. You watch.'

Charlotte watched. One of the men, in a peaked hat and threadbare shorts, picked up a sack of wet soya beans and emptied it into a wide funnel. He plucked at the engine and it roared to life, sending the nearby hens skittering. From the base of the

130

funnel, a milky liquid poured into the bucket below. When it was full, he picked it up and emptied it, in its turn, into a cement cauldron, where it began to bubble over the wood fire below.

'It must cook one quarter of an hour,' said Mr Harry, backing from the flames. 'Then it stay in the sun and get thick and then the women make snacks.'

The procedure continued. Another sack of beans was fed into the funnel, another bucketful slopped into the cauldron. There was a lot of noise, which appeared to please the men. They sat cross-legged on bamboo benches and sucked their teeth in absorbed contemplation of Miss Millichip's gift.

Presently, Charlotte turned to Mr Harry. 'What are the women doing?' she enquired.

'Please?'

'The women,' Charlotte repeated. She had noticed before that questions concerning the female sex had an oddly muffling effect upon her guide's hearing.

'They inside. They wait to make snacks.'

She scratched under one breast and tried to remember when or if she had taken this week's malaria tablets. It was the female mosquito that carried the disease, or so they said. An unsisterly insect. She said, 'So this is not the machine that helps the women make snacks?'

Mr Harry removed his gaze from the soya bean activities and regarded Charlotte, perplexed. 'Yes, of course. That it. That *it*,' and he waved towards the roaring engine.

There was a kind of bed beside the wall, laced with leather thongs. Charlotte sat down on it. 'If you don't mind,' she said, taking out her notebook, 'I just want to make sure I've got it right. Now. Before this engine came, the men had to grind the soya beans by hand.'

'Esactly,' Mr Harry said.

'And the women made the snacks by hand.'

'Esactly. Esactly.'

'Then Global Family Funding gave the engine to help the women.'

Mr Harry's esactlys trebled, encouraging his backward protégée.

'But, Mr Harry, the engine doesn't help the women, does it? It helps the men.'

In the pause that followed, a translucent butterfly settled on Charlotte's left hand. She and Mr Harry stared at it together.

'Oh my goodness my,' he said finally. 'It hot. It very hot.' This fact had evidently caught him unawares. He eased himself out of his jacket and folded it over one arm. Then he sat down beside her on the bed, which sagged slightly, nestling their shoulders close. 'You not understand too well, I think. The engine make many more tofu so women can make many more snacks. Miss Harlot, I tell you this before.' His voice held a restrained reproof.

Charlotte remembered the Mad Hatter's story of the sisters who lived down a treacle well. Now she knew how they felt. She did not want to continue this interrogation, sitting halfway up a mountain in the middle of a forest beside a man who might or might not have a low IQ. Mr Harry hummed under his breath. They sat shoulder to shoulder for a few more minutes until the headman of the village, a portly gentleman with his own photograph pinned to his lapel – was amnesia a tropical hazard? – indicated that the soya bean crushing could proceed without them and ushered his visitors into the interior of the building, where there were five wooden chairs arranged side by side. This made relaxed conversation tricky but, since it was expected of her, Charlotte did her best. Turning her head rhythmically from left to right, Wimbledon-fashion, she assured her hosts of her interest in their endeavours, to satisfied smiles down the line. Two women appeared and bobbed nervously in front of Charlotte, offering her food from a tray.

'Tofu snacks,' Mr Harry informed the room.

She nibbled her snack. It was bland but filling. As she ate, she glanced around. From every strut and beam hung stooks of rice, strings of dried corn-cobs and clay gourds, giving the bamboo room with its earthen floor the look of a country cottage done up by Laura Ashley. She could, she decided, be very happy here, if the whole could be transferred to somewhere cooler. Northamptonshire, say, via the North Pole. Mr Harry's elbow recalled her from a daydream involving a swift plunge into polar seas. 'Any more questions?' he asked.

'Yes,' she said. 'Why did Global Family Funding give the tofu engine to this particular village?'

'Ah *ha*!' He extended a finger into the roasting atmosphere. 'I will answer that. Because, dear guest, all women of fertile age here

132

are acceptors. All have IUD. Very good village, we pleased. We give them reward. We say to the women, if you put in IUD like our President wish, you get prosperous. When the women say to us, we have IUD, then along come' – he walked his fingers through the air – 'Global Family Funding to give good women tofu-engine. We keep our promise!' He gave himself a little hug at the moral logic of his story.

'I see,' Charlotte said. 'The women get the IUD, the men get the engine.'

'Esactly,' Mr Harry breathed and sat back in his chair, mightily relieved that his guest had at last understood.

The return journey was easier. By then, the mud had been baked solid and Charlotte only tripped once. In the van, as the driver revved up, she asked a last question. 'The men in the village. Do any of them use contraceptives?'

Mr Harry spoke around the edges of a white hanky as he dabbed genteelly at his temples. 'Ho no,' he replied.

'And why not?'

Mr Harry folded his hanky, tucked it neatly into a pocket and twinkled at her. 'Because our women no like,' he answered. 'They not like at all. And men not do what women not like. In Sulanasia men say, always' – and he placed a hand upon his sternum – 'the woman is Queen. You understand?'

A little light-headed, she turned to the window. As the van coughed itself awake, she watched a moulting hen scratch between the protruding roots of a tree. Then, fluffing out what feathers it possessed, it settled in the shallow depression and its little hen eyes took on a thoughtful look. Charlotte found herself worrying that if it didn't hurry a KNNA official would nip out of the forest, catch it round its skinny neck and contracept it.

'Push,' she urged it silently as the van drew away.

On the drive back to Tanjung, Charlotte's breathing apparatus seized up, refusing to expel the air it had inhaled with any sort of grace. The resulting sound of distant bagpipes caught Mr Harry's attention.

'Why your bosoms whistle?' he asked, focusing with interest on her palpitating chest.

She tried for nonchalance which, in the face of slow asphyxiation, was not easy, and grappled in her bag for the inhaler. Fortunately it was to hand and by the time her guide had become really concerned, his face approaching hers so closely she feared an attempt at mouth-to-mouth resuscitation, her lungs were going about their proper business and the maroon of her cheeks had subsided to pink.

'You very sick,' Mr Harry pronounced.

'No,' she gasped. 'It's nothing. Soon over.'

However, she could summon up no more breath than that, so Mr Harry kindly raised his voice to drown out her residual rasps and embarked on a detailed account of another bonus awarded mothers who accepted intra-uterine devices – the free immunization of their existing children.

'So now,' he concluded as the van left the mountain track for the asphalt valley road, 'our babies have no more the polio. No more the cholera or tetanus or typhoid. Also we have baby rehydration therapy, so no more dysentery. In old days this very bad. Kill many. Today, that all finish. No more infant mortality. Bam bam – gone,' and he chopped exuberantly at Charlotte's knee, causing her leg to give a congratulatory kick.

She remembered the boy limping after his companions on the improvised football field and told herself she must not lose sight of the wood for the trees. Sulanasian birth control might have its imperfect aspects but if the children gained by it, if little ones lived instead of dying and lived well and whole, then the work of Gordon Grant and even of Miss Millichip was a thousand times worthwhile.

'You mean,' she said to Mr Harry, 'that infant deaths are now far fewer? That if women have just two children, those children live?'

'Esactly,' said Mr Harry. 'Esactly, esactly. And now we eat.'

The van slowed down beside a cluster of houses and stalls and with a poignant gurgle, the engine died. Its occupants clambered out and Mr Harry directed Charlotte towards some plastic-covered tables set out behind one particularly well-stocked kitchen-on-wheels. Though the tables were arranged rather too near the dusty road entirely to suit her view of hygiene – a fine layer of diesel grease had already made the tablecloth tacky – she subsided on to her chair with a good grace, still cheered by what she had heard of the battle for infant survival. An elderly lady with cheekbones that swelled proudly above the indigo gums of betel addiction placed before them large glasses containing a pink liquid, copiously iced.

'Papaya juice,' Mr Harry said and raised his glass. 'Bottoms up.'

Charlotte chinked her glass at him and put it down again. Ice. Never touch ice, Elspeth had warned, unless you know where the water has come from. She looked anxiously at the stall. A mottled bucket stood there with, at its rim, a dripping hose. She craned round to track down its provenance.

'You no like?' Mr Harry said.

'Oh yes, yes. It's just' – and she gave a quick cough to clear her parched throat – 'I'm not actually thirsty.'

Melancholy settled on Mr Harry, weighing down his shoulders. 'You afraid Sulanasian water dirty. All visitors afraid so. I know this. I so shamed.'

His accompanying sigh shamed Charlotte in her turn. The pink liquid must be imbibed, no matter how uninhibitedly the germs of tropical disease might besport themselves therein. Noblesse, or whatever, obliged. She picked up her glass and gulped its contents. Having thus disposed of her remaining hold on health, she joined Mr Harry and the driver of the van in the further disposal of a large platter of noodles topped by wizened eggs and a bowl of some green leaves thickly pasted with peanuts. Her stomach, ignorant and blissful, licked its lips. Mr Harry smiled brightly at his doomed guest.

When the meal was over, Charlotte walked to the van and stood waiting for her guide, who had closed upon himself a battered door to the side of the stall. The midday sun exacted a fresh spurt of sweat from her as the price for every movement though it did not seem unduly to penalize the four or five customers eating and drinking with gusto at the stall. As she looked at them, she saw again the leprous bucket with its dripping hose and, without interruption this time, picked out and followed its snaking length with eyes shielded against the light. The hose ran along a gutter choked with the skins of bananas and other less readily identifiable remains, coiled around two of the outside tables and disappeared in a runnel of mud beneath the door that presently concealed Mr Harry.

At this unhappy conclusion Charlotte closed her eyes, moved herself a careful ninety degrees around and opened them again. This time, they alighted upon an edifice across the road. In front of it was a plot of earth wherein were laid out, in geometric rows, many white coffin-shaped tombstones, each neatly tailored to fit a future occupant aged between zero and approximately three years old.

Then Mr Harry was beside her, discreetly adjusting his dress. 'Please. Now we full, we go to other clinic.' He slid the van door back with energy renewed.

As darkness extinguished the orange roofs of Tanjung and the Christmas tree bulbs that looped along the shop fronts lit up in greens and blues and reds, Charlotte climbed down for the last time that day from the mud-streaked van.

'You not mind little walk to hotel?' Mr Harry asked through the window. 'I very busy with my Big Boss tonight and I late already. You *sure* you not mind?'

Whereupon the van lurched forward on spinning wheels, threw up a farewell chunk of road at Charlotte and sped into the night. Charlotte brushed herself down and began plodding towards the Hotel Puri, grateful for the mercy of a vanished sun. All along the pavements on either side, men and women squatted beside blankets and rugs upon which was arrayed a catholic collection of goods. No passer-by showed the remotest interest in buying any of it. Only the food stalls, aureoled in the glow of smouldering charcoal fires, were doing good business selling, Charlotte piously hoped, tofu snacks. With a view to encouraging the patient merchants, she proceeded to buy a rubber animal of doubtful species, a pair of flip-flops, a mangled John D. Macdonald paperback and a white T-shirt. As she paused with her purchases to gaze through a shop window at a stuffed mongoose, one of whose legs was stuck halfway down the wired-open fangs of an extremely shiny snake, a small figure trailed past. It was a young woman – a girl – whose face was glossy with sweat and whose hair, scraped back from hollow temples, rose at the crown of her head into a jaunty pony-tail. Her bare feet dragged in the dust and her fists were pressed into her stomach. Charlotte started after her, dodging through the honking traffic. It looks like the girl from the Happy People Party who had hobbled out after her

136

IUD insertion. She had had a pony-tail but, then, how many other girls in Tanjung wore their hair in that fashion? It was not difficult to catch her up but when she had, Charlotte could only walk alongside her, looking foolishly at her bent head, unable to offer a word of comfort. The girl was whimpering under her breath and Charlotte's stomach clenched with pity and frustration.

Just then the girl veered on to the pavement, halted at the back of a stall and stooped below Charlotte's line of vision. Charlotte stood still, jostled by the crowd. When she saw the girl again, she had a sack on her back crammed with bricks and the sweat dripped from her chin.

'Don't!' Charlotte exclaimed to nobody. 'No.' Her protest did not fall on deaf ears.

'You tired,' said a voice behind her, rich with commercial sympathy. She looked round. The man wore a torn straw trilby and his eyes, under a ragged fringe of hair, regarded her eagerly. 'Miss, I see you very tired. Where you want to go? I take you.' He nudged her thighs in a friendly fashion with the edge of his pram-bike.

Speechless, she shook her head and peered into the throng that choked the narrow thoroughfare. The girl and her impossible load were no longer visible. 'Oh *dear*,' she said.

'Oh dear oh dear oh dear,' the man echoed, pleased to have elicited a response. 'You have too many shoppings, oh dear. Please, you get in.'

The pram bumped at the back of her knees, buckling them, and before she could regain her balance, the man had scooped her up and was jogging her down the street, shouting merrily 'Where to?' She told him and sat sulkily until she was decanted at the bottom of the Hotel Puri steps. As she paid and gathered up her parcels, she glanced towards the brightly lit verandah and saw Kelly there, comfortably slumped in a deck chair, a long drink at his elbow and a group of squatting children at his feet, engaged in trying to sell him an assortment of bead necklaces.

From the merciful darkness Charlotte observed the honey-gold head, the armoured chest, the long slope of thigh. She heard his low laughter as he joked with the children and caught a flash of white teeth in the blunt lion face. It all added up to a display of looks so ostentatious as to give her no other option but to find her way into the hotel by whatever tradesman's entrance, staff door or cellar

137

ingress that presented itself. She began tiptoeing towards the corner of the building.

'Hey, Mrs M.' Kelly's shout ricochetted off the Puri's bathroom tiles. 'What you after, scuttling off like that? Got a fella back there?'

Charlotte stopped. Straightening up, she turned and mounted the steps with as much dignity as her sore feet would allow. When she reached Kelly's level, she raised a non-committal eyebrow. 'Oh, it's you,' she said. 'You made it, then?'

'Sure.' He got up, towering above her, and heartily bruised her hand. 'Christ, you look beat. Where did all the mud come from? Been skinny-dipping in the paddies?'

Charlotte experienced a fervent desire never to hear another comment upon her undoubtedly frightful but nevertheless personal appearance.

'I have been working,' she replied, putting some emphasis on the pronoun. There was no discernible dimming of Kelly's grin. 'If you don't mind, I shall go to my room and change.'

'Suit yourself,' Kelly said. 'I'll line up the lagers in the bar.'

The sight of herself in the mirror of Room 101 brought tears to her eyes. Sternly, she reminded her wrecked reflection that they were tears of vanity and self-pity, two of the pettiest vices and singularly abhorrent in view of the plight of the young woman on the street. Also in view of the fact that she did not give *that* much – here, she tried clicking damp fingers and failed – for what some overgrown beachboy thought about anything, least of all Charlotte Macanally, Cotterstock Director, UK Envoy of the SHWF, frequenter of ministerial salons and internationally renowned authority on birth control programmes.

She then showered, washed and blow-dried her hair, attired herself in her only frock, put on a great deal of mascara and two layers of Lypsyl, dabbed English Rose Eau de Cologne on her ears and made for the bar.

'You look great,' said Kelly.

To avert an attack of lash-fluttering, Charlotte put on her Princess Anne voice, said, 'So do you' and resisted a follow-up slap on Kelly's back. The afterglow of the compliment, however, persisted, giving her a rabid thirst.

'How does the local horse piss grab you?' Kelly asked.

'I'm sorry?'

He translated. 'You want a beer or what?'

She had what.

'Have another,' he said.

She had another. Then she returned the favours, under the Sex Discrimination Act.

'Kelly,' she said presently. 'You know what I've been telling you. About the Happy People Party and the clinics and so on?'

'Sounds great. I should get some really good stuff out of . . .'

Charlotte leaned confidentially towards him, keeping her voice low. 'There are some things I'm not entirely happy about. Some aspects, that is.'

'What are those?'

She tried to marshall the case for the prosecution but crucial departments of her brain appeared to have closed down for the night, leaving the rest in a communicative shambles. No sooner had she got the woman with the bricks to the witness box than a boy with a wasted leg took her place who then, without warning, turned into a gravestone. To this a smiling Mr Harry attached an outboard motor and chugged off out of court. It was all very cluttered and she had another drink to clear the decks.

'The thing is,' she said in a burst of frankness, 'some of these women can't walk out of their houses without having an IUD . . .'

'Stuck up them?' Kelly supplied, helpfully.

'I mean, that can't be right, can it?' She scrubbed at the corner of one stinging eye. Too late, it was becoming obvious that mascara and the tropics did not mix. 'I mean, what do you think, Kelly?'

'I don't,' he replied.

The alcohol in her empty stomach had on Charlotte the unusual effect of inflaming principles rather than relaxing them. 'Well, you ought,' she said, drawing herself upright. 'We're funding most of it, after all. The West. You don't want power without responsibility, do you?'

'Try me.'

His grin, the frivolous approach he evinced on serious matters and the absurd whiteness of his teeth could not be allowed to pass unchallenged. It was as she always thought. For a moment, she groped for what she had always thought.

139

'*Men*,' she said.

Two Sulanasian women came into the scented darkness of the room, teetering on stilt-high heels, giggling behind their hands. They flicked the long blue-black tresses of their hair at Kelly and settled themselves with much wriggling of their shapely hips upon the bar stools. Kelly eased himself backwards in his chair and looked them up and down.

'It's a question of pressure,' Charlotte said loudly. 'With a programme like this, how much pressure is a government justified in using? *Kelly?*'

He swung back to her. 'There's a lot of Sulanasians about. What would *you* do, Mrs M?'

Charlotte gazed into the amber fluid before her and concentrated all her attention upon this question that was so germane, one could say crucial, to her future report which might, in its turn and in its own admittedly modest way, affect the far-flung strategies of Small, Healthy and Wealthy Families, not to mention the day-to-day plans of the great and good Gordon Grant and others of his stature in Family Planning organizations worldwide. At last, she looked up into Kelly's blue eyes.

'I don't know,' she said.

After this they sat in silence for several minutes until one of the women at the bar edged herself off her perch and went over to a piano, where she began playing and singing in a lilty voice, turning her face to Kelly like a flower to the sun. Kelly picked his teeth. Charlotte, lulled by the harmonious pastels of the singer's cosmetic mask, wove three hanks of her hair into a long thin plait and when this task was completed, dropped off, to wake as Kelly placed a warm hand over hers.

'You paid for a bed,' he said. 'Don't you wanna use it?'

She stared at him out of gritty eyes.

'Go on. You go up. What are we doing in the morning?'

'Meeting Mr Harry,' she mumbled. Had there ever been a time when she had not been meeting Mr Harry?

'Let's have breakfast before. By the way, I picked up a letter for you in Balu. Came the day after you'd left. Here.' He fumbled in the pocket of his trousers and held up an airmail envelope.

Regaining her room, albeit after several false trails, Charlotte groped her way into her nightdress, squirted insect-repellent at the humming ceiling and coughed through its fumes to the bed. The envelope Kelly had given her was inscribed in her mother's handwriting and, seeing that familiar scrawl, she sickened momentarily for England, Home and Wintry Beauty. She smoothed out the letter inside and began to read.

'Dear Mr Binns. I was very surprised to receive a recent notification from Sainsbury's that one of my cheques to them has not been honoured by you. Now, Mr Binns, I have been banking with you, and shopping in Sainsbury's, for that matter, for many years. I particularly like their wines, they do a nice dry white and . . .'

Circumstances chez Mrs Wren had evidently not altered in her absence. Wondering what Mr Binns had made of her mother's opinions on the Far East, she felt beside the bed for her handbag and pulled out the John D. Macdonald she had bought that evening. A short immersion in its thrills would, she sincerely hoped, divert her attention from Room 101, which had taken on an imperious life of its own and was swaying about in a very undisciplined manner.

She focused intently on the first page and in a second or two unfocused again. Either she was very drunk indeed or the book was in Chinese.

'I thought this was a Moslem country.'

'It is,' Kelly said.

'Then they shouldn't serve alcohol,' she said severely.

They were having coffee in what Charlotte had only just realized was the hotel bar in its alternative role of breakfast room, and its poor showing in daylight did little to boost her confidence in her own morning-after appearance. There was a sound in her ears as of church bells ringing across an English meadow, and her tongue seemed to have been transplanted from a mouth a good deal larger than hers. Feeling an obligation upon her, she explained to Kelly – who was, she noticed, in disgusting fettle – that though he might have gained the impression that she was always three sheets to the wind, this was far from the truth and her present problem vis-à-vis liquor was a well-known syndrome attributable solely to the heat.

'Is that right?' Kelly said.

'Also I have heard that one should not drink while taking malaria tablets, since one is likely to suffer the same ill-effects.'

'Now what *I've* heard, dearie,' Kelly said in a gossipy soprano, 'is that if you drink your beer in a yellow submarine with a kangaroo bone through your nose, you're one hundred per cent guaranteed to get zonked right out of your skull.'

Charlotte gave in. 'What did you do, after I'd staggered off?'

'Apologized all round, told them your minder was on his hols, paid the barman to keep his mouth shut.' Over Charlotte's protestations he added, 'So what kind of bloke is this Mr Harry you've been seen about town with?'

'All right.' After further rumination, she said, 'Actually, he's pretty dire.'

'Oh well. So long as he doesn't get in the way of my trigger finger.'

A waiter appeared with more coffee. Watching him leave the room Charlotte asked Kelly why he thought all young men in Sulanasia wore flared trousers.

Kelly took up his light meter and peered round it at her. 'There, you've hit on a problem that has occupied philosophers for over two decades. What is it with the flare? Why has it become the national dress of every underdeveloped country? You solve that and you're on to something. No, don't interrupt me, Mrs M, this is serious stuff. I reckon flared strides caused the baby boom. So never mind your contraceptives. What you got to do is get the men into tight Y-fronts and drainies and you can wave your IUDs goodbye for ever.'

'What,' asked Charlotte, 'are you talking about?'

Kelly leaned closer. 'Not many people know this, sport, but semen becomes infertile if the balls are deprived of cool air. Now, flares allow a lot of air to circulate round the privates whereas your drainies . . .'

Charlotte caught sight of Mr Harry in the lobby and waved at him with unusual enthusiasm. In response, he covered the ground to their table in an Olympic burst of speed.

'Aha!' he beamed. 'You make friend, Miss Harlot. I so glad for you.'

'Yes,' Charlotte said, not entirely pleased at his amazement. 'Mr Harry, this is . . .' Here it dawned upon her that she did not yet know Kelly's first name but Kelly was already on his feet.

'Kelly,' he said, 'nice to meet you. I'm from the *Sydney Herald*.'

Ingratiatingly, Charlotte added, 'He's a photographer. He'd like to take pictures of your work for his paper. Is it all right if he comes with us today? Do you mind?'

Mr Harry didn't look as if he minded. His head at an acute angle to accommodate Kelly, he said graciously, 'Mr Kelly, you are my guest. I do everything for you, like I do for my other guest,' and he bowed at Charlotte. 'Nothing, for me, is too trouble. I am servant for you now, like for her.'

Charlotte thanked him profusely, anxious to make up for her ungenerous remark to Kelly. Kelly said, 'Ta,' and applied himself to his camera straps.

'Today,' Mr Harry said, 'we go to primary school. You come, dear guests.'

Four crudely moulded plaster figures capered across the concrete gates to the village. They had the same lavatorial aspect as the figures on Mr Harry's maps and were of a man and a woman hand-in-hand with two pipe-cleaner children.

'Family Planning symbol,' Mr Harry explained, leaping from the van, 'so all village people can see must have only two children.' He watched with approval as Kelly took several shots though, oddly, he wouldn't be photographed himself. Then he led them through the gates under a frayed arch of banana trees, causing three women who stood chatting nearby to become mute with astonishment at the sight of the giant Kelly.

'The school is over there,' Mr Harry said. His comment was superfluous. The glade rang with the sound of voices, as if a thousand starlings were roosting in the palms. They walked towards the sound and, mysteriously, the news of their approach preceded them, so that by the time the building was in view, children swarmed outside, their shrieks of welcome quite obliterating the hungover buzzings in Charlotte's ears. As they drew nearer, the shrieks became bat-like and the children jumped up and down and careened off each other and pogo'd about in a frenzy on their thin brown legs. The noise was such that it shattered Charlotte's usual reserve as high notes shatter glass and she cavorted with them, clapping her hands, until one small boy's eyes bugged out so far with excitement that she feared for his sanity and pulled herself together.

'Please,' Mr Harry said, composed and disapproving. 'Here is school teachers.'

They stood in the eye of the hurricane, bowing with doleful

dignity, a man with his lips in a nervous rictus and a grave woman with a veil pinned to her chignon, while all around them their tiny pupils leapt and screamed.

'How in the world do they make themselves heard in this . . . ?' Charlotte shouted to Kelly over the bedlam. As she spoke, the female teacher put up her hands and clapped once. The shrieks stopped on the instant, leaving only echoes to drift across the clearing.

In the silence, Mr Harry said, 'We go in now.'

The building was divided into four classrooms by low partitions. The classrooms were furnished with rows of wooden desks that faced towards a blackboard. Charlotte sat at the back of one of them while Kelly crouched in one corner taking pictures as groups of quiet children stood in front of the blackboard and began a recitation of its chalked contents to the rhythmic beat of the teacher's baton.

'This reading class,' whispered Mr Harry, squashed at a desk beside her.

'What are they reading?' Charlotte asked.

'Is very nice Government poem. Say children lucky today, not have too many brothers and sisters like in old days. Now only two children, like happy birds in nest.'

'I see,' said Charlotte as the children's voices rose to the bamboo beams above, where an extended family of sparrows hopped and fluttered. A textbook lay open on the desk beside her and she flipped through it. The first pages depicted a distraught-looking woman holding a baby while a number of emaciated children regarded an empty bowl. The last pages showed the woman grown stout and tidy while, beside her, two wildly grinning children stuffed themselves from loaded plates.

'Interesting Government book,' said Mr Harry.

The children at the blackboard wailed monotonously as Kelly moved down the aisle, Cossack-fashion. Mr Harry removed Charlotte to the next classroom, presided over by the male teacher. He had just placed a shelled egg in front of a little girl with her hair in bunches. The egg gleamed on the dark wood.

'This arithmetic class,' whispered Mr Harry. 'He say to girl, if you have just one brother and you hungry, what you do with this egg?'

Solemnly, the child took up the knife given her by the teacher

144

and pressed its blade to the egg. It bulged and fell into halves, revealing a brilliant yellow yolk. The teacher nodded and spoke again.

'Now he say, if you mother not do what Government want and she have two more baby, what you do with egg?'

Wielding the knife again, the little girl poked at the halves of the egg, coaxing them into quarters. The white flaked, the yolk crumbled. The girl regarded the mess before her with interest.

The teacher shoved at the egg, talking to the child. She looked up at him and laughed.

'He say,' Mr Harry translated, chortling in sympathy, 'if you hungry, little child, one quarter egg no good. Now you go home to you mother and say please, mother, no more babies, or I hungry and my brother!'

'Goodness,' Charlotte said, absorbing this moral tale.

'*And* he say,' Mr Harry continued as the teacher walked back up the aisle, 'must also tell to grandmother, please, grandmother, tell our mother no more babies or we have no eggs for our meal.'

The children tittered, entranced at the thought of lecturing granny.

Charlotte asked Mr Harry if the children were taught about the mechanics of birth control.

Mr Harry shook his head. 'They too small, in this school. They not hear these things. But' – and he spoke hastily in case his guest deplored this omission in her omnipresent notebook – 'in next school, right away they taught. IUD, injection, sterilization, everything. Is call Biology.'

Charlotte smiled down at the docile child beside her. 'And they teach the children at the next school about sex?' she asked Mr Harry.

'I just tell you so,' said Mr Harry in the patient voice he used when his guest had one of her ga-ga turns.

'No, *sex*,' Charlotte hissed. 'How babies are made.'

An iron pressed out his features. 'Maybe,' he said, gazing earnestly at the blackboard. 'I not sure.'

Charlotte bit at a nail, trying to work out how most tactfully to proceed. She must, she supposed, come to terms with this contraceptive force-feeding and the beleaguering of mothers and grannies. It was designed, after all, to combat disease and hunger and never having been hungry or seriously ill in her life, she was not in a position to criticize. Nevertheless, it would be easier to digest if she could find out how much general sexual knowledge was given alongside the nitty-gritty of family planning.

'I mean,' she said to Mr Harry's averted ear, 'what will the children learn about' – she began to flounder – 'men and women and how to . . . how to give each other . . . pleasure. So they know how to make sex enjoyable when they marry.'

Mr Harry lowered his eyes and an uneven redness invaded his cheekbones, 'In Sulanasia,' he informed the desk, 'we not talk about such things. Is not our custom. I very sorry.'

Her own cheeks uncomfortably warm, Charlotte gave up and scraped an awkward nail at a splinter of wood, wondering, before she could censor the lewd conjecture, whether Mr Harry had any idea where the clitoris was located or even that it existed. It seemed, on the whole, unlikely. Poor Mrs Harry. But then, she had often wondered the same about Bruce. Poor her.

After another hour of a writing class that, thankfully, seemed to have no connection with family planning and a half hour of the teachings of Islam that, in Sulanasia at least, did – 'Our God say He not like big family, he like only two,' said Mr Harry, piously translating the Holy Words – she was ushered off for jasmine tea. She caught sight of Kelly through the louvred window, tree-like among a group of laughing women, and knew *he* knew where the clitoris was, which thought, once introduced, refused to be exorcized until she was faced with the teachers, waiting expectantly for the ritual interrogation. Obediently, she asked about various aspects of primary school teaching and ended on a more intimate note.

'Please ask,' she said to Mr Harry, 'how it is that they can just clap their hands and the children are quiet. In England, that would not be so easy.'

A short conversation took place between her guide and the woman teacher. At its close, Mr Harry said, 'She say all children are so. They must listen. It is natural.'

Gloria Watkins' Jason slid into Charlotte's mind, a rubicund seven-year-old with fierce buck teeth who had once emptied the contents of a tin of Lyle's Golden Syrup over the Cotterstock lino and who regularly rioted in the waiting room, causing hitherto indecisive clients to plump for instant abortions. His mother not only clapped her hands but clapped Jason, frequently, hard and to

no effect whatsoever. How, Charlotte wondered, would Master
Watkins manage amongst these Sulanasian children whose exuberance was so easily quelled and who thereafter sat so obediently at
their lessons?

This thought brought on a compensatory chauvinism. Though
these children were biddable beyond the dreams of the average
English parent or teacher, there was surely a price to be paid. Rote
learning of the kind she had witnessed might be an excellent way of
grinding in arithmetical tables and the elements of the other two Rs
but it was not a rich compost for the anarchic and challenging mind.
Whatever else one could say about Jason Watkins – most of it
common abuse – no one would deny that he was challenging and
anarchic.

Charlotte said to Mr Harry, 'Is there anything they think could
improve the quality of their teaching?'

Once again, he conferred with the teachers.

'The lady say yes,' he told Charlotte. 'She say it better if more
discipline in school.'

'More discipline?'

'Esactly. She is frighten for the children in modern world. She
frighten what they maybe do.'

Charlotte asked huskily, 'And what might they do?'

Mr Harry lowered his voice. 'She think perhaps they drink
brandy. Or' – and now his voice sank as he prepared to enunciate
the unspeakable – 'or perhap maybe they do sometime break-
dancing.'

The woman teacher nodded mournfully at Charlotte in confirmation of these dreadful possibilities. At the door three small girls
stared at the adults with huge mild eyes.

After these revelations, the leave-taking was subdued. Outside,
Kelly was cajoling some of the children's mothers to pose for their
portraits. She imagined them being harangued about birth control
by one or more of the pupils within.

'Would you ask them, do they mind if their children tell them
they mustn't have more babies?' she said.

Mr Harry advanced towards the women and talked to them at
great length. When he had finished, the women said a few shy
words, shuffling their feet in the dust.

'They say no, they not mind at all. Is modern.'

'Is that all they said?'

'Is modern.'

Just then the children, released as from a spell, ran from the door and ringed their visitors, squealing with renewed vigour. Kelly made fe fi fo fum noises at them, sending them into convulsions of laughter, while Charlotte stood stroking the hands of the timid whom Kelly's antics had rooted to the spot. She looked at the sun-sodden clearing, at the neat bamboo houses in their palm tree groves, at an affable cow munching by a well and at the giggling women with their quiff-haired babies. Come to Sunny Sulanasia, she thought, Jewel of the Sula Sea. But please leave all questions at the airport as they tend to spoil the view.

Later, as the sun cooked the air to the soup of the day and Mr Harry, talking non-stop, ferried them from village to village, her mood darkened and hardened round the edges with envy of Kelly. There he was, free to look around him, free to absorb every fascinating detail of human life and landscape with his eyes and with his camera and, above all, free – because always out of ear-shot – of Mr Harry's bottomless fund of information that impelled her to write until her wrist gave out and then to listen, as she plodded beside him, for courtesy's sake and in the haunting fear that she might, if she let herself be distracted, miss some vital clue to a situation that became with every step she took more factually clear and more emotionally muddy.

'He Catholic,' Mr Harry said of a colleague cross-legged in a field among women generating income by embroidering blouses of the kind she had seen by the rackful, unbought, in Banabalu.

'Catholic? And he's an official of the family planning programme?'

'Esactly.' Mr Harry cantered out of the field at a great pace.

'But Catholics aren't *allowed* birth control,' puffed Charlotte at his heels.

'Oh no?'

'No. The Pope doesn't like it.'

'Here, he like,' Mr Harry said with simple faith and bent down beside the van to dust off his shoes.

In the afternoon, the van halted at the side of a track to allow a group of women to pass. Five young men, well-turned-out wisps in their flares and stacked heels, shooed them along like sheepdogs herding their flock to the dip.

'New acceptors,' Mr Harry remarked.

Charlotte combed back wet hair from wetter forehead. 'What

about vasectomies?' she asked, at pains to keep irritation at bay. 'Don't any of the men have vasectomies?'

'Some time. Oh yes.'

'How many?'

Of a sudden, Mr Harry's statistics deserted him. 'I not know exactly,' he said. 'But is not good, vasectomy. Our God not like.'

'God likes the IUD, does he? He like Depo-Provera?'

'Yes, these he like.'

'How useful God is to men,' Charlotte said. Her sarcasm washed over Mr Harry and left him bone-dry.

'Is true,' he said. 'God very good to men.'

Waiting at the van for Kelly who had last been seen photographing a small, tearstained boy perched on a stool in a market having his hair cut, Charlotte tried again to shift the silt in her brain.

'Why isn't the Pill used here?'

Mr Harry arranged surprise upon his features. 'The Pill? We have. Many, many.'

'They don't have it at the clinics.'

'Oh yes.' He blinked at her. 'They do.'

Charlotte took her query out of the interrogative. 'I have not seen or heard of any woman so far who has been given it.'

'Is not good for women, the Pill,' Mr Harry said in his caring voice. 'They not remember to take it. Every day, every day, is too hard for them. Also, our . . .'

'. . . God not like it.'

'Ah!' Mr Harry exclaimed. 'You Christian religion and you know so good about Islam. How is this?'

'They have a lot in common,' she said.

Towards the end of the afternoon, when the sky was white-hot and Charlotte's nose bloomed as redly as a flame-of-the-forest flower, they entered yet another gate upon which the family planning figures danced their interminable plaster dance.

'I've been here before,' Charlotte said, reduced to the whine of a package tourist trying to get a refund. 'This was where they had the Happy People Party.'

'But this time we see acceptor group make baskets.'

They saw the acceptor group making baskets – or, rather, Charlotte thought crossly, an acceptor group not making baskets, since all weaving ground to a halt on their approach and the women

149

brightened in anticipation of the strangers' questions. Hearing Charlotte's peevish mumble, Kelly came to her aid.

'Go on, treat yourself to a walkabout,' he said, his blue eyes undimmed by the day's slog. 'I'll deal with them this time. What do you want to know?'

'Not a thing,' said Charlotte, her conscientiousness quite boiled away, and she walked rapidly towards the village lanes. She had grown confident that, on the whole, the villagers did not appear to resent her presence. Faces that seemed blank and hostile would almost always, when smiled at, smile back so that she now permitted herself to look around, though never to stare. When she came to where the houses ended she found herself on a slope and scrambled down the rocky scree into a forested valley. There, within a vine-roofed grotto, stood the mossy ruins of an ancient temple, a Hindu relic of Sulanasia's pre-Islamic past. The undergrowth was strewn with a rubble of carved boulders fallen from the tower over hundreds of years. Crumbling steps, alive with lizards, led up the tower's flank to a hollowed-out alcove in whose dark recess reposed a large statue of the Elephant Goddess, Ganeesha.

In the quiet heat, Charlotte gazed up at her and out of the whorls of her wrinkles the Goddess gazed stolidly back, her great hooves tidily together and the coil of her trunk wedged into a stone bowl. The only sound was the coo of doves. Charlotte moved to the steps and climbed up. Ganeesha was black with age except for one burnished ridge on her trunk. Charlotte rubbed it thoughtfully, liking the smooth feel of the stone. How very different Ganeesha was from her own deity, with his man's body, his human face. What human could ever guess what went on under the adamantine hide of an Elephant Goddess?

The hopelessness of the task she had undertaken weighed heavily upon her. Facts, statistics, methods, aims, these she had access to in plenty, provided ad nauseam by any official to whom she turned, from Gordon Grant and his colleagues in London to Gina Millichip, Mr Harry and armies of others. But who asked the people what they felt; the women? They remained beyond her reach, hidden from her by language and by culture, enigmas among whom she could only blunder. Birth control, family planning, contraceptives – these were labels to be put on the drawers of filing cabinets or on the title pages of books and pamphlets. And why was it taken for granted that a woman like herself with no special expertise, had a perfect right to come here and poke in and out of Sulanasian lives, deciding what was good for them and what was not, without a word of common language with which to communicate with them, consult them? The impertinence, when you analysed it, was colossal.

With these unsettling thoughts, she climbed down the steps from Ganeesha's shrine and picked her way over the litter of stones. Slowly, as she walked, the calm beauty of the place and the somnolent snores of the doves soothed her so that, halfway up the scree again, she was the more startled when the first scream rang out, sending the birds crashing on panicky wings up through the palm fronds. A second scream followed and then a ragged series that twisted her guts. They came from close by, over the brow of the slope, and she slipped and stumbled upwards, breaking her nails on the rocks, until she was standing at the top from where she could see, clustered at the doorway of the nearest hut, the backs of several women, some bending, some squatting.

She ran towards them and paused, running with sweat, at the bushes that marked the boundary of the house. The screams had died away, to be replaced by long pitiful moans. An old woman shuffled past carrying a basket full of jars and ducked into the doorway without a glance at Charlotte. She turned away and flip-flopped as fast as she could in her loose sandals to where, beyond the rows of houses, she could see Kelly standing with Mr Harry.

'Christ, you look like you've been hit by a Bondi tram,' Kelly greeted her.

'Mr Harry,' she gasped, ignoring him. 'There's a woman scream-ing back there.' She waved back at the huts. 'It's dreadful. She's in pain.'

'I know this,' Mr Harry answered, arranging the collar of his shirt so that it lay flat on the neck of his jacket. 'It okay. They take care.'

'Who? What's the matter with her? Is it a . . . baby?'

'No baby. She sick. Somebody come soon, is okay.'

She looked at him. Smile-lines radiated across his temples and scoured his cheeks but there was no smile in his eyes. He brushed the air as if driving off insects and she looked away.

'Come. We wait long time for you. Now we go.'

He turned and walked towards the village gates, beckoning her to follow.

'We can't just leave her,' she said to Kelly. 'Can't we do something?'

Kelly took her arm. 'They've been sick before you came and they'll be sick after you've gone. Who do you think you are, Nanny Nightingale?'

She looked up at his face and saw, inches from the crown of his head, a foot-long gout of blood.

'Yeah,' Kelly said, following her quivering finger, 'banana flower. Creepy, eh? Let's go.'

'I've got the shakes.'

'You have,' he said solicitously. 'I expect you've got malaria. Did you know too much alcohol brings it on?'

Kelly's expectations were misplaced. Charlotte did not have malaria. Instead, she awoke in some baking stretch of the night under the impression that a small but determined python had wrapped itself round her abdomen and was trying to turn her into a tofu snack. As the coils squeezed ever tighter, popping beads of sweat out of her pores, she wondered hazily if the uproar taking place below was in some way psychosomatic, brought on by over-exposure to intra-uterine devices.

Her stomach, however, soon made its territorial claims crystal clear and she spent the next few hours lurching between bed and titanic bathroom, where the pattern of the tiles directly below the loo incised itself on her brain. In the intervals she fell into short and fretful comas orchestrated by phantom screams.

She was communing again with the tiles, groaning glumly to herself when she heard a bang at the door and Kelly's voice calling her name. Feverish as she was, she froze.

'Mrs M,' shouted Kelly, drumming on the wood. 'Open up in the name of the Law. What are you doing in there, having an orgy?'

Charlotte did not reply. After three increasingly ribald suggestions from Kelly as to her bedroom activities, said at full throttle, she realized that if she was not to be run out of town by the Tanjung vice squad she would have to respond. Holding her cotton wrap tightly around her, she shuffled to the door.

'Go away,' she whispered with as much ferocity as her debilitated state would allow.

The voice warmed. 'Oh, you're there,' it said. 'Harry and I are waiting for you. What's up?'

Charlotte explained in a low hiss that she was unwell and would Kelly kindly give her excuses to Mr Harry and proceed without her.

'Your time of the month, is it?' enquired the door.

Shocked, Charlotte said no, it wasn't, an avowal she quickly regretted.

'Got the trots, then? Oh come on, Mrs M, let me in. I'm a big boy, I can take it.'

She fumbled at the door knob, desperate to avoid drawing the attention of the entire Hotel Puri to her intestinal upheavals. Radiating health, Kelly strode in, held her at arm's length and scrutinized her. 'Dear oh dear,' he tutted. 'You look like a dug-up corpse.'

'I'm aware of that,' she said and the python squeezed drops of moisture from the corners of her eyes. 'Just leave me alone.'

'It's the Sulanasian squitters, right?'

Her head averted, she nodded.

'Any blood in your stools?'

She closed her eyes.

'Well, you've looked, haven't you?'

There had been times, since she had met Kelly, when she had indulged in the odd daydream concerning himself and her. Violins figured in it, as did palms and a full moon, strong arms and warm lips and herself, sun-kissed and dusky, with a frangipani behind her ear. But she had reckoned without Kelly the dream-buster. Moaning an affirmative, she sank to her pillows.

'Good,' he said briskly, 'you might live.' Picking up a jug from the dressing table, he filled it in the bathroom and put it on her bedside table. From his camera case, he took out two sterilizing tablets and dropped them in the water. 'I want to see that empty when I get back. And take this now.' He held out a salt tablet. 'Rehydration therapy. Otherwise you'll soon be as much use as a condom with a hole in it.'

He regarded the pillow that now concealed Charlotte's face. 'So long then, sport. I'll pop in when I'm back.'

The door slammed behind him and Charlotte removed the pillow. Her eyes were dull with shed tears.

*

153

The next morning she had recovered enough to eat the dry biscuits Kelly brought her and listen to his description of a day spent photographing women working in the rice fields. 'Bums in the air, all of them,' he said, 'in that stinking heat. They all had backaches. I asked.'

'Did they?' she said, vaguely surprised. 'I'd have thought they'd . . .'

'Get used to it? No such luck.'

'No.' She felt ashamed. They would have to work if they had what she had, too, and they probably had it often.

'I'll get up soon.'

He considered her, stuffing his tongue in his upper lip. 'Take a Lomotil. I don't reckon on them for the first day or two but you're on the mend and they'll cement you up good and proper. We don't want a nasty accident, do we? You know, I was at the Parthenon in Athens, one time, walking up the steps, and there was this woman lying full-length at the top in a pool of . . .'

'I'm not well enough,' Charlotte said despairingly.

'Okay, sport. I'll tell you when you're on your feet and that's a promise.'

'I can't wait,' Charlotte said.

'Right. Well, there was this woman lying stretched out with the flies buzzing all round her and this trickle of yellow . . .'

'Kelly!'

'Gotcha.' There was a fresh layer of tan around the whiteness of his leer.

'Fancy an evening out? Harry's got a concert on the menu, if you want to go.'

The Lomotil, hitting her insides in mid-slosh, had produced instant stasis. Faced with a concrete torso, the python had thrown in the towel. 'Concert?' she enquired.

'He's lassooed some of his acceptors into a band,' Kelly said. 'In this place, a lady can't get into a sing-song without showing her IUD. Hope you're suitably equipped, Mrs M? They give you a body search at the door.'

In his faded blue shirt and bleached pants, he looked like a heavyweight angel. Resigned by now to his coarseness, Charlotte made a gallant attempt to interpret his query as a tentative pass at her. Unfortunately, there was nothing tentative about Kelly, as she

154

knew to her cost. She was brooding on related problems such as why she had conceived only once in spite of being uncontracepted and why a man towards whom she felt so unlike a pal should insist on calling her 'sport' – no other Australian she had ever met used the word – when Mr Harry shot into the lobby on a tidal wave of cologne. He greeted Charlotte with the astounded gestures of one seeing Lazarus arise from the grave and, possibly as a result of her short respite, she was pleased to see him. He was, she decided, a good-hearted man, if a trifle hyperactive.

The musical event, he informed them after he had put away his hands, was within walking distance, if dear Miss Harlot could walk. Charlotte said she could and they set off together into the lush night, turning behind the hotel into a labyrinth of gullied lanes terraced with low houses whose carved doors and intricately wrought iron windows reminded Charlotte of old postcards of Hampstead before underground sewage came in. A million invisible cicadas were in full scratch and the aroma of roasting peanuts mingled to unique effect with Mr Harry's aftershave and a pervasive smell of urine. Within minutes they came upon a lamplit square and followed Mr Harry to a doorway whose threshold, piled with shoes, signalled a social occasion. The three of them also removed their shoes and were welcomed into a crowded room, where a courteous host offered them the best portion of floor. Charlotte, already lost in wonder at the scene within, bowed at the bowing heads around her and eased herself to their level on the ground beside Mr Harry, while Kelly, giving an appreciative whistle, knelt by the door.

The room was of modest size and its stucco walls, painted purple and patchily illuminated by neon strips, were bare but for a photograph of the President exchanging looks of mutual distaste with an infant in his arms. There was no furniture, which was as well, since some fifty men and women, along with a cumbersome collection of instruments of the kind Charlotte had seen at the Happy People Party, were packed into it, fitted as deftly as the interlocking pieces of a jigsaw. They squatted in circles that spiralled inwards to where, in the centre, the players knelt, tuning up. At one side, a 6 foot long yoke, its carved red frame supporting four great gongs as generously nippled as Amazonian breastplates, dwarfed the women who crouched underneath. The wooden xylophones, in contrast, were tucked round their cross-legged players like so many functional kitchenettes.

As the players communed with their scores and the crowded spectators chatted and smoked, Charlotte greedily savoured every rich detail of the clothes and faces about her, thankful that the flash of Kelly's camera at the door promised her a later and longer-lasting feast. How wonderful they all looked: the drummer ahead, his knee-caps peeping out beneath a checked sarong; a young brigand in a pink paisley shirt with a matching pink headband and a Fu Manchu moustache; an old lady whose frequent smile revealed a Royal Mint of teeth and, at the gongs, a Gauguinesque matron with a bosom so operatic that it partially concealed her neighbour, a shrunken gentleman who peered across its mounds with one bright black eye, the other sealed in a permanent wink. And then there were the singers, a kneeling row of women clutching pieces of paper, their net-covered buns a DIY triumph, their brown faces masked in festive white powder, the bones of their wrists touchingly fragile below lacy sleeves.

Charlotte felt her heart swell like a sponge with a flood of emotion that spilled out over everyone present, encompassing them all in its milky flow. The experience was humbling, transcendental, akin in breadth and intensity to that noblest of feelings, maternal love. She turned to share the precious moment with Mr Harry. Unfortunately, though still relatively upright, he appeared to be asleep. Just like Bruce, she reflected, at another such moment, the raising of her Kundalini. How strange men were, how tragically out of touch with the sheer universality of the universe, the incredible cosmic-ness of the cosmos, the awesome mystery of its mysteries. Women, fertile, womb-laden women, daughters of the Moon Goddess and subject to her waxing and waning, were the receptacles of life, and only they could comprehend the ultimate truth, sensed in one's every pore, that people everywhere were *people* and life, with all its wonders, was *life!*

She was fished up from these mystic depths by the opening strains of the music. The gongs clanged, the cymbals clashed, the xylophones began to burble and the women, kneeling as in prayer, opened their mouths and sang. Swaying gently to the rhythm, Charlotte sank fathoms deep again.

Two hours later, she trailed dreamily back to the hotel under a crescent moon and ribbons of stars. No sound disturbed the peace of the lambent night but the disconsolate croak of mating frogs and the murmur of voices from the two men ahead. Inhaling deeply of the creamy air, she wept one happy tear.

'Thank you for a wonderful evening, Mr Harry,' she said in the lobby, pressing his hand with grateful fervour. 'I shall never forget it.'

Mr Harry pressed her hand fervently back, and said, 'And, please, you also not forget letter to Minister of Women.' After this request, darkness engulfed him.

'Fancy a drink before crashing out?' Kelly asked, squatting over his cameras.

'An orange juice, perhaps.'

When the drinks arrived, Kelly took a long swig of his beer, wiped his hand across his mouth and said, 'Jeez, platypus piss again. Hey, I got some terrific pictures. Mind, I can't be a hundred per cent sure of them till I get to the lab. It's always a pain in the arse, waiting for . . .'

'Oh, Kelly,' Charlotte said, emerging from dreamland, 'wasn't that a marvellous evening? It gave me the most fantastic feeling. They were so wonderful, the people. I wanted to hug them all, just put out my arms and take them all in and *hug* them.'

Kelly regarded her over his glass. He put it down, inserted a finger into one ear and twitched it rapidly. 'Bloody awful noise they made though, eh?' he said. 'The frogs did better on the way home.'

'*What* did you say?' She could not believe she had heard him right.

'There, see? You're as deaf as a post and no flaming wonder. It was like being mobbed by a heap of mad cats.'

Charlotte eased her voice into its softest gear. 'I don't know what you're talking about, Kelly. The singing was perfect. The music was divine. It was all' – she clasped her hands to her breast – 'quite, quite beautiful.'

'You're joking.'

She answered stiffly, 'I am not joking. I cannot tell you what a privilege and an honour I consider it to have been so fortunate as to be invited to such an event. I am exceedingly grateful. It made me very happy. And now, if you don't mind, I shall go to my room.'

'Hang on,' Kelly said. 'Are you telling me that yowling turned you on? They were amateurs, Mrs M, and tone-deaf, most of them. Flat as a pancake on every note.'

'You obviously don't understand Sulanasian music,' Charlotte said, uncertain whether to go hot with anger or cold with disdain.

'And you do?'

'I appreciate other people's culture.'

'Fine,' he said, stretching up his arms and yawning, 'but you don't have to go ape over a lot of housewives tearing shit out of their tonsils.'

Once again, Kelly's animal magnetism had sidetracked her from the essential crudity of his nature, his impoverishment of mind. It was her own fault, of course. Animal magnetism was bound to have its darker side, yet she had deluded herself into thinking it was possible to have the one without the other. True, he was not the psychopath she had first thought him. He could be kind. It was his loss that he could not reach the emotional peaks she scaled.

'That's what they are,' Kelly went on. 'Village matrons on an IUD outing. The Little Friends of the Loop raising money for the church organ – if you can say "organ" here without being nicked. If you'd heard them droning away in Piddling-on-the-Bog or whatever you call your merry English hamlets, you'd have stuck cotton wool in your ears and broken the world record running the other way.'

'There is,' Charlotte said, 'no similarity whatsoever between the two.'

'No,' Kelly agreed, giving a thoughtful belch. 'In Piddling-on-the-Bog the ladies are pink and sit on chairs and here they're brown and sit on the floor. Worlds apart.'

'You know,' she said kindly, 'I can't help feeling sorry for you, Kelly. Those wonderful people, those warm-hearted human beings welcomed you into their midst, into a private gathering, and gave of themselves freely and generously to you, a perfect stranger. They created beauty. Yet all you can do is run them down.'

After this summary of her position on the matter, there was a pause. Kelly put in some work on his molars with a toothpick. Then he said, 'You know what you are, Mrs M?'

'Good night.'

'You're a nice, kind, sweet-natured, soft-hearted Pom lady. And you're also an un-bloody-reconstructed racist.'

'Good *night*,' said Charlotte.

But he came after her, weaving and dodging about her along the corridor as she stared stonily ahead. 'Want to know what they were singing about, your Sulanasian Sutherlands? Harry told me.'

'No, I do not,' Charlotte said without opening her lips.

Kelly sang in a mosquito soprano:

'Go in for Family Planning
Body and Soul
Family Planning is good for you
Body and Soul
You'll be happy if you do
You'll be well-preserved if you do . . .'

Charlotte shut the door of Room 101 in his face. It did not noticeably muffle his voice.

'I made a tape of the singing. It's yours with my best wishes. I'm leaving it outside, okay? Nightie night, snuggle-pie.'

After checking the silence, Charlotte opened the door again. Its jamb sent something skidding into the darkness. Shortly, she retrieved a palm-sized tape recorder.

In bed, she switched it on. It hissed for a second and then regurgitated the sounds of the musical evening.

One hour earlier than she usually rose, Charlotte went down to the bar-cum-breakfast room and ordered a bowl of fresh figs. There were many things troubling her, including the fact that her stomach, over-reacting to the Lomotil, had shut down the works and gone on indefinite strike.

As she spooned in the figs, hoping that their good offices would solve her problem, a shadow fell upon the bowl. She looked up in alarm, afraid that it was Kelly, arrived before she had prepared her speech. It was not Kelly.

'Hullo,' she said.

He looked thinner and shiftier than the last time she had seen him as he slid his narrow pelvis on to the edge of the chair opposite. He was still carrying his briefcase, which he placed beside the table. There were yellow threads on the whites of his eyes and a pinpoint of blood at one almond corner. Charlotte resigned herself to the fact that if he wanted to sell her another carved figure, she would have to buy.

'How's the English going?' she asked.

'My studies go very fine, thank you,' he answered with formal politeness.

'Good.'

She ate two more figs, resisting the urge to spoon one into his mouth. Poor boy, for he was not much more than a boy, he looked in bad shape.

'But my studies,' he added after a pause, 'are the only thing that go fine.'

'Why is that?' she enquired. The question, she immediately saw, was too direct. He caved in under its impact as if it had hit a rib. Hastily, she winkled out smaller talk. 'Goodness, it's so *hot* already. In England, it would never be this hot except, maybe, in the middle of one day of one summer in ten.' She made a pantomime of plucking her blouse away from her skin, in case he hadn't caught her drift.

'Hot,' he said.

After a longer pause, during which the student glanced about the room as if vetting its facilities for a future booking and Charlotte tried to think of some remark that was not in the interrogative, she said idiotically, 'It's a nice hotel.'

'Nice,' he said.

There was an eerie familiarity about this non-conversation that brought her mother to Charlotte's mind, perhaps because guess-work seemed to be playing an increasingly central part. She dislodged a fig pip from a lower tooth. 'Would you like to sell me something?' she asked at last.

His response, this time, was less monosyllabic. 'If that is what you think, please, I will go.'

'No. No.' Flushing, she touched his bony wrist. She had made a great mistake. Obviously, in her absence from Mrs Wren, her intuitive faculties had deteriorated. Silence, perhaps was a better policy. Let him talk.

Silence ensued. Eventually, after a final glance around him, the young man pulled his chair closer. 'If I say something to you, you will tell no one?'

Charlotte said she would not and waited rather nervously for a revelation.

'I am Moslem.'

'Really?' She tried, in this land of Moslems, to look properly surprised.

'Devout Moslem. I am always in contact with my God.'

His face was so close now that she could see the black hairs sprouting on his upper lip. Nodding in appreciation of his piety, she wondered vaguely whether the Jehovah's Witnesses had an Islamic branch. 'I have noticed,' she said, 'that Sulanasians are all very devout.'

This was another mistake, for his lips twitched. 'I speak of the *real* Islam,' he said in a heated whisper. 'Not official Government Islam. That is corrupt. That is a tool they use against my people and the true Sulanasian culture. It serves only the greed of the Western interests in Banabalu, who sacrifice our religion for American gold.'

'Oh dear,' Charlotte said inadequately.

'But All'ah will not be mocked.' He looked at her quickly. 'Is that how you say it?'

'Er . . . yes.'

'I do not want to be American.'

'Er . . . no,' replied Charlotte, who did not want to be American either. 'But how . . .?'

The dam was breached and there was no stopping him now. '. . . and I do not want All'ah to be American . . .'

'I should say not,' she agreed. The way he said 'Allah', with a glottal stop, made Him sound undisputably unAmerican.

'. . . but our Government, our President, they try very much to make us forget we are Sulanasians, true children of All'ah. They pretend they are Moslem and they use All'ah's name to make us do what they wish. But these things are evil. The Ko'ran speaks against them. The simple people believe these evil things because they are ignorant and the President tells them he is their good father. Also, they are afraid.'

Across the room, the morning sun lit up the lobby. It was shadier here but not too shady to see the patina of sweat on the young man's forehead and the way his fingers twisted together. The word he had used – 'afraid' – buzzed a warning in the back of her head. A light switched on.

'Are you telling me this,' she said, whispering herself, 'because I'm involved with the birth control programme? You don't like it.'

'I hate,' he said simply. 'And my God hate.'

She frowned down at the empty chair between them. Its padded leatherette seat was night-club smart but a stray sunbeam, gaining unauthorized entry through the crumpled slat of a blind, revealed upon it a large stain. Something had eaten through the surface of the leatherette, exposing gray tufts of kapok. God hate large families, Mr Harry said. God hate small families, the student said. The

161

Sulanasian God was not a picky hater. She removed her gaze from the kapok and regarded the moist face of the student.

'But Sulanasia is very over-populated,' she said gently. 'You are an intelligent, educated man, you know that. Too many people, too little food. Surely Allah hates that too?'

'You think wrong way,' he said and a plume of hair on the crown of his head stood up with emotion. 'All'ah give enough food for *all* the people. Sulanasia rich, fertile land. Only, now, landlords take. Big Western business take. Leave nothing for people.' Passion was massacring his grammar. 'We want give land to peasants, then can have many many babies, what All'ah want. You make report, you must *say* this. Sulanasians not want Western aid, it aid only West. Sulanasians want Islamic *revolution*.'

The genie of the Ayatollah Khomeini materialized before Charlotte, his features grim and grey enough to make Alladin regret his lamp. Arms spouted blood from handless stumps and the bright sarongs of Sulanasia grew chador black. 'Oh, no,' she said involuntarily, '*No*.'

Under the soft, almost girlish skin of the student's face, the bones set hard. For the first time, he smiled. 'Jihad,' he said. 'Holy War.' There was a lilt in his voice. 'You better go away from Sulanasia, you Christian woman, you Western woman. Take your con-tra-cep-tion from Islamic women, they not want.' Discarding caution, he spoke loudly into Charlotte's face. 'It not your business. American, English, you come here, stop Sulanasian babies, then go home and have babies how many you like.' Purring, he added the coup de grâce. 'But not *you*, I think. You too old for babies, you barren now. Maybe that why you want our women barren too?'

Charlotte's eyes snapped shut against the invasive boyish smile. Her heart, already in a state of unrest, made a final attack on the bars of her ribs and broke out, a fat cushion that sprouted wings, swooped across the room to the Puri lobby, dipped under its doors, trod air for a moment in the sky outside and then rocketed for home.

'Mrs M?'

She sniffed to siphon back tears and opened her eyes. The student and his briefcase had gone and in his place stood Kelly.

'What's going on?' He jerked his head backwards. 'I collided with some kid in a hell of a hurry. Did he nick something from you?'

There was a disabling constriction in her chest that prevented her

162

from answering. Kelly stuck a finger under her chin. 'Look, if that bastard took something, I'll . . .'

She expelled stale air from her lungs. 'He didn't,' she said. 'It's nothing. It's all right.' Nothing would have made her divulge to Kelly, of all people, what had been said. Her stomach, however, did not share her reticence. To her horror, she realized that it was on the verge of a violent expression of outrage. She rose and fled.

With the aid of another Lomotil, Charlotte managed the day's excursions without mishap but the student's speech had jarred everything out of kilter. A bad film unreeled before her eyes, out of focus and underlit, so that what had yesterday been bright and sharp became shadowy and sinister. She was distracted by sudden quivers at the edges of her vision, a ghostly flitting. Nothing was as it seemed. The show went on, the actors said their lines smoothly from the spotlit stage but in the wings she heard ominous creakings, inexplicable rumbles, muffled oaths. On a visit to another primary school, the children greeted them with the same exuberance but this time they seemed to her possessed, their excitement shot through with hysteria, their hands pecked at her clothes like the beaks of hungry birds and their chants at the blackboard were the mindless mouthings of idiots.

In the bare room of a clinic, the doctor's smile did not divert her from the bowls of bloody water on the floor upon which floated shreds of stained cotton wool and the women who stood at the doctor's desk no longer seemed merely timid but intimidated, poor frightened sheep. They were stripped of dignity, afforded no privacy. They lay wretchedly, knees apart, behind perfunctory screens that gave them no privacy from spectators who wandered in and out, the children who hung in knots round the door or Charlotte herself, the arrogant stranger whose white skin was all the passport required to cross frontiers of modesty barred to her at home.

Shaken, she went outside. The sky was a ruthless blue and the sun brazen. Where the hills began their luxurious curving above a fringe of coconut palms she could see water buffalo, sleek as grey seals, moving through the muddy fields. Long-thighed chickens strode purposefully about in the dust, their bodies tough and sinewy, without spare flesh. Charlotte, confronted daily with their corpses at the Hotel Puri, knew that to her cost and had thought nostalgically as she chewed away of their full-breasted counterparts at home. Today, she realized that this fatter meat was the flab of jailbirds penned up from birth to slaughter. If ever she was to be reincarnated in the Third World, she'd be better off as a hen than a woman.

As she was contemplating this unlikely eventuality, she saw Kelly on the other side of the courtyard in his usual crouched position, this time at the knees of a pompous-looking gentleman who stood with one hand across his chest gazing sternly ahead like Napoleon surveying the domes of Moscow. Well out of the picture, hands carefully screening his face, stood the camera-shy Mr Harry. Again she felt a sour envy for the photographer's job. Click, flash, pix, finis. Surfaces, innocent surfaces, that was what Kelly dealt in. If the face was enigmatic, he was only required to portray it; if it opened its mouth and shrieked, he snapped it; if it smiled, he filmed it. No one expected him to explain the enigma, discover what anguish caused the shriek or what lay behind the smile. If the *Sydney Herald* rejected his pictures it would be for straightforward reasons: too dark, overexposed, blurred, boring. They wouldn't argue with him. They wouldn't say, 'You got it wrong, it's not like that.' He couldn't be held responsible for what he photographed, only how he photographed it. Gordon Grant, on the other hand, and the hundreds like him across the world who might read her report, would expect analysis, argument, opinion, quotes as well as statistics and a well thought out conclusion. The more she thought about it, the more upset she became. How was it possible to write that report when she only had access to the birth controllers and not to the birth controlled? It was like being asked to assess the Third Reich by talking to the SS and ignoring the Jews.

This metaphor, rising unbidden in her mind, so distressed her that she put her head between her knees and rocked herself back and forth on the steps. Presently, she felt a touch on her shoulder and looked up. A woman sat beside her, old and scoured with wrinkles. Her breasts were two empty pouches under a loose shirt and her hand, resting on Charlotte's shoulder, was a charred claw. The old head nodded, the seamed face split into the filed-tooth smile of a small and kindly shark. Charlotte smiled back. The claw edged into her hand and she held it close. It was a frail bridge across a gulf but it, at least, could be trusted.

Mr Harry was scuttling towards her, throwing up a slipstream of dust. 'Kelly finish. We go on now,' he said, dabbing at himself with a hanky harmoniously tuned to his shirt. 'We go sightsee. Kelly ask me. I say why not? Very interesting for you.'

Meanly, Charlotte imagined this meant it was interesting for Kelly. The two men, she noticed, had taken quite a shine to each other. She contemplated raising an objection on professional grounds. M'Lud, I suggest the proposed sightseeing is an unnecessary diversion that would seriously handicap my client in the pursuance of her vital and world-renowned work. The suggestion was thrown out immediately on the grounds that there was nothing she needed more than a diversion. The more frivolous, the better.

But before she detached herself from her elderly friend she wanted some answers. Answers were all she could barter for kindness received.

'Ask her,' she said to Mr Harry, 'does she have grandchildren?'

Mr Harry confirmed that the old lady did.

'How many?'

He held up two fingers.

'Would she like more?'

'No-o-o,' he said, shaking his head with vigour. 'She happy only two.'

'*Ask* her, please.'

While they talked, Charlotte stared at the seamed face as if, by staring, she could penetrate the flesh and find the truth below. Surely the old lady wanted many grandchildren to warm her worn heart, cradle her old bones and ease her into death with hopes of earthly immortality. What else, after a lifetime's drudgery with nothing else to show for it, made sense?

'Nya,' said Mr Harry, the Sulanasian version of I-told-you-so. 'She say *of course* she happy only two.'

The old woman gave her beatific grin and Charlotte sighed so deeply that she had a coughing fit.

The sight to be seen – selected, Kelly assured her, not by him but by Mr Harry – was the tomb of a king. What king and when he reigned remained obscure. 'Long time ago,' was all their guide would or could vouchsafe, which was quite enough information for Charlotte who wished to be given no more facts and had, anyway, a tenuous grasp on the centuries. 'Long time ago' would do nicely.

Forty minutes of a tooth-splintering drive over boulders and pits brought them to a plateau where the van wheezed to a halt, raising a good deal of dust that settled in a cloud over a woman squatting amongst a curious collection of plastic toys. Kelly jumped out, lugging his film box after him, took a bandanna out of his pocket and dusted down the resigned and immobile woman while Charlotte bought a one-armed doll and a gloomy-looking fish to cheer her up. Mr Harry watched these philanthropic efforts with the indulgent smile of one from whom all blessings flow and then pointed ahead.

'There is tomb,' he said. 'Up we go.'

Charlotte looked up. She looked up and then up. Kelly did an impromptu soft-shoe shuffle in the dust. 'I'll build a stairway to Paradise,' he crooned in a pleasing baritone, 'with a new step every day.'

'Oh God,' said Charlotte. She had on a striped tent dress and stood wetly inside it like a camper taking a shower.

They walked to the bottom of the steps.

'Three hundred and forty-five,' Mr Harry said proudly.

'This sight better be worth seeing,' said Charlotte in a hollow voice.

Kelly sang out, 'Stand aside, I'm on my way,' and ran up the first flight in a depressingly agile fashion. His load of cameras and lenses bounced against his pelvis as if they weighed ounces.

'I stay with you. I help you,' Mr Harry said to Charlotte, as one saddled with an invalid en route to Lourdes. She ducked his proffered arm.

'Thank you. I can manage,' she said haughtily. 'You go on, you two. I shall climb at my own pace and observe the countryside.' Mr Harry, after all, could not be more than five years older than her and Kelly not more than five years younger. Did they expect to carry her up on a stretcher? Censoring the thought that if there had been a stretcher to hire, she would have hired it, she began the climb.

At the first landing, she paused and put her hand to her forehead, looking ostentatiously about as she struggled to regain her breath.

Mr Harry hovered, showing no sign of stress. 'Nice view,' he said.

'Very,' she replied, examining a banyan tree. 'Do go *on*, Mr Harry.'

At the second landing, she sat abruptly on the ledge beside the stone balustrade. Mr Harry tripped lissomly down from where he had climbed above her and, taking off his glasses, regarded her with some anxiety. His eyes, stripped of their usual shield, looked undressed and rather poetic.

'Is plenty time,' he said, 'you must go slow.'

'*Please*, Mr Harry. Forget about me. I'm perfectly all right.'

Five minutes passed and she began on the third flight.

Two hundred steps later, soaked from head to foot, she lay full-length with her back propped against the next lift of the balustrade, her breasts thrusting against the flimsy cotton of her dress as urgently, she thought as she helplessly rasped, as her toes thrust against the ends of her sandals. Mr Harry, who had run down again at her collapse, stood non-plussed at her side, looking down at the seismic activity with awe.

'I so sorry,' he said, his naked eyes glued to the moist circles of her nipples. 'You stop here, I not want you to be sick. You are, dear Miss Harlot' – and he bowed low over her prone form – 'my guest. And my guest is my Queen.'

Heat enveloped them, pinning Charlotte to where she lay. She looked up at Mr Harry and saw the skin of his neck and his chest, amber and without a hair, without pores, smooth as the burnished stone of Ganeesha's trunk. For a moment, she let her thighs, straight and clenched as a Crusader on a tomb, relax.

'My guest, my Queen,' murmured Mr Harry. The cicadas shrieked.

A distant shout made them both jerk upright. Kelly stood at the top of the steps with one arm stretched above him in the air, looking, Charlotte thought as she rolled off the balustrade, like a glamorous Führer addressing his troops. She clambered on, her footsteps still dogged by her faithful subject, whose momentary lapse from character she refused to recollect.

At last, giddy with exhaustion, she stumbled from the last step, sat down heavily under the nearest tree and spent the next few seconds wondering if an iron lung could be conveyed up the steps quickly enough to save her life. When this no longer seemed in imminent danger, she opened her eyes and looked round, determined to absorb every detail of what had cost her so much to attain.

She saw a square cement pool full of dirty water, a large dull urn and a small woman surrounded by Coca-Cola bottles of the type Miss Millichip had warned her against in Banabalu.

'You like?' said Mr Harry, offering her one with a straw at the ready.

The membranes of her throat parted long enough for her to gasp 'no' and closed again. After a while she expressed her disappointment at the lack of funereal equipment on the arid hill side. 'Where's the tomb, Mr Harry?' she asked crossly. 'I don't see any tomb.'

'There,' he replied.

She followed his slightly shaky finger to where a dirt track wound in a half-hearted way up a steep and craggy incline behind them. There were long gouges in the earth beside it – caused, Charlotte had no doubt, by the clinging fingers of mountaineers as they slid, bellowing hopelessly, to their deaths on the rocks far below.

'Good . . . *heavens*,' she exclaimed. 'If I'm expected to take another . . .' At this point, so pitifully was Mr Harry flinching from her wrath that she took a deep breath, swallowed the next few angry words and dragging herself up, trudged off to where Kelly was standing, a camera bolted to his eye.

'One of these days,' she said to him, 'that man will be found strangled . . .'

'Look,' said Kelly.

Charlotte looked and said no more for the time being. Far below the escarpment where they stood lay an undulation of emerald valleys streaked here and there with pink clouds. At the edge of the sky was the satin sea. A fragrant steam arose from the distant green bowl as rich and strange as if the world were still in the making. As she watched, transfixed, a violet stain seeped over the valley and in the rolling forest carpet seed pearls of light winked on and shimmered.

'That's it,' Kelly said, putting down his camera. 'Light's gone.'

'Heaven. *Heaven*,' breathed Charlotte.

'Better than a slap in the belly with a wet fish, I'll give you that.'

A stroll on life's highroad with Kelly, Charlotte saw, would be knee deep in the corpses of precious moments. Only half joking, she said, 'Why have you got no soul?'

'I only pack essentials when I travel. Find me a soul that's drip-dry, charges batteries and holds a six-pack of Foster's and I'll buy it.'

He sat with his arms wrapped round his knees. She had not known before that knees could be handsome. Also wrists. Kelly's were the size of another man's fists, flecked with gold hairs. The twilight painted violet shadows along the short bridge of his nose and there were smudges of the same in the recesses of his ears. When men were beautiful, things fell out of kilter. Rules were broken, peacocks swam and lions flew. It was some time since Charlotte had thought of Bruce but she thought of him now, with particular emphasis on his knees, his wrists and his ears. Her nerves steadied by this exercise in the obtainable, she felt in her sling bag.

'Here,' she said.

'What's this?'

'Your tape recorder.'

He looked at her. 'Still pissed off about that evening?'

'I listened to the tapes. The voices on their own don't sound . . . well . . .' She gave a reluctant laugh. 'But Kelly, saying I'm a racist. I can't accept that.'

'My treat,' he patted her knee.

'I'm not, you know. What made you say it?'

He got up and slapped his neck. 'Mossie time,' he said, 'we better get moving.'

Charlotte, already the possessor of two bites whose itching the presence of Kelly made easy to ignore, scrambled up beside him. 'Tell me, go on.'

'Oh, I don't know,' He looked as though he was swallowing medicine. 'You act too nice to everyone. Wanting to hug people. That type of thing.'

'That's racist?'

'Yeah, of a sort. In my book, there's two kinds of racists. One lot hate all tinted folk because they've got these huge pricks. The other lot love all tinted folk because they've got these inky dinky pricks. You're the second kind.'

This analysis rendered Charlotte speechless for five paces. At the sixth, she drew breath. 'That's an amazingly male-centred remark.'

'You're right. For women, it's the other way round.'

'I am not interested in men's . . .'

'. . . pricks,' supplied Kelly.

She ploughed on. 'It's the people in general. In the villages. They're so kind, putting up with us. They smile, they're . . . spontaneous.

169

The way the women take my hand . . . I can't help it, I think they're so sweet.'

'Some of them are about as sweet as a nest of rattlers. They're just people. Nice guys, bastards, same as us. They're most of them a lot poorer than you're used to, that's all, and you've got a bad case of the guilts. But don't let what I say get to you. Why give a shit what I think?'

They came in sight of Mr Harry. He stood drooping under a tree of whiskery flowers, swatting himself. With the remnants of vexation, Charlotte said, 'There's *one* Sulanasian I feel no guilt about.'

Kelly looked down at her and his eyes were as distant as the satin sea. 'Harry's quite a fella,' he said. 'I'm just wild about Harry.'

On the way back in a darkness streaked with fire flies, Mr Harry went into details of the next journey.

'We fly to Sinabaya, very nice town by the sea, you come also, Kelly' – he beamed at Kelly, – 'and day after, we visit *very* big factory.' He held his hands apart, indicating a factory building the length of a good-sized carp. 'Biggest factory in Sulanasia and many, many women workers. Make Sulanasian cigarettes. Kelly can take so good photos. You like, Miss Harlot?'

Charlotte, hunched in the back, said, 'It's not a question of *like*, Mr Harry. What relevance does a factory have to my current project?'

'Please?'

'Where does birth control come in, she means,' explained Kelly.

Mr Harry threw up his hands. 'Everywhere!' he exclaimed. 'Every everywhere! Factory have big clinic, all women workers have IUD, is special good place to write about birth control.'

Charlotte rolled her eyes and grunted. Mr Harry regarded her with anxiety. 'You sick again?'

'No,' she snapped, 'I'm in perfect health. But I won't fly. I don't like flying and I want to see the countryside.'

'Too far in train,' Mr Harry assured her. 'And countryside same as here.'

'It's nine hours, about,' Kelly added. 'I wouldn't advise it.'

'Then you're going to fly?'

'You betcha.'

'Well, you go with your . . . friend. Mr Harry, can you book me

170

on to the morning train? I want first class, please.' She sounded to her own ears like Miss Millichip at her worst but she had a lot on her mind.

'First class?' Mr Harry said. He added, absently, 'My guest, my Queen. First class, yes, good, I do.'

There was a sudden jolt, the van skidded sideways and stopped on a bank. The driver said something to Mr Harry.

'Is funeral,' he translated. Already the windows were blocked with passing heads, dark silhouettes against flickering lights.

'Where's my flash,' Kelly said, diving into his black boxes. 'I gotta get this.' He heaved back the van door and jumped out.

The sides of the narrow road were fenced with bicycles lying one against the other, three and four deep. Their owners, young men for the most part, stood quietly in groups, their white shirts neon-blue in the flare of torches held aloft by the mourners walking in the road. The procession was not long; a few muffled figures of men and women who trailed after a plank coffin carried on the shoulders of four men. Charlotte slid back her window and watched the coffin approach. As it reached her, she looked down. The coffin was open. Inside, between rough boards, lay the insubstantial body in a shroud strewn with torn flowers. Only the face was uncovered, a small ivory mask framed in petals.

Charlotte shut the window. 'It's her,' she said. 'It's her.'

'Please?' Mr Harry's face was pale, too, in the dark.

'The girl in the coffin. At the Happy People Party. The IUD. I saw her in Tanjung, in pain. I heard her screaming. I should have done something. Why didn't I do something?'

'I do not understand,' Mr Harry said. 'My English maybe not so good.'

Charlotte pressed her hands in her lap. 'It was the same girl. I know it was. Awful, awful.'

There was a silence. Mr Harry knitted his brows. 'You see her before? I think no,' he said finally. 'You make mistake.' He leaned from his seat and patted her shoulder. 'Too many women, you mix up. It hard for European lady. All Sulanasian people look same to you. Women, men. I too look same to you like other man. I know this. I understand.'

Charlotte scratched at a bite on her arm until it bled.

*

171

'It *was* the same woman, Kelly, I swear.'

'Sure.'

In the road in front of them, the drivers pedalled their pram-bikes up and down. Occasionally two would lock wheels, whereupon lengthy and on the whole good-natured altercations took place while the passengers sat with their parcels piled on their knees, patient babies waiting for their nannies to stop gossiping and trundle them home.

Charlotte nibbled at the green stuff in her bowl, hot from the cauldron that simmered beside them. She had not eaten a square meal for days and now felt faintly repulsed by the greasy smoke arising from the stall. Kelly, however, was vigorously ladling in his noodles. White worms hung from his glistening lips and Charlotte's stomach, once so omniverous in its demands, went into a maidenly swoon at the sight. It seemed there was nothing to be gained in pursuing the identity of a dead woman, so, putting down her bowl, she reverted to an earlier matter.

'This guilt I've got, Kelly. Why haven't you?'

Through strings of noodles, Kelly said, 'Never seen that it gets anyone anywhere.'

'But that's not true. You could say all Western aid comes from guilt.'

Calmly, Kelly repeated, 'Never seen *that* gets anyone anywhere, either. Except into debt.'

'You don't approve of the birth control campaign, do you?' Charlotte rubbed one wrist, raising Bruce-type flakes. 'Well, I don't either, the way it's run here. But there has to be birth control and we have to give aid for it. And for all the other things developing countries need. You approve of that, surely?'

Kelly made the sound of a cork with his lips. 'Don't approve, don't disapprove. I leave it alone.'

'You can't. If you do, people die. Like that girl. You can't just pass by on the other side. It's your *business*.' As soon as she said this, Charlotte saw the Moslem student before her and heard his lilting voice.

'Look,' Kelly said, 'I'm going to go on a weeny walkabout. I want to shoot some street scenes. Romantic Tanjung, moonlight over the chow stall.' He pushed himself off his stool and picked up his camera cases.

'Listen, Kelly.' Charlotte held his arm. She did not wish to retire

172

with these questions on her mind. 'Answer me for once. What do you *think*?'

A lock of hair hung over his forehead. He scraped it back and, studying the passersby, he said, 'What do I think? I think you aid people are like that old king. Everything you touch turns to gold and the poor shits on the receiving end can't eat gold. Also I think my business is to keep my snout out of other people's business. That's what I think. Now, if you don't mind' – and he looked as disgruntled as Charlotte had ever seen him look – 'me and my Brownie have got work to do.'

Hurt by Kelly's inclusion of her among the Midas people – she, Charlotte Macanally, paid a pittance, half as much in a year, probably, as he earned in a month – watched him step off the kerb. She called after him, 'You don't mind sticking your *Brownie* into other people's business!'

For some reason, this made Kelly laugh a lot.

On the morning of her departure for Sinabaya, Charlotte found she had lost so much weight that her boiler suit – once designer-baggy – now made her look as if she were skulking behind a curtain. With the aid of a belt, she managed to rope herself in. Despite a stain of unknown origin across one breast and an insect bite that had turned into a weeping sore, she smiled briefly into the mirror. Things on the appearance front were looking up, which was as well, for nothing else was. Thin or fat, there was the increasing probability that she was the wrong person in the wrong place. Pat Wilshaw, she felt sure, would not have given way to the doubts that assailed her on all sides nor had a recurring nightmare of dead women screaming. Pat had a proper perspective, a broad over-view, a commitment that would not be deflected from its aim by individual suffering. Pat was a General in a campaign, like Gordon Grant and Miss Millichip, and Generals accepted that you couldn't make omelettes without breaking eggs.

Brooding on her own lack of leadership qualities, she began to pack. By the time she was finished, perspiration drenched her. She took off her belt. Vanity stood no chance against one hundred in the shade.

On his own insistence, Mr Harry escorted her to the station.

'I'm really looking forward to this,' she told him. 'My first train journey in daylight. And the first class in the Banabalu train was very comfortable.' This was not entirely factual but she wished to cheer Mr Harry, who was looking unusually down in the mouth.

The station was packed with bona fide travellers and with families who appeared to have taken up residence within its portals and had not yet woken to face the day. Charlotte regarded their sleeping bodies with some envy as she and Mr Harry picked their way over the railway lines to where the train for Sinabaya stood. It was not, she noticed immediately, as big as the one she had taken from Banabalu. Indeed, it was altogether slimmer and a good deal more truncated, not to mention the fact that its pitted metal sides appeared to have been caught in crossfire during some short but vicious war.

'Is this it?' she asked her escort as she set foot on the boarding step.

'This it,' he answered pithily.

She entered the first carriage, followed by Mr Harry, and stood still with shock. Then, determined not to give vent to the tumultuous emotions surging within her before a thorough inspection, she stomped the length of the train, followed by Mr Harry. It did not take long.

'There is no first class.'

'All same class,' he said brightly. 'Maybe all first?'

'This . . . is . . . not . . . first . . . class,' Charlotte said. 'This third class. Maybe tenth.'

Mr Harry put his head down and grappled her luggage on to the inch-wide racks. The luggage fell back on to the bench beneath which, being too narrow to encompass it, passed it quickly to the floor.

'Right,' she said. 'You win. I'll fly.'

He shook his head. His features seemed to be responding to a strong vacuum from within. 'So sorry, Miss Harlot. Plane full now. No seat.'

'I'll fly tomorrow.'

'So sorry. Factory close.'

'*Close*?'

'Holiday,' he said meekly.

'Mr Harry. I asked you to book first class. Three times, I asked you.' She held up three trembling fingers. 'Why you not do what I ask? Why you not *tell* me?' Her English was surrendering its claim to mother tongue.

174

'You my guest,' said Mr Harry. His nose had almost vanished in the abject crumple of his face. 'You my Queen. I want please you.'

'This,' Charlotte intoned, setting her breasts aquiver, 'does not, Mr Harry, please me.'

There seemed no more to do or say. She sat down hard on the harder bench. Mr Harry deposited her luggage beside her, murmuring intimately to it as he patted it into place, 'Good. You stay there. Miss Harlot like you near to her. When Miss Harlot tired, she lean on you.'

The train gave a sudden shriek and recoiled violently, terrorized by its own voice. Charlotte's luggage flung itself to the floor again.

'I go now,' Mr Harry stammered, halfway down the aisle. 'I meet you nine hour from now. Four clock at station Sinabaya. Bye bye, Miss Harlot.'

'Nine hour,' she said through gritted teeth.

Half an hour later the train, recovered from its premature ejaculation, was still standing serenely in the station and Charlotte's bladder would brook no more delay. She pushed her way through the hordes of passengers who had staked their claim to benches and floor since she had arrived and sidled through an aperture insecurely screened by a warped door. Inside, she gave a grievous moan. Every wall was artistically stippled with the offerings of bygone occupants, the basin was thickly smeared with grime and there was hardly room for a foothold over the hole in the floor. Liquid seeped into her sandals and a stench as from the mouth of hell arose from the hole. She wedged her feet as far apart as she could and peeled down her jump suit, trying not to touch a wall or breathe at all. As she hoisted both arms free, the train began to move. Steadying herself by will-power alone, she peeped out of the small grill. Mr Harry had not gone. He stood immediately below. Catching sight of her, he started and gave a nervous wave.

Charlotte returned him a distant nod and sank regally onto her haunches.

By the time she returned to her bench, sadder and wetter, its meagre length housed two women, three men, a child and a mercifully underweight lad. Two of the men were already deep in a game of chess, their legs of necessity so interlaced as to form a useful table. In spite of the best efforts of these fellow-travellers, who goggled in understandable amazement at her choice of transport, there was

175

hardly room enough to accommodate even her new-model hips and the seat itself supported a mere sliver of her rump.

For a while she sat bolt upright and inwardly fumed at Mr Harry, upon whose absent head she called down the wrath of Jehovah, Buddha, Vishnu, several Greek deities with a nice line in revenge and threw in Mother Prayana in case Mr H ever ventured Caxton Hallwards. The voodoo served to keep her physical wretchedness at bay until the last corrugated shacks of suburban Tanjung had disappeared and the countryside of Sulanasia, upon whose transcendental qualities she had set such store, made its appearance. Or rather a fraction of an appearance since the windows, unwashed for several decades, revealed no more than passing smudges of green.

In protest at the collapse of the journey's central purpose, Charlotte's body renounced all pretence of stoicism. Her buttocks became catatonic, her thighs developed chronic sciatica, her neck went into spasm and her back, with a hitherto unsuspected acrobatic talent, stabbed itself through to the spine. The leasing of a rubber cushion from a passing vendor did nothing to alleviate her aches and pains. Its fist-like pressure under her upper legs threatened to cut off an important blood supply and Charlotte was forced to remove it before gangrene set in.

There was also the heat, an element that upped straightforward torture by several notches to the realms of unanaesthetized vivisection. The fans did not work, the windows did not open and the air quickly congealed to a torrid and odorous jelly. She soon learned that no human beings become totally inured to the lamentable aspects of their environment. In spite of a lifetime spent in their country's sweltering climate the other passengers looked as distressed as she felt. One woman lay folded in a torpor, the sweat trickling over her closed lids, another kept a phial of some strong-smelling liquid permanently under her nostrils. The mother with the child flapped a corner of her shawl at it and herself until her strength gave out and the two of them flopped in a tangled mound, half-fainting, half-asleep, while the two chess-playing men, no longer with the energy to lift their pieces, sat still and breathed sonorously through sagging mouths. The lad alone retained some spark of consciousness. Though the skin of his face had gone a sickly green and he never once moved his cramped limbs, his eyes flicked sideways whenever someone moved down the aisle.

176

It was the aisle that provided the only distraction from the torment of the journey. At every station – and there were many – a motley collection of sellers and beggars crammed themselves into its narrow confines, rousing the comatose travellers with the shouting of their wares. Baskets laden with brown-flecked bananas, oranges and other more mysterious fruit were passed under the passengers' noses and over their heads, peanut pastries and other savouries were shaken before their gummy eyes. There were tea vendors, Coke vendors and multi-coloured-juice vendors, on none of whom Charlotte dared bestow her custom, for though her throat was grainy with thirst and she had long discarded any fear of infection, a beverage would inevitably hasten a return visit to the hell-hole at the end of the aisle. Rather an impromptu bladderectomy than that. Rather public incontinence.

The beggars, sandwiched between the vendors, underlined a growing suspicion that her official tour had been sanitized in advance by the KNNA. Either the villages she had visited had been requested beforehand to keep out of sight their needier citizens, or the villages themselves were the most prosperous Sulanasia had to offer and she had been carefully diverted from the rest. Here, men dragged themselves along the aisle on stumps encased in leather patches of the kind used to reinforce the jacket sleeves of English gentry. A young woman yanked behind her a blind companion, directing the clouded orbs in a vice-like grip at the sighted to wrench a few ratah out of them. And they gave. They could not afford to pay their way out of nine hours of travail but they knew dire necessity when they saw it and gave, in grubby coins. Charlotte gave, too, from her comparatively infinite resources and thought of the first class carriage from Banabalu, where bouncers must have been hired to keep such annoyances out. What did Miss Millichip know of these downtrodden of her Global family, enclosed in her chauffeured limousine? What did Gordon Grant know, in his glass corn-cob on Threadneedle Street? Or Mr Harry, for that matter, polished as a brass button among his carefully selected rural folk?

At this spurt of moral outrage, enough adrenalin entered Charlotte's limbs to move her off her perch in the hope of finding somewhere a little more acceptable to spend the leaden hours. She sat for a while at a table in what passed for the dining car. The table's surface was gouged with cigarette burns. A wooden cup supported the stem of a greasy plastic rose. There was a box of toothpicks. The floor beneath her feet was thick with peanut shells and here, too, the windows were filthy. After staring at a sleeping child in a T-shirt lettered 'Donald and Goofy' and at the family next to her eating cold clotted rice, she got up and crunched over the peanut shells to the rear door of the carriage, heaved it open and came upon salvation.

Here she stayed, sitting on the metal ledge between the carriages with the wind ripping through her hair and the train's roar deafening her, in the friendly company of a bunch of stowaways who clung from every available handhold. Below her dangling legs rushed the Sulanasia she had gone to such lengths to see. Water buffalo lifted their swept-back horns to see her go. Geese stretched their necks and ducks poked up muddy beaks from ponds. A man, pulling down his shorts, mooned at her as he squatted in a river. Sheep, tethered near the train, bleated in terror as it tore past. At level-crossings the occupants of bikes and trucks waved and the pendulous jowls of brahmin bulls swung as they turned to gaze after the earth-bound comet. In the paddy fields, women stroked the mud with long paddles and behind them, distant volcanoes erupted clouds. A brown billy-goat, incensed by some grievance, butted another in its skeletal ribs and seconds beyond their stomping hooves the land on which they stood plunged half a mile into a ravine in whose rocky depths Charlotte, peering between her toes, could see the bending figures of women beating their washing in the foam of a pink waterfall.

From the bottom of her heart she forgave Mr Harry, whose maladministration had brought her these joys. As the boys around her leapt with seasoned skill from one impossible toehold to a worse, guffawing soundlessly in the hot blast of the wind, and a woman with no teeth took her outstretched hands at a stopping and held them, looking intently at her with wise monkey eyes, she blessed his name. He was good for her, Mr Harry. In some strange way, he provided what she most needed, whether she knew it or not, whether he meant to or not. A talisman.

For the rest of the journey, she sat on her perch or lay flat on the metal grid. Only when her bladder began to send out faint and then ever more urgent SOSs did her warm sentiments curdle. She hung on as long as she dared but as the countryside yielded to the urban sprawl of Sinabaya she gave up in the face of impending explosion and entered the carriage again. Approaching her bench, she saw two grey-shirted men talking to the occupants but, unable to pause, she sidled past them and squeezed herself once more into purgatory. She was still there, blue with oxygen deprivation among the spattered tiles, when a final jerk of the train signalled Sinabaya and soaked the last dry thong of her sandals.

It stood motionless, puffing, and Charlotte squelched back to collect her luggage. The two grey-shirted men had gone and in their place were two soldiers who gripped the chicken-bone elbows of the underweight lad. They hauled him from his seat and propelled him along the aisle, their shiny holsters bobbing at their hips. She had a glimpse of the lad – head high, skin stretched tight, hand clenched over some sort of card – and he was gone. No one looked after him but Charlotte. The passengers gathered up their baggage in silence, avoiding each other's gaze, and shuffled silently down the carriage to dismount.

'What could he have done?' she asked Mr Harry, recounting the incident as they drove into Sinabaya. He did not look at her and he did not answer her question.

'I pray to my God for your safe travel, Miss Harlot, and you come safe,' he said instead.

'But what could he have *done*? They had pistols. He was very young.'

'Robber, maybe.' He looked bored to death.

'Break-dancer, maybe,' Charlotte muttered to the window.

'Well, whatever he's done, they can't kill him,' Charlotte said to Kelly. 'They don't have capital punishment in Sulanasia.'

'No?'

'No. Miss Millichip told me. Not even for murder.'

'Goodie goodie gum drops,' said Kelly.

Sinabaya was a seaside town, wide and white and shady, and though the sea could not be seen from the KNNA van – the identical model that ferried them about in Tanjung and identically battered – it lay not far away, a benign and cooling presence. Rain had fallen minutes before Charlotte's arrival and the air was clean.

'I must have a shower,' Charlotte said, reminded of her own soiled state. 'What's the hotel like?'

Mr Harry studied his nails.

Kelly said, 'I chose it.'

Mr Harry said, 'My sorrow,' and laid a hand on his chest. 'I apologize many times.'

The hotel was in an alley off Sinabaya's main street, inaccessible to vehicles. Mr Harry made a gesture of helping Charlotte out with her luggage but his heart was not in it and as soon as she and Kelly had dismounted he thumped the door shut. His face at the rear of the van as it pulled away had the relieved expression of a man fleeing seconds before a dam burst.

'What's the matter with him?' enquired Charlotte, stumbling over the cobblestones.

Kelly, shouldering her rucksack, said, 'He doesn't approve. Thinks you ought to be staying at a grander place.'

Charlotte soon saw what Mr Harry meant. There could be few lodgings less grand in all the world, she imagined, than this one-storey hole in the wall where ferns had taken healthy root in the many and spacious cracks and what little she could see of the roof was all there was of the roof.

'Bloc,' she read aloud from a ramshackle sign. 'Is that its name? Very ethnic.'

'Thought you'd like it,' Kelly said.

'Are ·you staying here?'

'You're getting very suspicious in your old age, Mrs M.'

'About time, too,' she said crisply.

Bloc – even to add a 'The' before its name seemed pretentious, never mind 'Hotel' – was as delapidated inside as out but it had a purity of function and design that took Charlotte's breath away, though whether in panic or in admiration she would have been hard put at that moment to say. The rooms were bamboo cabins round a small square courtyard that contained one large potted palm, three webbed chairs and a television set. Towels and wet washing dripped from a low wall. Each room had a bed. Some had two beds. Testing the mattress in her room she reckoned that 'mattress' was too pretentious as well. Plain Bloc seemed the right word for most things here.

'*Well*,' she said.

Kelly, who appeared to have grown in bulk and height since Tanjung, smiled.

After she had unpacked he showed her the ablutions. They

consisted of a tiled tank full of water, a plastic ladle and a large pair of footprints placed on either side of the same hole in the ground that the train had possessed, but spotless and without odour.

'Well *well*,' she said. 'What more could I want?'

In the event, her mild sarcasm turned out to be exact. As the days passed, Charlotte became addicted to the modus vivendi of Bloc and found herself cherishing it. She felt she had spent too long hacking her way through a forest choked with vines and undergrowth. Now she had come upon a clearing and could see the sky. She had opened a gimcrack box and found inside something limpid and full of light. The possessions and facilities that cluttered her London life, bought or used for comfort and pleasure, somersaulted to expose their inner workings, noisy, demanding, polluting and an arm and a leg to run. Morality played no part in this judgment, Charlotte knew that much. There were no hair shirts or interesting instruments of self-flagellation on display, no painful renunciations were in order. Indeed, no sacrifices of any sort were on the cards. It was a simple reversal of the meaning of words. Now Bloc was comfort and pleasure.

Nevertheless, initiation into these monkish delights was, as all initiations are, stressful. It involved a drastic lopping away of superfluity and a pruning of much that Charlotte had previously considered vital. Bloc provided no sheets or pillows or covers or linens of any kind. There were no surfaces upon which to put things but the beds. There was no soap or towels or glasses or cupboards or mirrors or drawers or any hooks. There was no hot water or mats or lavatory paper. There were no lights in the rooms. What electricity there was served a courtyard lamp and the television set, extraordinary import from another planet. The thatch of the roof covered only the beds and those in no way officiously – elsewhere, when it rained, it rained, drenching everything. Only in Nature was Bloc well furnished. Lizards scurried across the walls, birds nested in the thatch and fluttered at will, insects, winged and otherwise, inhabited every part, tunnelling and weaving and mating and stinging and droning the sun-soaked hours away. Plants did well, too, and moss and lichens. Also fungi.

On that afternoon, Charlotte's first priority was to wash her journey off her. Since there was no dry spot for discarded clothes in the ablutions, she stripped in her cabin and put a dressing-gown on. Then, clutching her sponge bag, she hovered at the threshold until the coast was clear and scuttled across the courtyard to the dank washing cubicle. Paddling back, she passed in full view of Kelly stretched full length on his bed which, in Kelly's case, meant a fair bit of leg uncatered for.

'Feel better?' he called.

'Much,' she called back and made to paddle on, unaccustomed to being seen in a state of undress by any but domestic eyes. But Kelly was beckoning.

'What?' She stepped uncertainly nearer, relieved that her gown could now be held well across her.

'You know, you look good. Lost your puppy fat.'

'Some. Aren't we going to the factory?' She put in this reference to work to distract attention from her blush.

'Harry's changed his plans. He'll brief us tonight at the Grand Hotel Sinabayə.'

'Is that where he's staying?' she asked, suppressing a stab of envy.

'No. But he doesn't want to come here. Bad for his image.' Kelly sat up and patted his bed. 'Come and sit down.'

He was wearing only rolled-up shorts and his body filled the tiny room. Nina Kowalski wouldn't turn a hair. She would lope towards him, entirely unconcerned with the fact that she was naked but for a threadbare length of cotton.

A man with a broom came into the courtyard, preceding two other men. She dived for Kelly's cover.

'I can't stay long,' she said, keeping a stretch of mattress between them.

'No? Booked seats for the opera, have you?'

Embarrassed, she gave half a girlish giggle. 'Tell me about yourself,' she said. 'I don't even know your Christian name.'

'Keep 'em talking, eh?' Kelly nodded wisely. 'That way, they'll keep their hands to themselves. I know.'

But he talked anyway, for a while, astonishing her with the revelation that he had parents and visited them now and again. It was like hearing that the King of the Jungle partook of the occasional cuppa with his mum. She was less surprised that he'd had a wife.

'What went wrong?' she asked but he only shrugged. And he didn't keep his hands to himself. While Charlotte told him about her marriage in return, omitting irrelevant details such as Bruce's flakes, baldness and beret, her own lumpishness and her recent return to Mrs Wren rather than a gay divorcee's pad, he stroked her ankle on the bed beside him and then began to massage her feet. It was a friendly gesture and the fact that his touch threatened her with electrocution was not, she told herself, his intention or his fault.

'So,' she said, shrugging as casually as Kelly, 'three months ago, we split. You know how it is.'

He cracked two of her toes and ran his fingers down her instep.

'It's groovy, really, being on my own. I like not having to bother with cooking and that . . .'

He was doing extraordinary things to the back of one calf.

'. . . it's cool. I mean, like I've got some personal space, you know? I can let it all hang out . . .' Why, exactly, an American appeared to have taken her over, she could not say, but she battled on. 'Bruce was a swell guy, all my girlfriends freaked out . . .' And an *old* American, at that. This simply would not do. She extracted her legs from his fingers and lowered them to the floor.

'It's been nice talking to you,' she said, wrenching her voice out of her nasal passages where it seemed to have taken up roost. 'See you around.'

As she dashed for her room, Kelly called after her, 'Have a nice day, mind.'

A few minutes later, when she was at that delicate point between frocked and unfrocked and still pink with the shame of her Stateside excursion, the outline of Kelly loomed behind her bamboo screen.

He said, 'I am your friendly neighbourhood postie, my name is Peeping Tom,' and pushed a folded newspaper through the interstices. It dropped on the floor by Charlotte's feet. 'Have a look at Foreign News.'

He had marked the article in the three-day-old *Times* with a cross. In the safety of her clothes again and relatively composed, Charlotte read it.

'Three men were executed by firing squad yesterday in the remote Parabam District of Sulanasia's eastern peninsula. The men, who had been imprisoned for six years under Sulanasia's 1975 Control of Terrorism Act, were said to have been leading members of the banned New Jihad Party of Islamic insurgents, recently described by the Sulanasian President on a visit to the US as "hysterical fanatics bent on discrediting the progress of our Government in the eyes of our people and of our allies in the West".

'In an interview on French television after the executions, the exiled founder of the New Jihad Party attacked the Sulanasian

Government's pro-Western stance as a corrupting influence on Sulanasian culture and religion and deplored the damaging effects of dependence on World Bank funding. He said, "They are selling our land from under our feet and teaching our people to act against the will of Allah." This last comment is thought to refer to Sulanasia's highly successful birth control programme.'

She took the newspaper clipping with her when they set off for the Hotel Sinabaya. Mr Harry was in the lobby to meet them, his white shirt outshining the gleaming white ceramic floor. He looked as scrubbed and polished as a prep school boy on Parents' Day.

'How is your room?' he asked Charlotte.

'Fine.'

Mr Harry's glasses winked sympathetically at her. 'Not so fine, I think. Very terrible, this place. I shamed for you. You important lady of London. *This* where you must live.' His glance at Kelly was full of reproach but Kelly was already aiming his camera at a spectacularly glamorous woman posed beside a marble pillar and did not see.

Their tray of orange juices was brought to them by the pool, whose bikinied European occupants so over-excited Mr Harry that Charlotte was glad he had spectacles to keep his eyeballs in. When he was calmer, she took the opportunity to ask, disingenuously, if there were people in Sulanasia who disliked the idea of family planning.

'No . . . oo,' Mr Harry said. 'Everyone like. Everyone know is too many people in Sulanasia.'

'What about Moslems?'

'We *all* Moslems. We *all* like.' He spread out his palms in an oceanic gesture.

'I was told in Banabalu,' Charlotte lied, 'that there were some Moslems who objected. Who didn't like.'

His face, at first a parody of amazement, shifted into impassivity. When he had finished making noises with his straw he said, 'Maybe some. Only few. These few very old people. Old people not like change.'

'But there are young people too. Young men and women,' she said, piling on the agony. 'A Minister informed me of this in Banabalu.'

At this fresh evidence of metropolitan indiscretion Mr Harry's juice became greatly agitated. 'Some, yes, perhaps, maybe.' Then, he rallied. 'In *every* country some fanatic. You have fanatic in England, too. I see on television. Bomb Missus Tatcher in hotel. Woof! . . .' and he gave a spirited rendition of the English Prime Minister falling through the air in disarray. 'These Irish peoples, *very* fanatic. Yes?'

His confidential nod shared out equally between himself and Charlotte the awesome burdens of rulers. She wished he hadn't introduced the Irish dimension, that familiar muddier of English waters. Once, she had pressed a book about Nicaragua onto an American visitor. 'And what about Ireland?' the American had said triumphantly. But two wrongs did not make a right. Charlotte pressed on.

'What do you do about these fanatics . . . if you find them turning the people against birth control?'

'I talk,' Mr Harry cooed. 'I go in mosques. I say to priests, you naughty men, you must listen to what our President say. You must preach what he ask.' He wagged a reproving finger to illustrate his sales technique.

'And if they won't?'

Mr Harry's smile had remained gallantly in place during most of Charlotte's interrogation. Now it wavered for a second before he wrenched it back into position. This was the moment to whip out her cutting and deliver the coup de grâce, but the tenuous grasp her victim had on his features stayed her hand.

'Ah, Kelly!' Mr Harry exclaimed with huge enthusiasm. 'Please, you sit down. Miss Harlot and I have finished nice talk. Now is time for brief.'

Nothing about the heat-soaked days that followed was brief. Often Charlotte felt she was crawling along at the bottom of a lake. But the change of air had galvanized Mr Harry, redoubling his already prodigious energy, generating sparks from his hair and his eyes and buffing up his polished shoes so that they whisked across the bumpy landscape like shooting stars. Charlotte failed to stop him in his pre-ordained tracks even with a quite alarming asthmatic attack. He paused to allow her exactly two gulps from her inhaler and accelerated. Her lungs, seeing no future in their bid for attention, gave up and let her go. Kelly, as tireless as Mr Harry, loped in circles around them, clicking.

Fields of sugar cane and rice, teams of water buffalo, villages, clinics, bowing headmen, timorous women and children flashed past Charlotte, leaving her only with images: white overalls and the whites of women's eyes; suckling babies pressed to their mothers; a village midwife, puckered like an old fig, flinging up her arms in fright against Kelly's camera; enamel bowls; steel instruments; an ulcer festering on a soft breast; the sore skinny legs of children; swollen bellies rising above wrapped sarongs.

'More women pregnant here,' she gulped at Mr Harry once, racing after him to shake more outstretched hands.

'Some more, yes, Sinabaya is strong Moslem. Was very terrible area to overcome. You see . . .?'

The schoolgirls who approached were as decorous as nuns in long grey skirts, their hair concealed under cotton balaclavas. The younger girls wore shorter skirts, but their legs were swaddled in woolly stockings that made Charlotte, in that heat, sob inwardly to see. Most women had their heads veiled and no frangipanis lodged coyly behind ears.

Another time Mr Harry darted sideways into an acacia-roofed alley that had vast carved doors at its end.

'Mosque,' he said. 'I speak to priests. You see.'

Grateful for every respite, she had watched him advance upon the priests who sat along the steps of the verandah, their old necks scraggy above the folds of their garments. Mr Harry stood, finger wagging, while the priests swayed their necks slowly towards him like basking lizards.

'Is okay now,' he said on his return. 'I tell them they leaders of community. But if preach against President, then no more leaders!' And he sliced at his throat and took off again, chortling. Catching him up, Charlotte panted, 'What do you do if some woman who wants more children than two won't accept an IUD?'

'Make home visit,' he said, steaming along. 'Talk, persuade, make shamed.'

'And still she won't?'

'Make more home visit. More, more, *more!*'

The thought of Mr Harry's twinkling specs turning up day after day on her doorstep would, she knew, send her screaming for an IUD. She stopped and leaned against a banana tree.

'Where do the *men* come in?' she shouted after him. 'The husbands. Don't they take their share of *any* of this?'

Mr Harry walked back to the banana tree and stood regarding her, his face suffused with patience. 'Of course,' he said. 'Of course

186

husbands take share. They give permission for wife to have IUD. *That* is their share.'

Charlotte let herself slide down the trunk of the banana tree to the ground. 'Tell me, Mr Harry. Do you honestly think so few men should have vasectomies? It isn't fair on the women, you know. It isn't *fair*.' Despairingly, she wondered what she was doing, squatting at the root of a banana tree arguing the case for vasectomies. Wouldn't everyone be better off if she were watching her washing go round in a Kentish Town launderette?

Mr Harry had bent over her, smiling happily. 'Husbands will not have vasectomies because they want to please *wife*. Wife not want. Because – ' he paused for dramatic effect – 'wife know if husband have vasectomy, he go with other women!'

An acute pain tore from Charlotte's heart up her throat and released itself in a loud screech. To her relief, it was a screech of laughter. Mr Harry examined her helpless writhing. Then he laughed too.

'I make joke for you in *English*,' he spluttered, hopping ecstatically from foot to foot. 'I not so low IQ! My father, see! I laugh in *English*.'

Four days later, after putting in a bruising twenty miles of pot-holing in the van, Charlotte pleaded for a rest. Mr Harry held up a reluctant hand to the driver and she crawled out, trying to keep her many green fractures in place for easy setting. She stretched herself wearily, took a deep breath and let it out again, fast. An unparalleled funkiness pervaded the air. Looking around, she saw the corpse of a large dog lying a few yards away, at the portals of a ruined temple. There was another dog above the dead one, a stone dog, its fanged jaws stuffed with orange petals. Had she come upon some sacrifice to an ancient canine god? Could death stink so?

Such questions, she decided, were better asked a long way away and holding her nostrils closed she turned to walk back to the van. Too late. They came from nowhere to mob her. A draggle of children calling like birds, dirty little hands outstretched. Beggar women, nudging at her body with their bowls, eyes glazed and unblinking. One, with a forehead bound in brilliant tatters, flapped in her face a fan of postcards. Another, heavily pregnant, her cheekbones ridged above sunken cheeks, took a hold of Charlotte's dress and yanked. A third, also pregnant, hair covered with a torn pink cap, clawed at her arm and, at their feet, a young man, handsome, with no legs, elbowed towards her in the dust and grabbed her ankles. Above them came the bats, wheeling and diving at her, darkening the sky, their chitters mingling with the human cries. They whizzed in their thousands from the reeking maw of a cave that reared up behind the temple, flicking Charlotte's hair with their bony wings, fluttering so close that she could see their open rat mouths and the pink of their hairy nostrils. With a shriek that outdid any other on the scene, she flung up her arms round her head and ran.

Mr Harry slammed the van door behind her. 'I sorry for you,' he said with profound satisfaction. 'I not want to stop. This very bad rural area, KNNA programme not come here yet.'

As the van pulled off she stared down at the IUD-less souls, stock-still in a whirl of bats. It was hard to think of any programme, however draconian, that could further blight their lives.

'Poor things,' she said.

'Poor poor,' Mr Harry's voice rang like mission bells.

The days filled Charlotte's notebooks and emptied her. Each evening she fell through the doors of Bloc like a soldier home from the trenches and became civil again between the ablution walls, scooping gallons of water over herself. In the courtyard the television was always on, watched by the same three men, their chins propped on twig brooms.

'What's it all about?' she asked Kelly once. The figures on the screen were fast becoming familiar: a family coming and going, some sort of serial, a Sulanasian soap.

'You get one guess,' he said. 'Come *on*.'

'Not family planning?' she said, awed.

'What else?'

They dined al fresco at a roadside stall where they dined every evening on noodles pungently spiced with diesel. Here, Charlotte's daytime confusions reached a nightly crescendo.

'How am I going to write this report, Kelly?' she wailed. 'I can't make head or tail of this country. Every time I decide the programme is good, something ghastly happens. Every time I think it's ghastly, something good happens. Everyone believes in Allah but some say Allah wants this and some say Allah wants the opposite, and the one who guesses wrong gets shot. The women are bullied into contraception when they don't need to be because all women *want* contraception. Which do you reckon is worse,' she appealed to him, 'compulsory childbirth or forced IUDs?'

Kelly's teeth gleamed in the darkness. 'Two weeks in Alice Springs,' he said.

'Oh, Kelly. Don't you take anything seriously?'

'Tried it once,' he said, hoovering up the last of his noodles. 'Didn't like it.'

She went to bed, leaving Kelly as always to mooch off with his cameras on one of his late-night forays. And as always she was awoken two or three hours later by the voice in her head. On the first night this had happened she had stiffened with fright, feeling the voice drill into her brain. It seemed to come at her through the metal pipes that made up the bed and was, as she well knew from reading of Mr Pinfold's fate, the precursor of madness. Incomprehensibly but with a prophetic power, the voice buzzed tinnily on, rising and falling as she tossed on her damp pillow, grieving already at Mrs Wren's distress, expecting a daughter home and receiving a loony instead. Abruptly, the voice halted and she fell into a restless sleep.

'The muezzin.' Kelly had said in the morning. 'The bloke in the minaret calling the Faithful to prayer. There's one just outside. Sounds like an earful of mossies. It's okay, your screws aren't any looser than usual.'

Three days before Charlotte's planned return to Banabalu, she and Kelly kept their daily rendezvous with Mr Harry at the Hotel Sinabaya – he had remained unswerving in his resolve not to darken Bloc's doors. He was not there; they found a note from him instead. 'My sorrows,' it said in a flowery script, 'I do business this day. Toomoro I see you, kind sirs.'

'Well, we'll have to talk amongst ourselves,' Kelly said, grinning.

'Goodness, how sad,' Charlotte said, beaming back.

'Swim?'

'Let's.'

I have become, Charlotte thought, pulling on her swimsuit back at Bloc, the sort of woman who says 'let's' to swimming. Cry your eyes out, Kowalski. There wasn't a mirror in which to survey the effect but she felt reasonably sure it was endurable. Her thighs still hillocked below the grip of the elastic but her hands told her she now possessed a distinct concavity at the waist and a not untoward convexity at the bust. To avoid undermining her new confidence, she left her bottom strictly alone.

Kelly hailed a taxi and they headed away from the one tourist beach, following an arm of the sea until they arrived at a stretch of sand that was utterly deserted. While Kelly paid and reassured the incredulous driver that they could do without hot dogs or even tofu snacks for at least an hour without keeling over, Charlotte got out and stood by the track.

There was the sun. There was the dimpled turquoise sea, patting the bright white sand. There were the green palms, laden with golden coconuts. Four long fishing boats were drawn up from the frothing surf, carved and painted to resemble marlin, with round gold eyes at the bows. All was silence but for the gentle slosh of the sea.

Kelly came to stand beside her and, together, they surveyed the scene. It presented in every aspect the accumulated dreams, past, present and future, of every Western city-dweller trapped in brick and concrete and traffic jams. It was the antithesis of civilization and its apotheosis, the earth in crown and sceptre. It made Charlotte feel humble, unworthy and deeply moved. The hairs on Kelly's arm stirred against hers and she caught her breath. My cup runneth over, she thought.

But Kelly was at hand to take up the overspill. 'Right, got the picture,' he informed the seascape. 'Bit heavy-handed on the Robinson Crusoes. Scrap the palms, too bloody predictable. Okay, next slide please.'

Upon which he whipped off his T-shirt and shorts and set off towards the sea, leaving a spoor of fat prints from his rope-soled sandals on the shining sand behind him.

Jarred, Charlotte recovered as she watched him because she couldn't help it. Now Adam had entered her Garden of Eden, a Mr Universe Adam in a green elastic fig leaf who stood against the luminous sky with his ankles in foam and turned his glittering head to Eve, beckoning.

'Come on in, the water's lovely,' he hollered.

And Eve, with the confidence born of an ancient biological imperative, divested herself of her dress and her thongs and stood poised for a moment in her pink paisley cossie, a child of Nature and Nature's willing pawn. Then she tripped lightly down the sand towards her Fate.

190

Her first few steps were as graceful as those of a young gazelle. At the fifth step, a searing pain hit the soles of her feet, her knees shot up and with an ululation that rang round the quiet bay she galloped at full speed across the white-hot sand and crash-landed in the water, where she lay, neighing.

Kelly dragged her out and dumped her on her bottom with her legs stretched out to where the surf could minister to her blistered soles. He put a comforting arm over her shoulders and when she had stopped quivering and bleating she felt his tremors.

'You're laughing,' she accused.

'No . . . I'm . . . not. Jeez. Oh . . . you should have . . . oh, shit,' he said.

'Quite,' Charlotte said. She had received the message. She had been warned. Those who got above themselves the gods brought low. Bruce and his flakes might constitute a bottom line but Kelly was definitely over the top. It was regrettable that she had not heeded her own advice from the start. At home she would never have met him, men of his sort did not frequent the Cotterstock Trust or the Red Line bus to Kentish Town and to snatch at a shipboard romance with such a man was undignified, showed a pathetic lack of self-respect, and was, anyway, a trivial pursuit in surroundings of Third World poverty. There were certain things she, Charlotte, had to offer a man but it was unlikely that Kelly would appreciate any of them. Indeed, there were attributes of Kelly's not to her liking. She had no wish to be the rowing boat that an ocean liner passed in the night and capsized in its wash without even noticing. Therefore, that, thank goodness, was that.

At this point in her self-lecture, Charlotte became aware that Kelly had ceased his intemperate laughter and put his arm round her shoulders again. The arm tightened. Then he moved across her. On the other hand, she thought, as she found herself being lowered to the sand, should one not heed the poet's advice and gather ye rosebuds while ye may? Not to mention Pat Wilshaw's oft-expressed view that que sera, sera?

That, thank goodness, being that – and Kelly's lips almost upon hers – Charlotte was about to close her eyes in thrilled surrender when she saw a face. It loomed behind Kelly's face wearing a large baseball cap and an intrigued expression. She winched herself out from under Kelly and sprang to her feet.

'What the . . .?' said Kelly, rolling over.

'You like massage?' said the face. 'Very cheap, very nice?' There were three of them now and more coming, women in sarongs bearing baskets packed with the oils of their trade.

'No!' Charlotte said, flushed with lust and embarrassment. 'Please go away. Not want massage. Not want.'

'Oh, I don't know,' Kelly said. 'Now they're here, might as well. I'm in need of a bit of R and R.'

Her worst fears were confirmed. Rest and recreation. For the troops. With tarts. That is it, she told herself. That is *it*.

Kelly laid out his towel and rolled himself on to it. 'Come on,' he said to Charlotte, 'have one. Relax.'

'I do not wish to relax,' she said. 'We should send them away. It would be obscene to lie here, two rich tourists, and let those poor women work on us. I couldn't do it.'

'Two rich tourists? Who they?'

'You know very well what I mean.'

'Massage, nice massage,' wheedled the women, circling Kelly. 'Good for you, nice, cheap.' Their hands were already on him, stroking.

'Okay,' he said. 'Come on, girls, take me.'

Outraged, Charlotte watched the woman in the baseball hat dribble oil on her new client and smooth the liquid slowly, with both hands, up from his concave belly to his chest and his shoulders. Then she began kneading his biceps.

'Aaaw,' moaned Kelly, 'great. Oh, great.'

'Really,' Charlotte said. 'I don't know how you can. She probably earns less in a year than you do in a day.'

'All the more reason,' he said through his groans. 'She could do with the money.'

'Well!' said Charlotte, 'just give it to her. *Give* it to her.'

One of the other women, foiled by her fellow-masseuse, was running her fingers over Charlotte's neck. 'You like too, Missie. Lie down, lie down.'

'No!' Charlotte pulled away. 'Thank you.' Her feet burned. 'Go on,' she hissed at Kelly, 'give her the money.'

He looked at her for a moment, his eyes repellently blue, before he rolled over on to his belly. The masseuse sat astride him and ran the heels of her hands up his neck.

'It's the exploitation I mind,' Charlotte explained. 'They don't *like* doing what they're doing, you know. They'd all rather be back with their husbands. They've probably got lots of children at home, waiting for them. Crying.'

'Ooow,' said Kelly. 'Two.'

'Too what?' she snapped.

'Children, Mrs M. Or else you better report them to Harry. He could do with the commission.'

'Surely,' Charlotte cried, 'you can see it's awful, lying there while they work. For a pittance, I dare say. *Kelly.*'

'Aagh,' he said. 'Woof.'

On the way back to Bloc, on benches in a passenger van that had drawn up at the roadside, she sat with every muscle tensed, bobbing stiffly up and down. Kelly, his skin glossy with oils, lolled.

After a while he said, 'Look, Madam M. I have made one Sulanasian woman richer by one hundred ratahs today. What have you done?'

She cradled her tender feet. 'Like I said, you could have given it to her.'

'She wasn't a beggar.'

'Oh . . .' Charlotte said. 'It's the whole thing, you don't understand. I couldn't lie there like you did and let a woman that poor with all sorts of problems we don't know anything about and never will make me feel good as if she were some sort of servant I mean especially because I'm a woman myself and who'll ever massage her and I expect her back's breaking after what she's done for you and . . .'

Presently, she said, 'Nothing. I've done nothing.'

In the evening, they went along the main street of the town to where it spread into a broad plain with benches and souvenir stalls and men leaning on their pramchairs chatting under the insect-haloed lamps. The old palace, seat of long-dead Sulanasian kings, rose pink behind flowering trees.

'Why are you always right, Kelly?' Charlotte asked.

'I've wondered about that myself.'

'Perhaps because you have no soul.'

'Could be.'

They turned into the palace gardens, dimly lit and fragrant. Their path was intersected by long open-fronted verandahs and carved god-beasts with scarlet tongues and tinder-box eyes.

'I saw Ganeesha in that village where the woman screamed,' Charlotte remarked. 'In an old temple. There was a bright spot on her trunk, as if it had been rubbed for hundreds of years.'

'Women. Barren women, asking Her Elephantship for kids.'

'Oh,' Charlotte said.

In front of the shuttered windows of the palace, a Gone-With-The-Wind mausoleum full of dark oil paintings of darker kings and queens barnacled with jewels, there were dancers on a platform. Numbers of European tourists were sprawled on the steps, watching.

'I know what I meant to ask you,' said Charlotte to all-knowing Kelly. 'What's Mr Harry got to do with commission?'

'He gets it for rounding up acceptors. He's got a target, haven't we all. IUDs pay his rent. Hey, I've got to get this . . .' and Kelly, vaulting on to the platform, went into his cossack crouch.

'But that's *disgusting*,' Charlotte called after him. A beetroot-red man took his camera out of his eye and looked at her. Then he moved off and Charlotte wedged herself in his place, simmering. Surely even Kelly couldn't dodge this one. A commission every time Mr Harry or his KNNA mates managed to . . .? Like door-to-door salesmen using every . . . underhand . . . technique . . . to . . .

It dawned on her then that the dancers were wonderful. They stood across the platform like angular statues, the women masked in colour, cocooned in gold, moving the tips of their painted fingers. But the men – the *men*. Charlotte gazed at the nearest, some yards away, in open-mouthed admiration. He was a Samurai warrior carved in mahogany to a drawing from an ancient parchment, hard as stone and as still. His sarong swept across his splayed thighs and wrapped his narrow loins where a kris curved down, padded and tasselled. His chest was bare and sketched with muscle and a folded turban crowned his head. To the solemn beat of gongs, he shifted his weight an inch at a beat from one foot to the other and from the ball of one foot to the heel. The long straps of muscle on his calves and his thighs moved as he moved, turning slowly around, controlled as the works of a clock that had almost run down. The gongs clanged and he lunged forward, the kris held high. The infinitesimal shifting began again, heel, toes, heel, toes, muscles rippling under the surface of the smooth skin, arms in a frozen arabesque, the silver kris gleaming.

They were at the palace gates again before Charlotte emerged from her trance. 'Kelly,' she sighed, 'even you have to admit it. That was glorious.'

Kelly admitted it. 'Fan-bloody-tastic.'

'The man nearest me, he was superb. Such stoicism, such control. He looked grand, like a prince, and terrifying too. A graven image. A warrior-king.'

'Yeah,' Kelly said. He moved his film box to the other shoulder. 'A real pro, all right.'

As they came out into the crowded square and crossed at Sinabaya's sole traffic lights, Kelly took Charlotte's arm. 'That was Harry,' he said.

'Where?' She turned to scan the passing faces but he pulled her on.

'The man. The dancer. It was your Mr Harry.'

At the nearest stall, Charlotte sat down and drank two cups of thick strong coffee in quick succession, scalding her tongue to match her scalded feet.

'Unbelievable,' she said eventually. 'He was . . . another man.'

'He is.'

She looked sharply at Kelly. 'You know things about him. What do you know?'

'Aw. Boy talk.'

For once, his voice was devoid of humour. He scrubbed his chin, frowning, and did not seem disposed to say more. Charlotte had to insist and, even so, he would not speak again until they had left the stall and started back along the road to Bloc. Then he pulled her close to his side and in a lover's murmur told her about the man called Hariyono Premendongerum, student of Tanjung University who joined a party opposed to the military regime, a party that believed in a self-sufficient Sulanasia, free from foreign interference, where the land belonged to those who tilled it. He had worked with the party until it was banned and then gone underground. For two more years he and his comrades had led a twilight existence, moving in the nights from village to village, printing and distributing the party literature and talking, endlessly talking to the villagers – 'Harry's a poet, you know,' murmured Kelly, 'he went around reciting his flaming poems and I mean *flaming*.' Then, one night, the army caught up with them. Five of his comrades had been shot as they ran, Hariyono had been captured, beaten, tortured and interned. In his fifth year of imprisonment, there had been an uprising against the regime. The President's men had massacred still uncounted numbers of people, rampaging through the countryside, killing as they went, clogging the rivers with blood and bodies. When Hariyono was finally released, all his relatives and friends were dead.

'That was it,' Kelly said. 'Population cut in half with fucking machetes, everyone scared shitless, the best brains in the country pasted all over the walls. They kept it under wraps and the West didn't ask any awkward questions. What do we care if a lot of gooks get their families planned into flaming extinction? So there's Harry, poet, one of the living dead. What can he do? Covers his tracks, meets a woman, marries her. The father-in-law wangles him a job in the civil service, about the only employment around. He knuckles under, the poor bastard, toes the line, salutes the bloody flag. All he wants in the world now is a son, to keep the dead family's name alive, continue the fight, etcetera. But they won't let him. He'd be sacked if he had a third child. Two is enough, right? Poor fucking bastard.'

After a long silence, Charlotte said, 'Unbelievable,' again, her vocabulary shrunk by shock.

'But too bloody true.'

'I mean,' she said unsteadily, 'I can't believe how badly I . . . I've misjudged him. I thought he was a kind of . . . clown.'

'Good cover, a clown.'

They had reached the door of Bloc and Kelly held it open for her. 'Don't mention this to Harry when we see him tomorrow.'

'Why not?'

'If he'd wanted you to know, he'd have told you.'

This seemed unarguable and came as a relief. She needed time to recover, time to fit the bits of Mr Harry together again – dancer, poet, guerilla fighter, servant of a hated regime. Easier if he didn't know she knew. Easier to sort it out on her way home.

'I wanna use up the rest of this film,' Kelly said, his head half out of the door. 'Don't wait up for me, Mrs M.'

During the night Charlotte awoke, badly short of breath from a dream of unprecedented nastiness involving soldiers and butchered bodies, all of whom smiled while they bled and wore glasses like Mr Harry. She sat up in the hot dark. Nearby, another of Bloc's inmates was snoring – a light, lonely sound – and somewhere above her head a gekko gave its sepulchral quack. Wheezing, she reached for the handbag beside her bed but could not find her inhaler in its cluttered interior, nor a torch. As she fanned air into her starved lungs and instructed herself on the futility of panic, she heard footsteps on the stones outside and the shadow of Kelly extinguished for a second the dim coutryard light. It would have been comforting to call out but the necessary breath was not forthcoming. The door of his cabin squeaked open and shut.

Lying down again on the gyprock roll that served as mattress and stretching to give her lungs maximum blow-out room, she mourned the passing of her woman's intuition. It was not one of her outstanding characteristics, except with her mother, and now it was obviously defunct. The history of Mr Harry was proof of that. She had seen something moving in him, once or twice, and dismissed it, accepting without question that he was what he acted. As, in a milder way, she had done with Kelly. He acted flippantly, he appeared unemotional, uninvolved, even cynical. Yet Mr Harry had chosen to confide in him, not in her. Both of them had hidden dimensions, depths, longitudes, latitudes. Beside them, she felt flat, a millimetre thick, like her mattress.

For the first time it occurred to her that the visceral emotions which caused her so much upset yet which, it had to be admitted, she endured with a sort of pride, might not be quite as worthy as she had imagined. It was important to have a heart for a variety of reasons but to allow it to bleed too freely over everyone in its path was careless and, unless rinsed immediately in cold water, left unsightly stains. Mr Harry hadn't bled, he had taken action. Or rather, he had bled *and* taken action. Kelly was bloodless, at least in public. Whereas she dripped all over the place, an emotional incontinent. And what good did that do anyone? She wasn't even working as hard as Kelly, crippled by her angst about the job.

The gekko was still quacking as she closed her eyes. Just before sleep engulfed her, she realized that she was breathing easily again without recourse to the inhaler.

Mr Harry was not at the Hotel Sinabaya the next morning either. A younger man with a face so upwardly mobile that he could have been hanging upside down met them instead and conveyed Mr Harry's apologies in much better English than his predecessor.

'Mr Premendongerum has many meetings so I am here to take

you to the factory,' he said and Charlotte felt a painful relief again. Kelly was leaving tomorrow at noon and she the same evening so the less time there was for difficult farewells all round, the better.

The factory, reached after a two-hour jolting that loosened Charlotte's eyeballs in their sockets, was a small town in its own right, complete with avenues, staff houses, clinics and a swimming pool whose waters poured from the mouths of two viciously scaly dragons. Men walked and talked in the cool, marble-tiled executive halls, men tended machines in air-conditioned buildings. The women, more women than Charlotte had ever expected to see in one place at one time, worked in an unair-conditioned hangar large enough to house two Concordes nose to nose.

'Why are there only men at the machines while the women work with their hands?' she asked the guide.

'Women like better to work with their hands,' he replied.

'And why is there air-conditioning where the men work and not where the women work?'

'The air-conditioning,' he replied, 'is for the machines.'

They were led through the clinics to a salvo of statistics about the factory's family planning programme. Any woman whose village did not provide contraceptives could obtain them at work, said the guide. Charlotte stared across the green rice fields that surrounded the women's hangar to the villages beyond.

'Out of the frying pan . . .' she said.

'. . . into the stirrups,' said Kelly.

The upside-down man agreed, taking their words for gynaecological comment. He added, 'And if a woman has children already and will not become an acceptor, then we use peer pressure.' This, he explained, involved offering a village a television set or perhaps a sewage system . . .

'. . . or an engine to make tofu,' Charlotte suggested.

'Certainly,' he said, 'but it is offered only if all fertile women are acceptors, so the woman who will not, then her neighbours give her much trouble.' And he laughed heartily.

'Is it true,' Charlotte asked, 'that only acceptors can get jobs at the factory?'

'Not true,' replied the upside-down man, smiling.

'And if a woman is going to have a third child, will she lose her job?'

His smile became forgiving. 'No, *no*.'

Charlotte smiled too. It was much the same experience as watching politicians on television at home. They might be lying or they might not. Either way, it was best to view them with detachment or, if that got too depressing, switch them off.

The guide, made ill-at-ease by his guest's switched-off eyes, looked earnest and said, 'Sometimes, it is necessary to put pressure on women here. Maybe you do not need that, in England. In Sulanasia, yes.'

Incisively, Charlotte said, 'Mmmm.'

On the way back, Kelly asked the driver to drop him off at a market a few blocks from their lodgings.

'More pictures?' asked Charlotte.

'You wanna come?'

But her feet ached and she stayed in the van until it stopped at Bloc's alley. The guide handed her politely out. 'Mr Premendongerum will come to say goodbye to you tomorrow, before your journey to Banabalu,' he said.

'Here?' Charlotte was surprised. 'He will come to Bloc?'

'He say so. Also I have this to give you. It is for Mr Kelly.' And he handed her a piece of folded paper.

In Bloc's courtyard, the television flickered to an audience of one old man with a bucket and a mop. He was staring intently at an ample matron who was staring intently back at him. Charlotte, hoping that this TV personality, at least, was not lecturing him on the dangers of an activity that was well past his powers, headed for the ablutions, where she doused herself liberally with the life-giving waters. She emerged feeling refreshed and squeaky-clean, very far, she thought, from Kelly's condemnation of her race as The Great Unwashed, and went back to her cubicle.

On the bed was the piece of paper the guide had given her. She picked it up so that she could lie down and saw that it was a computer print-out bill from the Hotel Sinabaya, made out to Kelly. In computerese, it said:

Ent.Rm. . . . . Aus.$300.

As she was looking at it, she heard footsteps outside, then saw Kelly through the bamboo slats, the neck of his T-shirt rendered decolleté by the weight of his cameras.

'This is for you,' she said, at the door.

Kelly took the piece of paper and glanced at it.

'I couldn't help seeing,' she said. 'How on earth did you run up

199

a 300 dollar bill at the Hotel Sinbaya? They must have made a mistake.'

'Yeah,' he said. 'I'll sort it out.' He picked up his film box again.

'You haven't much time if you're leaving tomorrow.' Charlotte followed him to his room, towing one of his cameras. 'You're flying out in the morning, aren't you?'

'Yeah.' His back did not look accommodating.

But the questions would not go away. The next morning, mournful but resigned, she stood guard over Kelly's luggage while he went to pay his bill at the Hotel Sinabaya. When he came back, she gathered herself. 'Kelly, 300 dollars? It's none of my business, but what . . .?'

'I got a taxi outside,' he said. He was preoccupied.

She said 'What's an Ent.Rm.?' before she could think about it and, as she said it, she knew what an Ent.Rm. was.

There was a thin line between his brows. Under her stare, his tan darkened.

'Kelly?' she said.

'Charlotte?' he echoed but his grin wouldn't hold. 'Oh, come on, sport. I've been four weeks here, what else d'you expect?'

'Those evening walkabouts. You went to . . .?'

'You got it. An Entertainment Room.' His voice was light but his eyes were not. 'They lay on girls at all these hotels, if you'll pardon the expression. For tired businessmen and I reckon I qualify.' After a pause, he said, 'Jesus Christ, Charlotte, you're not my mother.'

'No.'

'And you and me, we never . . .'

'No.'

'Well, then. How about giving me a hand-out with my gear?'

At the taxi, blocking the narrow alley, she said flatly, 'It's very different from massage. Kelly . . .'

'Not a lot in it,' he interrupted, trying for a laugh.

'. . . how could you? After all you've said?'

He spread his arms out in an exaggerated gesture. 'What have I ever said? They're nice girls, they get bloody well paid and everyone has a good time. What's wrong?'

She looked up at his beautiful face in silence. The taxi gave an impatient snort.

'I gotta go. Listen, it's life. I didn't want you to know but now that you do, I'm sorry you're upset. You're a real cuddle-pot and it's

200

been great knowing you. If you're ever in Sydney, consider my place yours. Eh, sport?'

For a moment, she felt his body massive against the length of hers. Then he tilted her chin, kissed the corner of her lips, ducked into the taxi and was gone.

The bottle she bought had a label the shape of the eagle's wings on Bruce's forehead. On it was printed 'Jack Black's Essence of Whiskey'. After Charlotte had thrown her possessions into her suitcase, she sat on her bed and gave Jack Black her undivided attention. She was soon rewarded. The room grew mellow, the mattress beneath her slowly unBloc'ed. She lay back and listened to the rustles in the thatch. A dragonfly whirred in through the door, darted about inquisitively and then stood in the air an inch from her nose, casing her. She cased it back. Its wings were rainbow slivers, its bulbous eyes speckled with amethyst. 'I want to be alone with my grief,' she told it. 'Buzz off.' There came a louder rustle and she craned her neck at the door.

Mr Harry stood there, plucking at the bamboo slats.

'Hullo,' she said, no longer capable of feeling awkward. 'Come in.' Since there was nowhere else for him to sit, she patted the bed. He came in, closing the rickety door behind him, and perched himself on the edge of the mattress. 'Mr Harry? Are you all right?'

He looked all wrong. For the first time since she had met him at Tanjung Station, he was less than perfectly groomed. A label stuck out from the collar of his shirt, his trousers had yielded up their knife-edge and one of his shoes was almost unlaced. It even seemed possible that he had not shaved. His smile, however, had lost none of its phosphorescence. His face was quite screwed up with it.

'I completely fine,' he said. 'I come to say you sad goodbye.'

'Where have you been?'

'Much business. My Big Boss come. I very sorry.'

'Something's happened,' she stated, made acute by drink and certain movements of the heart.

His lips became so overstretched as to threaten a split.

'*What's* happened?' she said grimly and yanked at his sleeve.

The smile went into eclipse with a suddenness that made the room seem darker. 'You go home to England now. You not want to know.'

'I do.'

He turned his head and shocked her with the emptiness of his eyes. 'Maybe I lose my job.'

'They've found out.' The words were said before she could prevent them.

'Found out?' he repeated, his voice neutral.

She hesitated but Jack Black drove her on. 'Kelly told me. About what you did. You were . . . brave, Mr Harry. Very brave.'

A glimmer kindled in the emptiness. The smile, when it came, was crooked and bore no resemblance at all to smiles gone by. 'No, I not brave. Because I not dead.'

Gripped by a maternal anger, Charlotte said, 'And a good thing too.' She took his hand and held it in both of hers. 'Now, what have they done to you? Tell me.'

He told her. A rumour had been heard by his boss. There had been a confrontation. He had denied it, many times – 'You see? I not brave.' But if he lost his job, there would be no other for him in Sulanasia, there would be nothing. His wife and his children would have no house, no food, no future. Disgrace. Despair.

She stroked his hand.

He held his head as erect and still as a Warrior-Prince and only the tear-drops moved on his impassive face. 'I all wash up,' he said. 'Is that correct, dear Miss Harlot?'

'No,' Charlotte said and comforted him as best she could.

Early that evening, her researches in the field completed, Charlotte departed for Banabalu. This time, she flew. As the plane rose through clouds cunningly tinted to resemble the best smoked salmon, she mused on all that had befallen her since leaving that city. The presently undigested mass of information and impressions would require thoughtful pruning before her report, particularly of those off-shoots that were purely personal. Kelly, for instance. All very well to be laid-back about Third World problems in general but not so well to be rather more literally laid-back in a Sulanasian Entertainment Room. She still felt tender about him but the tenderness verged on the sore and that, too, had to be sorted out before useful conclusions could be reached. Mr Harry was another case in point. Dear, heroic Mr Harry. The myriad injustices done him would not be forgotten – she had already mentally written a dozen letters to Banabalusian bureaucrats recommending his work and his person in terms effusive even by Sulanasian standards – but how much should his plight influence her view of the birth control programme? Was it peripheral or central? There was also the question of the withdrawal from public life of her stomach, her wheeze, her spare tyre and her urge for nicotine. Very peripheral indeed, this, but the well-being thus engendered must not be allowed to sneak, under the guise of optimism, into the report.

These ponderings left Charlotte feeling strangely mature, though whether in the accepted sense or in the manner of an over-ripe Camembert, time alone would tell. Miss Millichip certainly wouldn't. Reached at home by telephone from the Sulanasia Plaza – to whose bosom Charlotte had returned for fear her one remaining discount voucher would discount even less at another hotel – the pillar of Global Family Funding wasted no energy on greetings or superfluous enquiries as to Charlotte's field experiences.

'How *lucky* for you,' she said, her voice crackling in the receiver as if it were radioactive. 'You're just in time to catch the annual KNNA show.'

'I'm afraid,' replied Charlotte, who had finished and posted the last of Mr Harry's testimonials and was already in a half-doze on the bed, 'that I'm far too . . .'

'. . . exhausted, of course, but then, I always am. No sooner had I got you off my hands than I had to set to and organize this. Naturally, without the help of Miss Irma Schultz. Would you believe, she's *still* in Sumino?'

Given Miss Millichip as a colleague, Charlotte could believe that Irma Schultz would choose to die in Sumino, but she made polite sounds of incredulity before pressing on. 'I only telephoned to say goodbye, Gina . . .'

'. . . perfectly resigned by now to carrying my own workload plus everyone else's. I always have and I dare say I always shall. As Mr Suyono said to me the other day, Gina, he said, if you will do things so efficiently, what can you expect? People will take advantage.'

Diverted by this evidence of Mr Suyono's newly acquired fluency in English, Charlotte was about to renew her refusal of the night's entertainment when the receiver chittered again.

'So we'll expect you in the lobby in half an hour. I'll send the chauffeur. Have you got that?'

'Gina, I'm leaving for London tomorrow and I'm dead tired and I've hardly any Sulanasian money left and . . .'

'It's on me,' said Miss Millichip bountifully. The line went dead.

In a dress marked by many vicissitudes, Charlotte crept into the appointed conference theatre and took a seat on the back row. Every other row in front of the curtained platform was packed with KNNA officials and their wives and families, interspersed here and there with the pear-inscribed uniforms of honoured field-workers and a number of expensively clad and made-up women whom she took to be the city's crème de la crème, contraceptively speaking. Among them she recognized various of the more loquacious Kartikis, a half-dozen of the bureaucrats she had interviewed and, snuggled in a nest of admirers, the chiselled profile of the Minister for Women's Affairs. Everyone in this last act of the pantomime seemed in the best of spirits, chatting to each other and smoking with abandon. Charlotte kept her head well down, planning a moonlight flit under cover of darkness.

At last the curtain rose, revealing an empty stage lined with wrinkled paper. It was not empty for long. To excited applause the Chairman of KNNA, Mr Zakir himself, advanced to the footlights, flailing his arms. Charlotte was unexpectedly pleased to see him again – somehow, she had come to think him a figment of her imagination – and clapped with everyone else as he bowed to his assembled disciples. After a longish speech directed to two cameramen snapping away in the front row and several jokes received with joyous laughter, he introduced a brisk-looking businessman in a grey striped suit and white shoes. The businessman extended his arms widely and began to sing in a soulful tenor.

'*There* you are,' hissed Miss Millichip, gliding to Charlotte's side. Silk whispered round her kneecaps as she sat down.

'Here I am,' replied Charlotte, inserting a temporal note into the words, 'but I can only stay a few minutes . . .'

'Sulanasia's top male vocalist,' said Miss Millichip, indicating the warbling man. 'A good friend of mine and of Global Family Funding.' Something in her tone intimated that the same could not be said of Charlotte.

The businessman ended his sentimental interlude and introduced six children who tottered from the wings clinging onto each other and were patted hard by Mr Zakir. He held up blobs of metal to tumultuous applause and deposited them in the hands of the children, who looked understandably crestfallen.

'Winners of a country-wide competition for the best school essay on family planning,' Miss Millichip informed her guest.

'Good heavens,' exclaimed Charlotte, 'they look too young for the birds and bees, never mind . . .' She was cut off by Miss Millichip's scornful breathing and remembered where she was. Birds and bees were not useful examples to Sulanasia's youth, being overly sexy and quite shamelessly unplanned.

A curly-haired girl bounced on to the stage in neon-pink tights and a silver tunic. She was partnered by a small boy in large trousers. The two of them simpered to the audience and, holding hands, emitted a prolonged series of piercing trills while sticking two fingers each into the air.

'Two children are enough,' said Miss Millichip.

'They are indeed,' said Charlotte in heartfelt agreement.

'I meant the *content* of the song,' whispered Miss Millichip, ice caking up her vocal chords. 'I presume you came across the slogan on your various jaunts?'

'Came across it? I waded waist-deep in it,' Charlotte reassured her. Gina was sawing on her taut nerves and a rapid exit became mandatory before snapping occurred. But just then a burly and splendidly moustachioed male took over from the trilling infants and set Charlotte's breastbone throbbing with a passionate baritone. She warmed to the way he massaged the air as he sang.

'A love song,' she remarked to Miss Millichip. 'Funny how you can tell, in any language.'

'This,' answered Miss Millichip without turning her head, 'is a family planning show. Therefore he is singing about family planning. Every singer here has been or is or will be singing about family planning.'

Charlotte examined the Millichip profile, a minuscule wiggle in the gloom. 'One gets to a point in this country,' she said carefully, 'where a song about a hole in a bucket dear Liza dear Liza would be most welcome. Except that someone would doubtless commandeer it for a contraceptive ditty.'

'Doubtless,' said Miss Millichip, imperturbable.

A man modelled to the approximate shape and muscularity of a soft-boiled egg waddled in to replace the moustachios. His belly bulged over a sarong, a woman's bodice strained across his pulpy chest and a wig as unkempt as a crow's nest adorned his fat head. Other adults stumbled after him, dressed in giant children's clothes. They looned about, sticking straws in their hair and tripping over their feet. Badinage took place. The huge children grunted and grinned, the fat man boxed their ears and the audience rocked in their seats. Miss Millichip gave several delicate snorts of appreciation and explained to Charlotte that the troupe represented a recidivist family, lost to the planners.

A svelte young woman, tastefully rouged and mascara'd, presently joined the reeling dafties and more badinage followed. The svelte woman pointed a jeering finger at the man's tidal belly and smacked her slim shanks.

'She is saying,' Miss Millichip translated, 'look at you, stupid woman, with your six children. They have made you old and ugly. I have only two. See how pretty I am? See my waistline? Where's yours?'

The woman took out a jewelled compact and started piling more make-up on her face. The man-woman gawped, rolls of lard dripping from his jowls. The men-children swivelled their eyes and drooled.

'She says you have too many children, your mind is confused. Where is your husband? He is gone and no wonder. With all these children, you have no time to make-up.'

Charlotte observed the woman primp. She watched a man-child yank his beret over his face, leaving his ears to flap comically. She saw the man-woman scratch his hairy armpits. 'I think it's disgusting,' she said.

'Now she is saying look how stupid your . . . I *beg* your pardon?'

'I said, I think it's disgusting,' Charlotte repeated. She had to speak loudly to make herself heard over the laughter.

'Might I ask in what way?' Miss Millichip inquired, studying her guest's earlobes.

Outrage and fatigue made Charlotte bold. 'Certainly,' she said. 'The message is – please correct me if I'm wrong – that having children is a female self- indulgence, a whim, nothing remotely to do with men. Women who have more than two are either selfish sluts or certifiably insane. They give birth to cretins and shortly thereafter turn into obese transvestites. At which point, we all laugh ourselves sick.'

A cretinous child bounced off his man-mother and fell flat on his

206

face. The svelte woman rouged herself furiously, her rosebud mouth pursed. Miss Millichip's was pursed to non-existence.

'What's more,' continued Charlotte, anger popping in her veins, 'all those IUDs you throw about like confetti *and* the injections, they're *bad* for women. Do you tell them that? Would you have them yourself? I saw a woman die after an IUD insertion. Have you seen a woman die, Miss Millichip? Or don't they do much dying in the military circles you frequent?'

Miss Millichip unpursed her mouth and opened it. Nothing emerged.

'They're being exploited, Gina. You and the KNNA and Global Family Funding, you're exploiting them all for your own ends.'

The thunderous claps of the exploited drowned out her voice. On their feet, they cheered and waved as man-mountain Mum, goofy kids and Beauty Queen exited left. Then, from stage right, to a roll of loudspeaker drums, sailed a galleon of a woman in full regalia. It was Deborah Doody, with Mr Zakir chugging in her wake. The two embraced in so far as their uneven statures would permit, after which Mrs Doody manoeuvred her bosoms stage front. She fixed the audience with a brooding eye, raised her voluminous arms and began to address them in a low and thrilling bellow.

The windows vibrated, the rafters rang, the seats twanged. Mother Doody bellowed on. Down in the bowels, something stirred; stirred and uncoiled and came alive. For the second time in its existence, quite uninvited, Charlotte's Kundalini rose. It struck at the base of her spine, setting her buttocks atingle, and reared straight as a poker upwards. Charlotte reared with it.

'Rubbish!' she shouted. 'Codswallop.'

A hush fell upon the conference hall. Two hundred faces turned, pale discs in the gloom. Mr Zakir stood paralyzed. The great plaited head of Mother Doody swayed from side to side. The faces of the idiot group gaped round the curtain and the fat man's wig, recognizing an emergency, flattened itself across one alligator eye.

Charlotte's Kundalini did not flinch. It stood erect upon its tail and went on shouting loudly into the silence. 'What does she know?' the Kundalini shouted. 'I bet she's got eight children at home and Old Mother Doody doesn't live in a shoe, not her. She's got no right to be here, what you do with your bodies is your business. Go home, Deborah Doody. Pack up your IUD kitbag, and go *home*.'

There came creaks as Miss Millichip recoiled on her seat. Then she unleashed herself upon Charlotte and downed her in a flying tackle.

'Communist,' yelled Deborah Doody from the platform, flapping her sleeves wildly. 'Red under the bed.'

Miss Millichip clipped Charlotte's arm in a half-nelson and hustled her to the exit.

'Marxist-Leninist,' screamed Deborah Doody. 'Stalinist-Trot. Fellow Traveller. Enemy Within.'

'Come *on*,' said Miss Millichip without moving her lips and shoved Charlotte through the door.

'Fascist pig,' Gina Millichip said pleasantly.

She lay on the other bed in Charlotte's hotel room, her stockinged feet side by side. Her silk dress hung in the cupboard, her shoes were heel-to-heel on the coffee table and she herself was virginal in a white lawn slip trimmed with broderie.

Charlotte sprawled on her own bed, her dress rucked up around her in permanent pleats. She lifted her damp face from the damper pillow, groped for a tissue and blew her nose.

'Communist. Fascist,' she said and hiccuped. 'I'm not even a member of the Kentish Town Library.'

'My dear Charlotte,' Miss Millichip propped herself on a sharp elbow and surveyed her sodden companion. 'The birth control business in the Third World is a minefield. If you don't wish to become a basket case you have to tiptoe. You stamped.'

'But *Communist?*'

She waved a dismissive hand. 'Oh that. A knee-jerk reaction, nothing personal. Mrs Doody's American, like me. Wind her up, she shouts Commie.'

'But you,' Charlotte sniffled, 'called me fascist pig.'

'I'm rather more sophisticated,' said Miss Millichip modestly. 'Your views, you see, are identical to those of the extreme right in the States. Our beloved moral majority. They'd like to see us all out of a job and no more aid. Is that what you want?'

Heaving herself off the bed, Charlotte padded over to where her suitcase lay in an explosion of clothes. She retrieved Jack Black's Essence of Whiskey from a padding of knickers and took a swig. The collapse of her Kundalini at the instant of Miss Millichip's tackle had made her identify with invertebrates everywhere, flabby, unboned and defenceless. She supposed she had been possessed.

Then, she had been vacated. All this bustling to and fro in her body had taken a lot out of her.

She gave a colossal sigh. 'What *are* my views?' she asked the room.

'You don't care for what we're doing out here,' Miss Millichip stated, pointing the seams of her slip over her scanty A-cups.

'And you think it's fine.'

Miss Millichip gave a sigh of her own. 'When I was a student, I sold aluminum blinds in the vacations, to pay my college fees. They were tacky blinds in terrible colours. Nobody needed them, very few people wanted them. I wouldn't have given them house room myself. If I'd had a house. Or a room.'

This confirmation that Gina Millichip had not sprung fully formed and plasticized from a box of detergent affected Charlotte. It also confused her.

'You mean, Global Family Funding is just a job to you?' she said, not ungently.

'I have never understood,' replied Miss Millichip with asperity, 'why it is so generally believed that one requires a spiritual vocation in order to administer birth control in less developed countries. I do not, myself, find it elevating work and I do not bring to it a missionary zeal. In my humble opinion, those who do should be regarded with suspicion and urged to spend time on a psychiatric couch. All jobs are a mixture of good and bad. I simply feel that mine is more good than bad. And yours?'

'Mine?'

'Your job.'

A vision of cold Cotterstock cubicles close-carpeted in Kleenex came to Charlotte, laced with a ghostly whiff of semen. Living jelly under a fun-fur coat. Dead jelly in kidney-shaped basins in Redhill.

'I am not in a position to judge,' she said, retreating into pomp.

'There you are, then,' said Miss Millichip with satisfaction.

A thin line of Whiskey Essence yellowed the bottom of the bottle. Charlotte disposed of it and sat down again on her bed. She was still surprised that Gina had not dumped her outside the hall after the Doody débâcle and gone, never to return. An hysterical English protégé would not add kudos to the Millichip name. Yet instead of receding into perma-frost, Gina had thawed. Roses had bloomed on the polar cheeks and the wee eyes had grown two sizes larger. It was as if the Kundalini, quitting Charlotte, had nipped over to establish squatting rights in Miss M. Nevertheless, this embryonic humanity must not be allowed entirely to mist over the issue.

'My women choose,' she said, 'yours don't. That's the difference. All the difference.'

Miss Millichip scrutinized the fly-blown lampshade. 'We have an educational job to do here.'

Charlotte, restless with the flux of argument, walked over to the wndow. 'What I saw,' she remarked to it, 'wasn't educational. It was IUD or else.'

'Oh, field-workers. They tend to get a little carried away.'

'It's not them I blame. There's no other job and they need the money.'

Frost was forming on the voice again. 'Sulanasia, Charlotte, is not jolly old England, you know. It's a small over-populated island in an under-developed part of the world. The average woman had eight to ten children before we started here. Is that your picture of a perfect life? How many children have *you* had, if I may ask?'

In the alley beneath the window, a dog had mounted another dog. They stood, joined, looking dismally about them. 'None,' Charlotte said, 'and I'd give my eye teeth for one. I'd have ten if I could and I wouldn't want you telling me I couldn't.'

Miss Millichip made a sound with her tongue like the first stone before an avalanche but when she spoke, it was softly. 'I shouldn't dream of telling you anything. Except that I fear you've left reproduction too late.'

The melancholy dogs became blurred at the edges. Charlotte blinked hard to spare her cheeks a further watering. The air-conditioned room was cool, almost chilly. Moving stiffly past Miss Millichip's bed, she lay down on her own and pulled the blanket up. Her stomach took hold of her intestines and began to churn them about like clothes in a washing machine. She attempted to jam up the agitator with her fists but the cycle went on. I must have my say, she thought. I must speak out. You're not planning families, Gina Millichip, you're giving aid and comfort to a dictator, buying his friendship. He doesn't give a hoot for his people. He just wants less of them, especially the poor, and that suits you, too. What he wants is power, tanks and guns to play with, soldiers to move about and wave flags at him, tame civil servants to clap him. Who's going to criticize that? We all think there are too many blacks. Except, perhaps, the women, but nobody, *nobody*, listens to them. They're just a lot of targets for your womb police. Half the world makes a living off them in one way or another – researchers, scientists, developers, doctors, arms salesmen, bankers, politicians, you. I've had a free trip out of them. But the woman doesn't even get a commission. She just does what she's told. If the Moslems got into power tomorrow, or the Pope, bingo, her womb would be uncorked and she'd have to produce as many kids as she could squeeze out before she dropped dead. One way or the other, she's given no choice at all. Choice, Miss Millichip? *Huh.*

This inner monologue was therapeutic. The agitator had spun to a halt and, inside, there was only a peaceful gurgle. Now she was in control, as Kelly would have advocated; now she could criticize without emotion, her shafts all the more powerful because detached. She sat up and looked with calm authority at the neighbouring bed. Gina lay there, white and tidy, her toes pointing upwards, her eyes closed. As Charlotte watched her, she gave a contented snore.

'One more thing,' Charlotte said to Miss Millichip recumbent. 'I didn't actually see a woman die of an IUD. She might have done but, then, she might not. Just thought I ought to clear that up.'

Miss Millichip appeared to take her confession in good part.

Part Four

'But I don't *want* a man,' Charlotte Macanally said.

She looked down at her hands. The sight of them comforted her. They were no longer brown but they were slim and ringless. You're half the woman I married, Bruce had said the day before, and asked her to stay for a TV dinner. You could do with a bit more flesh, he'd said. She'd told him not to worry, she'd soon put it on again.

'Well, goodness knows how you expect . . .' Pat Wilshaw was distracted for a moment by the screech of brakes outside and Charlotte got up. Pat examined her. 'You're sure you don't want . . .?'

'No,' said Charlotte.

'And you won't go back . . .'

'No,' said Charlotte.

Pat drummed her fingers on a pile of papers. 'This report.'

Charlotte sat down again.

'Unorthodox, to say the least.'

'My own impressions,' Charlotte said. 'That's what they asked for and that's what they've got.'

'Very one-sided. No attempt at balance.'

'Well,' said Charlotte cheerily, 'everyone else seems to be on the other side. I'm the balance.'

'And all this' – Pat flicked through the papers – 'about leaving it to the women. You can't leave family planning to the *women*.'

'Why not?'

'Are you sure you went to Sulanasia? Didn't stop off for a dirty three weeks in Paris, did you?'

Pat's sarcasm was withering but Charlotte remained unwithered. 'You mean, Sulanasian women are too ignorant, superstitious and bloody-minded to limit their child-bearing without being forced. Is that what you mean?'

'Education,' Pat said through her teeth, 'is necessary. They have big families because they think they need them. For the wages. For old age.'

'And they're right.' But she did not want to be aggressive. She was too happy for that. 'Look, Pat, all I'm saying is what Gordon Grant said to me. Give the women a choice. Set up the clinics, make contraceptives freely available, tell the men to shut up one way or the other and leave their wives to it. All through history these ignorant, superstitious, bloody-minded women have been willing to half-kill themselves to get abortions. Kill themselves, if necessary. They've soaked themselves in alcohol and poisonous brews, they've stuck sticks up them, they've chucked themselves downstairs, they've had rocks piled on their bellies and other women jump up and down on them. Can't they be trusted to take a short spin to a clinic for contraceptives, once they know they're there?'

'I suppose you're aware,' Pat Wilshaw said heavily, 'that this clinic, the one you work for, relies on funding from Gordon Grant? In part. And Mr Grant isn't going to like *this*.' She drummed again.

Charlotte's intuition, honed by two months back with her mother, made her look hard at her superior. 'Won't you get your trip to Peru?' she asked.

Vinegar contracted the Wilshaw features to Millichip dimensions. 'I am talking of the good of this clinic, Charlotte. Presumably your new philosophy doesn't include its closing?'

'I'll leave, if you like,' Charlotte said, wondering at her own jollity in the face of long-term unemployment. 'Then you can wash your hands of me and my report. I'll give it to Mr Grant as an ex-employee. Nothing to do with the Cotterstock. You can tell him I was always unstable and now I'm into a full-scale crack-up.'

Pat's face registered total belief in this statement. However, she merely said, 'Don't be smug. I'll do some tinkering with . . .'

'No. No tinkering.'

'Life,' Pat said, 'is full of compromises. Balances and counter-balances. A little more here, a little less there.'

216

'Not for Sulanasian women, it isn't,' Charlotte said.

'Lucky them,' said Pat, bitterly.

When Charlotte returned home in the evening, her mother was enthroned in the basket chair clashing two knitting needles together.

'What do you feel about this?' she enquired of her daughter, holding them up.

Charlotte inspected the outcome of the battle. 'Isn't it *woolly*,' she said.

'You know, I've been thinking, Charlotte.' The needles flew at each other again. 'I'm very fond of Diana and also Sybil. Do you like Sybil?'

'Yes,' said Charlotte, who didn't. 'But what if it's a boy?'

'In that case, would you consider Alan? Your dead father's name, though he couldn't stand it himself. Said it always made him feel he ought to be a Morris dancer, I can't think . . .'

Charlotte, kneeling beside her mother, laid a hand upon the needles to put them out of their misery. 'Tell you what, Ma. If it's a boy, we'll call him Harry Alan. How about that?'

'Harry.' Mrs Wren considered. 'I knew a Harry once. An odd man. He could only pee in his own house. A great handicap for someone in the Foreign Office. In the end they had to move him to Internal Affairs and . . .'

Placidly, Charlotte listened, her hands folded over her stomach .

THE
CAT OWNER'S

SURVIVAL GUIDE

SOPHIE JOHNSON

ILLUSTRATED BY **TATIANA DAVIDOVA**

summersdale

THE CAT OWNER'S SURVIVAL GUIDE

Illustrations by Tatiana Davidova

An Hachette UK Company
www.hachette.co.uk

Summersdale Publishers Ltd
Part of Octopus Publishing Group Limited
Carmelite House
50 Victoria Embankment
LONDON
EC4Y 0DZ
UK

www.summersdale.com

Printed and bound in China

ISBN: 978-1-80007-401-9

Substantial discounts on bulk quantities of Summersdale books are available to corporations, professional associations and other organizations. For details contact general enquiries: telephone: +44 (0) 1243 771107 or email: enquiries@summersdale.com.

TO ....

FROM ....

INTRODUCTION

If you are a seasoned cat owner
you'll understand the idiom,
"It's like herding cats" – they
are their own person and little
you can do will ever tame them.
You'll know that they pretty
much rule wherever they roam.

So here's your survival guide to living under Chairman Meow's rule. Tips, tricks and advice for making your life as a cat parent as wonderful as can be. Because, although they rule the world, they do so with such wonderful grace and attitude that it's a pleasure to serve under them.

THERE IS A SECRET
NUMBER OF TUMMY
RUBS YOUR CAT
WILL ALLOW BEFORE
THEY TURN INTO AN
UNCONTROLLABLE
SCRATCH MONSTER.
AND IT CHANGES

EVERY TIME.

YOU MUST ACCEPT
THAT YOU NO LONGER
HAVE ANY PRIVACY.
YOUR HOME IS
THEIR HOME.

YOUR CAT MAY LOOK
CUTE AND INNOCENT,
BUT SECRETLY THERE'S
AN EVIL MASTERMIND
AT WORK BEHIND
ALL THAT FLUFF.

YOU CAN

FORGET

SITTING DOWN

TO READ

THE SUNDAY
PAPERS.

YOU'LL NEED TO PRACTISE YOUR GRATEFUL FACE FOR THOSE INEVITABLE UNWANTED GIFTS. THERE'S NO STOPPING THEM.

THIS IS NOT YOGA.
THIS IS A BIG SICKY
MESS IN 3... 2... 1...

ITEMS PLACED ON A SURFACE ARE HIGHLY OFFENSIVE TO CATS AND WILL BE QUICKLY DISPATCHED TO THE FLOOR

WHERE THEY BELONG.

CONGRATULATIONS ON YOUR NEW ROLE AS YOUR CAT'S P.A. (PERSONAL ASSISTANT) AND P.D.O. (PERSONAL DOOR OPENER). IT'S EASIEST JUST TO ACCEPT IT.

BE PREPARED TO WEAR
CLOTHES THE SAME
COLOUR AS YOUR CAT.
THEY'LL END UP THAT
COLOUR ANYWAY.

YOUR CAT'S

TIMEKEEPING

IS BETTER
THAN YOURS.
THIS IS

JUST A FACT.

NEVER DISTURB YOUR SLEEPING BABY, NO MATTER THE GYMNASTICS YOU NEED TO DO TO KEEP THEM COMFY.

YOU'LL SPEND A FORTUNE ON NEW, IMPROVED, FARM-TO-TABLE, ORGANIC MEATY CHUNKS – TO FEED TO THE BIN.

THERE'S NO EXPLAINING THE SCIENCE OF CATS

IN BOXES.

THEIR REAL NAME MUST
BE PRONOUNCED THE
SAME WAY A SHAKEN
BAG OF TREATS SOUNDS.
IT'S THE ONLY THING
THEY RESPOND TO.

**MESS-BLINDNESS
IS A COMMON
SIDE EFFECT OF
CAT PARENTHOOD.**

KNITTING?

IT'S JUST
NOT A THING

YOU CAN DO

ANY MORE.

YOU MIGHT HAVE
HOUR-LONG DISCUSSIONS
WITH YOUR FUR-BABY,
BUT BEAR IN MIND
ALL THEY WANT IS
MORE TREATS.

LEAVE ROOM IN
YOUR HOUSE FOR
YOUR CAT TO
SPARK JOY OF
ITS VERY OWN.

SUDDENLY, YOUR CAT
WILL SPOT SOMETHING
TERRIFYING AND
INVISIBLE — A GHOST?
A HUGE SPIDER? —
AND YOUR DAY

WILL BE RUINED.

DON'T LET YOUR CAT IN YOUR HOME OFFICE, OR YOU MAY END UP TELLING YOUR BOSS HFUEIJSJEIOWIRW EJIOFRWOIAQWQ.

THEY ARE
UNTRAINABLE.
JUST ACCEPT IT.

SECURITY DEPOSITS ARE BASICALLY

CASH GIFTS

TO YOUR

LANDLORD.

YES, THE LITTER TRAY
IS AN OPTION, BUT IT'S
NOT THE ONLY ONE.

OF COURSE THEY
LIKED THE NEW FOOD.
(UNTIL YOU STOCKED
UP, THAT IS.)

ON TOUGH DAYS,
YOU MAY BE TEMPTED
TO HUFF SOME
CATNIP YOURSELF.
IT DOES NOTHING,

HONESTLY.

YOU'RE
ONE OF THEM.

**GET USED
TO REASSURING
FRIENDS THAT
EVERYTHING
IS OKAY.**

ONCE YOU ARE A

CAT PARENT,

THREE WILL ALWAYS

BE A CROWD.

AND ALL BECAUSE
THEY ONCE SAW A
DOG (A DOG!) DRINK
FROM A BOWL.

WATCH OUT FOR
ANGRY LETTERS
FROM BIRD
CONSERVATION
CHARITIES.

SPECIAL MAT,
SPECIAL LITTER,
SPECIAL TRAY.
THAT STUFF
WILL STILL GET
EVERYWHERE.
ADD GLITTER
AND INSIST

IT'S A FEATURE.

CHRISTMAS
DECORATIONS
MUST BE HUNG
WITH NOTHING LESS
THAN SUPERGLUE.

GARDEN WITH CAUTION.
TURN YOUR BACK ON
A FRESHLY DUG BED
FOR A SECOND AND...

NO NEED
TO WATCH

WILDLIFE
PROGRAMMES

ANY LONGER –
YOUR CAT NOW
PROVIDES ALL THE

ENTERTAINMENT

YOU NEED.

THE MORE EXPENSIVE THE BED, THE LESS IT IS USED.

USE ALL THE SPRAYS
AND OINTMENTS
AVAILABLE TO KEEP
THE TINY ITCH-
DEVILS AT BAY.

YOUR CAT DOES
NOT CARE FOR

YOUR ADORATION.

BEFORE LONG, YOU'LL BE USING THE TERM "DISPOSABLE SOFA".

IT'S QUITE NATURAL
TO OBSESS OVER
FINDING THE BEST
CAT-HAIR REMOVER.

BE PREPARED
FOR YOUR CAT
TO MAKE A

STAR APPEARANCE

DURING

**REMOTE WORK
MEETINGS.**

IT IS NO LONGER
SAFE TO LEAVE FOOD
UNACCOMPANIED.

YES, YOU
INSTALLED A CAT
FLAP, BUT DENNIS
PREFERS YOU TO OPEN
THE DOOR FOR HIM.

SCANDI CRIME DRAMA
HAS EXTRA MYSTERY
WHEN YOU CAN'T
READ THE SUBTITLES.
TAKE THIS AS YOUR
CAT'S HINT THAT IT'S
TIME TO LEARN A

NEW LANGUAGE.

AT LEAST YOUR HOUSE
WILL ALWAYS BE FREE
OF SPIDERS NOW.

YOU'LL HAPPILY PUT
UP WITH ALL OF THIS
(EVEN THOSE TINY
DAGGERS ON THEIR
FEET) – BECAUSE
YOU LOVE THEM.

Have you enjoyed this book?

If so, find us on Facebook at
Summersdale Publishers, on Twitter
at @Summersdale and on Instagram
at @summersdalebooks and get in
touch. We'd love to hear from you!

www.summersdale.com